KEEPER

Keeper

by

Sydney Quinne

2020

KEEPER

ISBN 13: 978-1-63555-852-4

This Trade Paperback Original Is Published By
Bold Strokes Books, Inc.
P.O. Box 249
Valley Falls, NY 12185

First Edition: October 2020

Credits
Editor: Cindy Cresap
Production Design: Susan Ramundo
Cover Design By Tammy Seidick

Author's Note

In this book, there is a somewhat convenient solution to the emotional challenges Isabelle Templeton faces. This is, however, a work of fiction. I encourage anyone with similar challenges to reach out to someone capable and qualified to assist them. It is always okay to ask for help. Please do so if you or your family feel you need it.

Also note that I somewhat reinvented the NYPD Major Case Squad for the purpose of this book.

My sincerest thanks to the team at Bold Strokes Books—Len Barot, Sandy Lowe, and Cindy Cresap in particular—for their patience, guidance and expertise. It is much appreciated.

Dedication

For Catherine

CHAPTER ONE

The wiry, twitchy guy at the end of the bar was going to be trouble. He was too drunk to care who he messed with and too small to end the fight quickly. Then again, she'd often seen the short, stupid ones outlast the Goliaths. They were like bull terriers. Just couldn't let go, even if it killed them.

Andy took a frosted beer glass from the fridge behind her, filled it from the Heineken tap, and slid it across the counter to a woman who'd been sitting alone for most of the evening.

She didn't like the woman either. She was also American, and she had made sure Andy knew it. She was too inquisitive. Too friendly—flirting almost. She was older than Andy by about ten years or so, which put her in her late thirties. She had shoulder-length chestnut hair, unreadable brown eyes, a delicate face, and a trim, fit body, as if she trained religiously. A white shirt showed the swell of pert, perfectly rounded breasts, the invitation clear, especially when she pushed them in Andy's direction.

Andy had dealt with enough bullshit in her life to recognize it sitting at her table. And at six foot two, she could see most things coming.

"Thanks." The woman lifted her glass, smiling broadly. "When did you say you're knocking off again?"

"Didn't say." Andy took the twenty-pound note from the woman.

"Keep the change. A handsome woman like you deserves more." The woman tilted her chin in the direction of the almost empty tip jar.

Andy said nothing. She was saving her energy. Trouble was brewing. She could sense its soft-footed approach. She just wished she knew which direction it would be stalking in from.

She checked to see if the baseball bat was still under the counter.

Yeah, there it was.

Yankees, it said in red scrawl. It was one of the few remnants of her previous life, miles away from SoHo, the miserable London weather, and this place. The Black Sheep was not your typical English pub with its creaky floors, wood paneling, and green carpets, but a proper old-fashioned raucous New York-style bar with a touch of neon lighting and big screen TVs.

The twitchy guy at the end of the bar bit into the thumbnail on his right hand, then shouted at the TV screen where Manchester United was losing to Liverpool. Behind him a crowd of red-jersey supporters stood four-deep, watching the game.

"Come on, you bastards! This is fucking bollocks!" he shouted. "Useless pieces of shite. You play worse than my mother."

A woman in a red Man U shirt leaned forward and gripped the man's shoulder with long red fingernails.

"Shut it, you sod. There's still twenty minutes on the clock."

The man turned to face the sea of Manchester supporters, glaring at them through greasy bangs. "Fuck you. They're playing like girls."

"Watch your mouth," the woman shot back. "I know a girl or two I'd put on that team."

Now would be a good time to back down, Andy told Twitchy Guy silently, but the man jumped off his chair as if it was on fire. The woman, big-breasted and surly, took a step back, watching him as if she couldn't decide whether he was worth the trouble.

He glared at her, grabbed his beer from the counter, and tossed the pint at her face. She ducked and the glass sailed over her head, hitting a tall guy in a Knicks sweater.

Fuck it, thought Andy. Where the hell is Jimmy?

As if hearing her silent prayer, Jimmy, the Black Sheep's assistant manager, stomped through the crowd from the men's bathroom, moving swiftly for a former pro-wrestler with a bad knee. It took him two seconds to separate Twitchy Guy and the man in the Knicks sweater. He looked at Andy, lifting his one eyebrow in a question mark. Andy pointed at Twitchy Guy. Jimmy pulled back a fist, opening his hand midair to slap him on the shoulder and bounce Twitchy Guy off the bar counter.

Jimmy knew not to leave a mark.

Twitchy Guy turned, yanking a knife from his pocket and flipping it open in a single fluid moment.

Yep. Always the little ones.

Andy grabbed the Yankees bat and smashed it down on the bar counter. Glass shards and beer flew into the patrons of the Black Sheep.

Everyone went quiet.

"Get out," Andy said, her voice throaty, level. She gestured at Twitchy Guy. "Now."

"No way," he argued, waving his knife nervously from her to Jimmy.

She shrugged and pointed the bat at him again. "Get out now, or I call the cops."

"Bloody hell! I didn't start it."

"Yes, you did." Andy leaned over the counter, tapping the bat against the knife. "And why the hell bring a knife to a gun fight?"

"I didn't…you don't have a…" He eyed the bat in her hand.

Andy smiled coldly and dropped her gaze to the empty space below the counter. "Says who?"

Jimmy snatched the knife from Twitchy Guy and yanked him to the door by the collar.

"Thanks, Jimmy," Andy said.

"No problem, boss."

Jimmy tossed the guy out and slammed the Black Sheep's door shut.

"Lock it," Andy called over the sudden resurgent din of the crowd. The sooner this night ended the better. "We're closed. If anyone wants a drink they can go look for it somewhere else."

She put the bat away, opened the fridge door next to her with the toe of her boot, and grabbed a shot glass from the top shelf. Time for some ice-cold vodka.

Chapter Two

The woman with the chestnut hair and the veiled eyes was the last to leave. Maybe she got stood up, or maybe she'd come trawling for someone to warm her bed. Andy didn't care. The only thing she was interested in was for everyone to leave so she could cash out for the night.

The woman lingered at the bar, watching as the last cheering Manchester United fans left. Their team staged a last-minute comeback to win 2–1.

"You're handy with a bat," she said as the door closed. She stared at Andy's chest, her hips. Lower.

Andy continued wiping down the dark wood counter, the white towel whipping from edge to edge. "Look, I'm not interested. You're beautiful, and you seem nice, but I'm too old and tired for you."

"My name's Claire. And you're twenty-seven."

The woman stood up from her barstool. She smiled, but it didn't reach her eyes. Andy froze, the hair on the back of her neck standing on end. She looked down at the woman's black slacks, her black heels. She could take her. She wasn't super fit anymore, but she was still strong. Could still run a mile in four-forty.

"Do you really keep a gun under the counter?" Claire pointed to where Andy had stowed the bat earlier.

Andy kept a straight face, mirroring Claire, and continued to wipe down the bar surface. "It's closing time. You better leave."

"I thought knives were more your thing. From what I've heard you could have thrown the knife out of that guy's hand with your own blade."

Andy stood back, clenching the dish rag in her fists. "Where is she?"

Twitchy Guy hadn't been the trouble she'd felt stalking her earlier tonight. It was far, far worse.

Claire stared at her with surprised eyes that grew colder by the second. Andy counted ten seconds on the wall clock before Claire answered.

"She's close." Claire walked to the Black Sheep's front door and unlocked it.

Andy hadn't seen Kate in a long time, but the sight of the woman not quite as tall as her, with the same wavy black hair as hers, longer, but graying, still startled her. She had the same strong chin, high forehead, olive complexion, and simmering dark eyes that turned black when provoked.

Her high heels sounded like muffled gunshots as she strode to the bar.

Always had to make an entrance.

Kate handed her red coat and black scarf to Claire and sat on the barstool she'd vacated. Claire moved to the entrance, as if standing guard.

"Hello, Kate." Andy sighed.

Kate smiled slightly as she peeled off her black leather gloves. "Whatever happened to calling me Mother?"

❖

"Whatever it is, whatever crisis you've invented, I'm not interested. Don't even waste your breath explaining." Andy stood back, resting her butt against the fridge. She waved to the door. "You can leave. Right now."

Claire remained standing at the entrance, Kate's coat and scarf in her hands. She looked at the now mute television where a panel of experts were dissecting the earlier football game.

Kate ignored her with equal success. She pointed at the sound system behind the counter. "Sticking with jazz, I hear," she said, flashing Andy a quick, slick smile. "Who's this? Miles Davis? Still sounds messy to me. It lacks the structure of a Debussy or Beethoven. I can never quite figure out where it's going."

Andy didn't answer. Talking would just prolong the agony of getting her mother to leave.

"Ah, and there's the Duke." Kate nodded as the music changed. "Duke Ellington. You love women, but you prefer men when it comes to music. Why is that?"

She was wrong, but Andy didn't want to tell her that, so she turned and poured herself a Scotch from the expensive bottle she kept behind the counter. She gulped it down in an effort to calm the rising unease in her stomach, then wiped the sweat from her hands on the front of her jeans.

"I'll have one too, darling. Don't be inhospitable. I raised you better than that."

"You raised me to kill people." The words slipped past Andy's tongue before she could stop them.

"I raised you to protect innocent people."

Here we go again.

Angry at herself for being baited, Andy emptied her glass and poured another Scotch. She felt blindly for a second crystal tumbler under the bar counter, filled it and slipped in one small block of ice—only one, otherwise it bruised the whiskey. Heaven forbid.

She turned and handed it to her. "Does your little errand girl also want one, or has she drunk enough for one night?"

"Claire is fine, thanks." Kate sipped from her glass. "Lovely, thanks." She put the whiskey down, tapping the rim of the tumbler with a long red fingernail.

Andy could almost hear the words strain at Kate's throat. The mental ordering, reordering to make sure she didn't sound like she was pleading.

Andy waited. Listened to the clock.

Kate dipped her head and stared at the amber liquid in her glass. When she looked up her eyes were soft, hopeful.

Damn it. What the hell was going on?

"She's twenty," Kate finally said. "She's the first dreamer we've found in four years. And I need you to come and take care of her."

CHAPTER THREE

Seventeen days ago

"Shit," Isabelle swore.

She sucked at the blood seeping from the cut on her thumb. She put down the knife and pushed the tomatoes to one side. She'd been distracted all day, her mind wandering all over the place.

If she could just get a good night's sleep, she'd feel like a normal person again. She'd be more alert; human, almost.

She looked at the textbook next to the tomatoes and groaned. She had a finite mathematics paper due later this month and she hadn't completed it yet. She knew she'd be okay, but she wanted to do more than okay, especially if she was to work toward an early finish on her degree next year and move on to a master's after that. She needed the best scholarship good grades could buy.

She looked at her finger. The bleeding had stopped. She always bled so easily. She pushed her hair back from her face and tied it up. Maybe she should go boxing. It should exhaust her enough to manage a few hours' sleep.

She ate the tomato she'd already cut, put the remainder back in the fridge, and started the hunt for her gym clothes in the tiny one-room apartment in Jersey City. She dressed quickly, pulling on only a hoodie for warmth, even though it was freezing cold outside. The gym was close by. She'd be there before the wind could cool her skin.

❖

Isabelle ducked below the long arms of her much taller trainer. She jabbed him once, twice in the side. Horace Gibson was a lean African-American with the reach of an octopus.

Former WBA heavyweight champion Horace the Hammer.

Isabelle was the only woman Horace trained. The rest of his clients were suits with money, wanting to look mean in the boardroom, and wannabe fighters still hustling their way up the rankings. Horace trained only one true boxer who would this month, after ten years in the ring, finally call it quits.

Isabelle danced back from Horace's bulky body, her skin slick with sweat after thirty minutes in the ring. Her calves ached, clenching as if they wanted to cramp, then eased up again.

"How the hell do you know what I'm going to do before I do it?" Horace puffed. "Fuck, woman. You make me look bad." He leaned forward, gloved hands on his knees. "Enough. You're giving my kidneys grief. I'm gonna piss blood for a week."

"You big softie." Isabelle grinned. She felt good. Alive.

Not at all tired.

She dropped her gloves.

Horace shot forward, his fist stopping inches before her face.

She startled and retreated in a quick shuffle.

"If the bell ain't rung…" he said.

"…never stop fighting," said Isabelle, taken aback. "Cheater."

"Slacker."

Isabelle's calves threatened to seize up again, but there was no way she was going to admit that to Horace. "Ding-ding?" she offered.

Horace moved back, stretching his back. He grinned. "Old man will take the bell so young girl can go study. But that's the only reason."

❖

Isabelle inserted the key, then lifted it to the right until she heard her front door click open. Always been a funny lock.

Her neighbor's door swung open. Jam, a short, purple-haired tattoo artist, emerged, laundry basket in hand. "Good session at the gym?"

Isabelle could never shake the feeling that Jam liked her, and not in a best friend kind of way either, but she didn't quite trust her. She was forever asking questions, wanting to know more about Isabelle's private life. Whether she was dating someone. If she slept well. Ate well. Enjoyed the boxing.

"Yes," Isabelle said, managing a smile. "Nothing clean to wear?"

She'd seen the inside of Jam's apartment. It was a mess, mirroring the colorful parachute pants and Pac-Man T-shirts she favored.

"Yeah. Can't put it off any longer. My mom is coming to visit. She's Japanese and she'll have a heart attack if she opens my closet. And she's going to do exactly that, make no mistake." Jam gestured down to the basement. "Are you sleeping better these days? No more dreams?"

She'd woken up screaming one night, Jam frantically knocking at her front door to see if she was okay.

"Much better," she lied. "And my math paper is due soon anyway, then I can breathe again."

CHAPTER FOUR

Twelve days ago

Isabelle slept fitfully. The violent dream that had been haunting her for the past week again pushed its way through the fog of sleep. A tall, older man was walking down the street, his hands jammed in a worn coat. He walked quickly, shoulders hunched against the cold. She still couldn't make out his face, his features hidden from view by the upturned collar of his coat.

Two men appeared. They wanted the tall man's wallet and phone. He stopped, shook his head, and strode away from them. The men followed, like eager street dogs promised a meal.

The night smelled of stale food and wet tar.

Everything about the dream was clearer tonight, sharper, more in focus than before.

The thinner man flicked open a knife. The other one, a snake tattoo curling up his wiry right arm, did the same. The men circled the tall man, looking for a gap to launch their attack. The thin man jumped forward and stabbed him in the back. The tall man turned and punched him in the face.

The thin man staggered back, blood on his face. His partner with the tattoo jammed his blade in the tall man's lower back, again and again. The tall man fell onto the sidewalk, hands blindly seeking the wounds in his back, trying to stem the bleeding.

The moon was so bright, the light from the streetlamps and the shopfronts so prominent, Isabelle could see everything in detailed slow-motion.

A door swung open. Someone ran down the sidewalk, screaming.

It was her. Isabelle.

The two men fled as she screamed.

She rushed to the tall man on the cold concrete and cradled his head in her lap.

For the first time in a week of dreaming the same jumble of images, she could finally see who it was: Horace Gibson, her boxing instructor.

There was blood on her hands, red, slick, and thick. The smell of copper stuck to her tongue, slid down her throat, and made her gag.

She screamed again.

Woke.

Her breath rushed over her lips, hurried and full of panic.

Breathe. Just breathe. She sat up, head between her knees.

She was too scared to open her eyes. Last night, when she did so after the dream, the room closed in on her, then spun away like some computer manipulated image from a B-grade movie.

If she'd maybe be made more of an effort with Jam, her next-door neighbor, she could go for help, but she'd never been good at asking for help or making friends.

She felt the bile rush into her mouth. She stumbled blindly to the toilet and threw up the tomato soup she'd eaten earlier. She heaved over the bowl, eyes still closed. Her legs were too shaky to hold her. She sank down to her knees next to the toilet.

Get up. Open your eyes and get up.

She had to find Horace. She'd recognized the sidewalk where the mugging had happened, the bright red neon sign of the sex shop next to the boxing gym.

The dream was too vivid not to be real.

She wiped at her mouth and stumbled to the front door, her eyes closed against the nauseatingly bright light. She padded down the hallway on her bare feet. The stairs were to the right. She felt for the railing, almost tumbling down the first step.

Focus. You can do this.

"Probability theory," she started to recite as she descended the stairs one by one, "is a branch of mathematics concerned with analysis of random phenomena. The outcome of a random event cannot be determined before it occurs, but it may be any one of several possible outcomes. The actual outcome is considered to be determined by chance."

The concrete under her feet told her that she'd made it downstairs. She breathed through her nose, bile rising in her throat again. She fumbled out the building door and onto the sidewalk.

She knew it would be quiet on the street. Didn't know how she knew it. Same way she knew it was three forty-five, although she had no watch to tell her the time.

She walked, trailing her hand over one cold shopfront window after the other. She counted the shops. Three, four, five. She opened her eyes.

The sidewalk was empty. No Horace. No blood. No bad men.

The city and its buildings collapsed onto her, the lights exploding into her mind. Her chest tightened, her breath raced. She knelt down, digging into the sidewalk.

A man stepped around her. "Fucking junkie."

She started to shiver. She was freezing. The cold crept through her bare feet, up her legs and into her stomach, her head. She struggled upright, leaned against the nearest shop window, and started to stagger back to her apartment.

Inside her building, she fell onto her hands and knees and crawled up the stairs.

She opened her front door, threw up on the threadbare carpet, curled into a ball, and waited for darkness to descend.

Chapter Five

Nine days ago

Isabelle was late. The measure theory class she was taking at NYU had wrapped up later than usual, and now she was late for her session with Horace. Damn subway was no help either. Seemed there was always some kind of holdup on the line lately.

She ran up the stairs, unlocked her door, and ran to her bed. She rummaged through her closet, threw off her coat, jeans, and boots and put on sneakers and a tracksuit. She grabbed her boxing gloves, ran from her apartment, and jogged to the gym, her feet pounding the wet sidewalk. It had been three days since the dream in which Horace was murdered and, despite the lies her mind had told her, he remained completely fine.

She picked up her pace, the night air cold, her breath a heavy fog as it escaped her mouth.

A knot of curious onlookers blocked the sidewalk. She zigzagged through them, halting abruptly when she saw the blue and red lights bouncing off their faces. An ambulance and two police cars were parked in front of Bonnie's Sex Shop.

She knew instantly. Knew from the light of the full moon above her and the sweet, sickly smell of stale food drifting toward her, that it was Horace.

She fought her way through the throng of people, catching snippets of conversation as she struggled to the front. "Mugging…poor guy… the boxer…bastards…"

She walked up to the yellow police tape and ducked underneath.

"Wait. Miss!" yelled a uniformed policeman from across the secured area.

She ran to the body on the sidewalk, the paramedics around him packing up their gear.

"Horace!" She knelt beside the body, touching the still warm face with her hand.

"Miss!" the policeman shouted again. "You can't be here."

She stared up at his face, no older than her own. "I know who did it," she said angrily. "I know who killed him."

❖

Detective Jane Wright stood in the observation room and listened to a gorgeous young woman with copper-colored hair give an amazingly detailed description of the two men she said had murdered Horace Gibson. Jane's partner was doing the interview. By now it was clear the woman was a complete nut job, but it didn't seem like Russo minded spending time with her.

Patrol had brought her to the Major Case Squad from the crime scene in Jersey City. Horace Gibson was a former WBA heavyweight champion. His death was already trending on social media, thanks to some look-at-me fucker with a cell phone and eager Twitter trigger finger. Whoever had posted it hadn't even stopped to consider whether Horace had family who wouldn't want to read of his death on a cold, blue screen.

Jane sighed. There was little doubt Gibson's death would lead the news cycle tomorrow, the newspapers announcing that NYPD's finest had no lead yet. Lieutenant Monaghan was going to be up her and Russo's asses as soon as he heard about the murder.

She hated the slow news days when the politicians kept it in their pants. Always made the media gun for the nearest crime scene looking for a story. And muggings were already bad enough. They were random, with no connection between victim and perp. It would take a boatload of luck to track these assholes down.

"So, let me get this straight," Russo said slowly. "You didn't actually see the men. You dreamed about them." His short sausage fingers were splayed in the air, his wide eyes mocking her. "Like you see the future, or something."

The redhead, Isabelle Templeton, didn't move a muscle. It was clear she regretted telling him she knew who killed the gym owner.

Jane had seen Templeton when she'd arrived at 1 Police Plaza. She'd seemed angry, mostly at herself, Jane felt. It was as if she believed she'd messed up somehow, as if she'd missed something important.

At first, when Russo had started the interview, Jane couldn't quite grasp what Templeton was saying. Then she'd realized the implication of her words. She was talking about a dream she'd had. A premonition. Woo-hoo voodoo stuff.

Fucking hell.

Russo was probably right. Templeton was a bullshitter, someone looking for attention in a city full of people craving the spotlight. Pity though. She was beautiful. Those green eyes were like something out of a fairy tale. The body, however, conjured up far more grown-up fantasies. Lithe, supple, with full breasts and long legs. Strong cheekbones, full mouth. Slightly askew left eyetooth. A nervous habit to bite a full lower lip when she was angry.

What was more interesting, intriguing even, was the way she held herself. She seemed unwilling to touch anyone or anything. She kept her hands covered by the sleeves of her black sweater, but not in a nervous way. It was more like she didn't want to pick up some kind of disease. And she sure as hell didn't seem flaky or unsure. Her story was logical, told from beginning to end. More importantly, it had remained the same, from A to Z, the three times she'd told it, Russo unable to shoot holes in it.

Interesting, and a looker.

Jane adjusted the Glock on her hip, resting her right hand on the butt of the gun. Then she clipped her phone from her belt and dialed a number she knew by heart.

"Any luck?" she asked, rubbing a hand through her messy hair. She stared at her tired eyes in the two-way mirror in front of her.

The man on the other side didn't even ask why Jane had called. She wasn't known for her patience.

"Nope. So far CCTV corroborates the woman's story. She's clean. Showed up only after the mugging. Probably just another whacko looking for a headline."

"Whacko? A woman doing a degree in advanced math at NYU?"

"Yep. The crazies can be smart too. You know that as well as I do."

Chapter Six

I'm not interested," Andy said. "I told you. I'm never working for you again. I'm done."

She drained the whiskey from her glass—her fourth shot if she remembered correctly.

"Please." She looked at her mother. "Just leave."

Kate reached for Andy's hands across the bar counter. Andy's hands became fists. She retreated, shoving her hands into her pockets. "Get it through your head. I'm done. No more looking after women with visions that will save your little world."

Claire looked up from where she was standing guard at the Black Sheep's door. Her hand reflexively traveled to her hip, dipping underneath her coat and searching for the weapon she no doubt hid there.

Andy guessed she carried a Glock. Probably a .22. Smaller, more concealable than its bigger brothers. She didn't look like the type who would want to ruin her outfit with a big, bulky pistol.

"She looks nice," Andy mocked her, jerking her chin in Claire's direction. "What is she? Your fifth keeper? And isn't she a bit too young for you?"

Her mother rarely dreamed anymore. Rarely needed someone to watch over her while she struggled to consciousness. Someone to interpret her dreams, to execute or prevent them. Somehow she had managed to let the dreams fade to black. To an occasional inconvenience she had to deal with in a day filled with other, more important things.

Their lineage went back thousands of years, to before Joan of Arc, when women still had to exert their influence from the dark. When they still had to work subtly by being wife, sister, lover, and daughter. When they'd tried their damnedest to protect the innocent from the rage-fueled destruction of power-hungry men.

Kate turned the glass in front of her, looking at the single melting ice cube. "You drink too much."

"Go away."

"Watch your mouth." Kate's black eyes—her own eyes—flared backed at her. "The goal is bigger than you and I. Than any of us, and you know it."

Kate pushed the glass in Andy's direction, tucking the graying hair behind her ears.

She was still beautiful, Andy thought. Still immaculately dressed and groomed. Still unmoving in her beliefs, convinced of sacrificing everything for the greater good.

Andy had also been like that when she'd started out, a lifetime ago.

Andy didn't want to refill her mother's glass. She didn't want Kate to remain at the Black Sheep one minute longer. Then she did it anyway. Poured herself another shot too, ignoring the concerned look from Kate.

"Isabelle Templeton is twenty," Kate said. She leaned back, crossing her legs under the white and black dress. "We don't know when she started dreaming. She fell through the cracks in the system without us knowing about her. She was a foster kid. Brilliant. Genius in math." Kate smiled. "She's building an algorithm that predicts human behavior. I think she's trying to understand herself better. Trying to grasp who she is."

Kate sipped her whiskey. "She's lost and scared. If somebody doesn't help her soon we're going to lose her to a mental institution, or the street. She's very strong, but this could kill her." She sighed then held her breath. "As far as we can see, the dreaming is intensifying. It's looking for a way out, even if it kills her."

Andy remained unmoved. She waited for her mother's trump card. The one she'd play in the hope it would sway Andy to give up her new life. Her carefully constructed, safe, orderly, predictable life. Away from what happened, what she'd lost.

"From what I hear she can dream four days into the future. At least."

"Four days?"

Andy spoke in spite of herself. Normally, there were twenty-four hours' grace to try to solve the puzzle, to put it all together before something awful happened—maximum a day and a half. Nothing more.

Kate nodded, pleased that Andy reacted. "It may even be more. Think of what we can do with that. Of the lives we can save."

"How close does she have to be?" Andy asked.

She hated herself for sounding interested.

"I don't know. I don't know anything about her. Which is why I need you. Women trust you. You have this thing that makes people believe in you."

Andy backed away from the bar counter. "Nope. Forget it. Not interested. Find someone else. You probably have ten keepers in training at the moment. Use one of them."

"I have six, the rest are all already bound to dreamers. None of them are right for Isabelle. I need someone experienced. Someone I trust. Isabelle could be the most powerful dreamer we've ever seen."

"I'm not that person. I'm retired, remember? If you lose your dreamer, you're allowed to retire." And she'd lost two. Not that it had stopped her mother. She'd been here before, begging her to return.

No. Not begging. Kate Bouchard never begged.

Kate looked over to Claire, shrugged, and tilted her head. She smiled slowly, ruefully. Claire pushed her body from the door, Kate's cashmere coat still folded in front of her body.

"Well, it was worth a try." Kate got up. "Come on, at least give me a hug good-bye."

"Sorry," Andy said, and maybe she even meant it. She took a deep breath and walked around the bar counter. "I'm happy. I need...I want a normal life. It was nice seeing you though. If you're in London again stop by for a cup of coffee."

And maybe ask me how it's going. Like a real mother.

"Happy? You? Really?" Kate asked. "Aren't you bored to tears?"

Claire stepped forward and lifted the coat as if to give it to Kate.

Andy caught the glimmer of black steel underneath the cashmere.

Shit. Didn't see that coming.

She jumped onto the nearest barstool, gunning for the Sig Sauer P266 hid in her office when the Taser zapped her in the back.

Chapter Seven

Andy struggled to consciousness, fighting the tendrils of darkness that lured her back to sleep.

"Hey, you okay?" a woman's husky voice asked.

She was close by but didn't touch Andy. Andy wet her lips and scraped her throat. She opened her eyes slowly. She was in a room with soft lighting, a light green ceiling. No windows.

Never a good sign.

She closed her eyes again, remembering what had happened. Kate's betrayal. Again. Couldn't even—ever—trust her own mother. Fuck it.

"Hey," the voice insisted. Whoever it was, remained outside her line of vision. "Do you need anything? I can try calling, maybe someone would come if I ask really nicely."

She could hear the woman moving closer. Her scent was that of a forest, pinecones and trees. Wet soil after the rain. And jasmine, unexpectedly.

Andy tested her voice. "Th…" She coughed, then wished she didn't. The sound rolled around in her head like a bowling ball. "They won't come."

"You sound as if you know them. Whoever they are," the woman said in a flat tone, distrust slipping into her voice.

"I do." Andy tried to sit up, her eyes still closed. She didn't need to open her eyes to know who the woman was.

"Let me help," the woman offered, in spite of the fear Andy could sense in her.

"No! No, don't touch me."

"Okay," the voice said again, distrust gearing up into anger. "As you wish."

"It's for your own sake," said Andy, her tone softer. "Things happen when you touch people. That's why you don't like doing it."

"How do you know that?" Footsteps, barefoot, stumbling back from her.

Knuckles—a fist?—rapped against glass, as if admonishing her.

She gave in and opened her eyes. Where…There. The reprimand must have come from behind the two-way mirror.

Andy sneered at the glass. "I'm going to tell her about you. I'm not going to win her trust and play your game."

She turned her gaze to the left. Blinked twice. The woman was beautiful. Full, deep-red hair, ivory skin, tiny freckles on her nose. Stubborn chin. Gorgeous mouth. Emerald eyes. She was taller than Andy had expected, but still a few inches shorter than her own six-feet-plus.

The woman looked at Andy, hands on her hips, cocking her head as if demanding answers from her. She wore a soft, flowing white dress with a slit up to her knee.

Isabelle Templeton was twenty, Kate had said. She looked older. Those eyes were much, much older.

"Who are you?" the redhead insisted.

"You're Isabelle Templeton?" Andy asked, managing a smile. Isabelle wasn't to blame. It was all her mother's doing.

"Yes." Her voice was ice cold. "Who are you?"

"Andy Bouchard."

"And who's that?" Isabelle pointed to the mirror. "You say you know the people who took us? Why are we here?"

Andy looked past her to the couch in the corner, the double bed across from it, the concrete walls, the green steel door, and the yellow light from a single, old-fashioned bulb swaying from the ceiling. The pitcher of water standing on a dinner table, set for two.

Cozy. Prison in a velvet glove.

She licked over her dry lips. "I'll tell you as soon as I've had something to drink."

❖

Andy emptied the glass and poured another. She held the water pitcher up in the air. “Do you want some?”

“No.” Isabelle remained rooted to the spot, hands on her hips.

“Do you know where we are?” she asked Isabelle.

“No. I was taken in New York. That’s all I know.”

Shit. “I was in London.”

“London? I can’t be in London. I have a finite math paper due in…I don’t actually know what day it is.”

Isabelle sat in one of the two chairs at the table and hid her face in her hands. Andy expected tears when she looked up, but there was nothing, only bright eyes and the thin line of a normally full mouth refusing to give in to helplessness. She sat across from Isabelle, reached out, and touched her arm where the long-sleeved cardigan protected her skin. She let go instantly as Isabelle’s gaze swept her away. Her eyes were burning like a forest on fire, angry and determined.

Andy turned toward the mirror. “I hate you,” she called.

Again, the rap of knuckles against the two-way mirror.

“Who are you talking to?” asked Isabelle.

“The people behind the mirror.”

“Who are they? Who are you? Not your name. Who are you?”

Andy didn’t answer. She stood and strode to the mirror. “I’m not doing this.”

Silence.

“No way,” she said again.

A speaker crackled from the roof above her. “Then you’ll stay there, both of you, until you do,” said her mother.

CHAPTER EIGHT

Isabelle knew the probability that she would escape from this room was infinitesimally small. They were in a locked room being watched 24/7, it seemed. The arrival of the other woman, Andy, had momentarily given her some hope, but that had since evaporated.

It had been three hours since Andy had been dragged in here. It was clear she knew who'd taken them, but she wasn't prepared to share that knowledge. In fact, the stubborn woman said nothing as she sat in the corner, head tilted back against the concrete, eyes closed.

Isabelle stood and walked toward the bed.

Andy shot to her feet. "No. Don't sleep."

"What? Why?"

Andy looked around her, fixing her eyes on the dinner table. "Let's eat instead. You must be hungry. I'm hungry."

"Eat what?"

Andy looked toward the mirror, her hands in a silent question.

Five minutes later, a different voice than before crackled over the speaker. Still female, it was lower and rounder, younger. "Stand against the opposite wall."

Andy motioned Isabelle to step clear of the door.

"Hands in the air, fingers locked above your head," the voice said.

They both complied.

Ten minutes later, the door opened and a chestnut-haired woman in an elegant red dress walked in. She placed a tray on the table, then nodded in Andy's direction.

"Andy. Hi. You okay?"

"Claire. Tell her I'm going to kill her."

"Tsk, tsk," said the intercom voice.

"What's going on?" Isabelle demanded, anger bubbling up inside. "Why am I here?"

"Ask Andy," said the voice.

The woman—Claire—walked out and the door slammed shut.

Andy sat at the table and motioned for Isabelle to do the same.

Isabelle's stomach rumbled. She couldn't remember when last she'd eaten. She sat down. There was one tea, one espresso, two cups of tomato soup, and two roast beef sandwiches on the tray.

Andy handed a sandwich to Isabelle. "Whole wheat is for me. That means rye is for you."

Isabelle looked at the paper covering the sandwich. "Jamie's Deli is in New York."

Andy nodded, somewhat despondently. "Good to know."

Isabelle reached for the espresso.

Andy stopped her, her hand over Isabelle's. "The tea is for you."

Isabelle looked at the hand on top of hers. She felt a pull inside her to a place she didn't know existed, a time beyond this one. Her breath quickened involuntarily.

Andy pulled her hand away as if it was on fire. "Sorry. But coffee is bad for you."

Isabelle swallowed, her mouth dry. "I love coffee."

"You shouldn't drink coffee. It makes the dreaming…Fuck it. Please just take the tea."

Isabelle wanted to argue, but then took the cup and tasted the light brown liquid. She pulled a face. "What is this?"

Andy drained the coffee in one gulp. "No doubt something with no caffeine."

Isabelle licked her lips as if she wanted to wash the taste from her mouth. "It's awful."

Andy opened the tomato soup and dipped into it with a plastic spoon. "You like tomatoes, though."

"Yes. How did you know?"

Andy opened the sandwich and studied it. "And red meat?" She frowned. "Rare."

"I try not to eat meat, but yes. I get these cravings. Why?"

What the hell is this place? And who was this woman? The man and two women who'd grabbed her on the way to NYU had told her not be scared. In fact, they'd been almost reverent in the way they spoke to her, handled her. Then the man injected her with a clear fluid. When she'd opened her eyes again, she was inside this concrete room with its green steel door and green ceiling, as if meant to calm psychiatric patients.

She opened the soup and started eating. Delicious. As she cleaned out the bowl she surreptitiously looked at Andy. She wasn't what people would call beautiful, but definitely handsome. Lean, muscled body with broad shoulders and big hands. Strong, angular jaw, dark eyes, prominent nose. A wide mouth that she somehow knew produced a magnetic crooked grin that promised "trust me." Not that she smiled much. The lines around her eyes said she was more prone to frowning.

She could do with a haircut, the black wavy hair was a bit messy, especially around her eyes. There was a small scar under her right eye. Every time she was angry—and she'd been angry ever since she'd been here—she'd touch it, as if it reminded her of something that had happened a long time ago.

Isabelle realized Andy had caught her in the act. She blushed slightly and looked to her feet. She'd always hated it that her face betrayed her like this.

"Sorry." She put the sandwich down.

A smile, barely noticeable, played around Andy's lips. "No, please. It's okay. I'd also worry that I'm locked up with a mass murderer."

Isabelle liked the smile. It softened Andy's face, ratcheting the anger down to something more palatable. "Well, are you?"

"A mass murderer? How many people do you need to kill to be one?"

Isabelle frowned.

"It's a joke. Well, half a joke." Andy pushed the soup in Isabelle's direction. "Have mine too."

"Thanks."

Andy wiped her hands with a napkin, then poured water from the pitcher for both of them. "What else do you like?"

Isabelle chewed, swallowed. "Food-wise?"

"Yes."

"Strawberries."

"Just like that? Nothing else thrown in there?"

How did Andy know to ask that? Isabelle blushed again slightly and pointed at the sandwich in her hand. "I like to make a sandwich with mushed up strawberries, beef, and tomatoes."

"Ah." Andy nodded. "Could have been worse. At least it's not anchovies."

Isabelle managed a smile, then said softly, "How do you know so much about me? Who are you? Why am I here? Please tell me."

Andy's mouth regained its hardness. She pushed her chair back from the table and stood.

"Please don't make me beg. I'm also…I also don't want to be here." Isabelle also stood. "Please tell me what you know."

The world around her tilted suddenly, her head swimming, her eyes unfocused. What was happening? Was she that tired? No. This was all wrong…

"Isabelle?"

Andy shot around the table, catching her just as she sank to the ground.

CHAPTER NINE

The dream was different from the ones before. It was more vivid, saturated with color.

She was in front of a closed door. Number 45, it said in elegant copper numbers. She tried the door. It swung open. The apartment was big, with hardwood floors, deep red walls, high, white ceilings, and beautiful original, colorful art against the walls. The art was from all over the world. West Africa, Australia, South America.

She gave one hesitant step into the airy space. Another.

Something was wrong. Something was…

The metallic smell was familiar. It was blood. Fresh blood. She wanted to turn around and run away, but her feet refused to obey. She kept going, down the hall and into the living room.

The body was on the floor, lying in a steadily growing pool of blood. It was clear the woman had tried to run to the window—probably to the fire escape—but died before she could reach it.

Isabelle didn't know the woman, but she sat next to her and held her hand as the day faded, murmuring assurances and saying a prayer for a life lost.

❖

The rage was blinding. It boiled inside her like lava. Andy smashed her fist into the mirror with little success. She picked up one of the chairs and threw it at the glass where it simply bounced off the surface.

"What did you put in the soup?" she yelled.

Silence.

"Cowards," she shouted.

The intercom finally sprang to life. "You know what you have to do. You are the only one she has now."

"Has? She doesn't have me. You don't *have* me."

"There are some things you cannot walk away from. Some things you were born to do. To be. It's no use trying to be someone else."

Her mother's voice was soft and soothing as if Andy was six years old.

"I cannot do this again," Andy said. "You know that. You *know* that."

"We've all lost people we've loved."

"You've never loved anyone in your life."

"Andy. That's not true. I lo—"

"Don't. No one believes you."

"Then do it for Isabelle. She has no idea what's happening to her. Help her find her purpose."

"Purpose?" Andy scoffed. "That's such an overused word. And why? So you can ruin her life too?"

"No. So that she can save someone else's life. If she knew the truth, Isabelle Templeton would tell you that your little equation on this, us—me—is all wrong, I can promise you that."

CHAPTER TEN

It was clear Isabelle was dreaming. She was thrashing on the bed, fighting her way toward consciousness.

Andy didn't know what it felt like to wake from dreaming. From what she'd been told it was like wading through black mud, struggling to breathe while the thick liquid seeped into your ears, mouth, and nose.

From what she'd observed, slipping into the dream was easy, living through it okay, but getting out was like escaping from a prison that did everything to keep you there.

She'd hoped Isabelle wouldn't dream when she'd put her in bed. But now she was.

Fuck it.

Andy sat on the floor in the corner, glaring at the mirror on the opposite wall.

The intercom crackled. "Help her."

It was her mother.

"You come and help her," Andy said, crooking her finger to invite her mother into the room. "You put her here."

Silence.

Isabelle screamed.

Andy closed her eyes.

"Help her. Dammit, Andy!" her mother shouted.

The scream became gargled, as if Isabelle was choking.

Andy swore, stood up, and rushed to the bed. She slipped in behind Isabelle, catching her arms by the wrists, crossing them over her breasts and holding her tight.

"Shh," she whispered. "Breathe, just breathe. Take a deep breath and come back."

Isabelle's body stiffened at the invasion, then fought hers. Andy tightened her grip, anchoring her legs around Isabelle's feet. She held on as Isabelle bucked, shouted something, and then finally calmed down.

"There you go. Come back. Come back."

She listened to Isabelle's breathing as she relaxed in her arms, the feverish heat seeping into Andy's skin. She smoothed the white dress down around Isabelle's legs.

Isabelle was a natural, snug fit against her own body.

"It's okay to come back," Andy whispered. "It's okay. You can let go and come back."

Isabelle's breathing slowed, becoming deeper. Then she drew one single sharp breath and Andy knew she was awake.

Her eyes remained closed.

"Are you nauseous?"

Isabelle managed a single word. "Yes."

"What if you open your eyes?"

"Rather not." Her voice was like gravel.

Andy looked at the two-way mirror, realizing she'd lost the battle. "Let me out so that I can help her."

Claire waited outside for her, Taser in hand. Her mother was nowhere to be seen.

"Don't worry, I'm not going to run."

"We'll see about that." Claire pointed to somewhere behind Andy. "Kitchen's that way."

❖

The arms holding her had been nice. She missed their strong, comforting presence. Same for the calm, steady voice that had lured her back from the thick sludge that had threatened to drown her. That had made her claw her way back to this room with its green door and double bed.

Isabelle lay perfectly still, eyes closed, world reeling, her stomach in uproar, until a wonderful smell stirred her senses.

"Can you sit up and take a sip?"

It was Andy.

"I'll try."

She didn't know why, but she trusted her. She struggled upright, the sheets tangled around her legs.

"Take it easy. Slowly." The voice was gentle, concerned.

She sipped the thick, lukewarm liquid that hit her stomach like a bolt of medicine. She sighed in satisfaction, opening her eyes. The world eddied, then settled, much sooner than was usually the case.

"Oh, this is so good. What is it?" Isabelle reached for the glass in Andy's hand.

More. She wanted more.

Andy stood back so that she couldn't reach. "Can you try to get up?"

Isabelle looked at the glass, the gray, muddy liquid swirled with red. She frowned. "What is that?"

Andy smiled, her eyes traveling from Isabelle's face to her body as if she were making sure she was okay. Isabelle smoothed down her dress, pushed up around her hips, blushing. She didn't want to think why this woman made every nerve stand on end.

She swung her bare feet over the bed.

Andy edged closer. "Here, put them on my boots."

Isabelle looked at her as if she didn't understand.

Andy shrugged. "Don't ask me why. Sometimes it helps."

"We've got…" Isabelle struggled to get the words past her lips. "We've got to talk about you and all of this. Seriously."

"I know."

She placed her bare feet on Andy's shoes. She felt anchored as Andy handed her the glass, her proximity providing the comfort her body craved. She reached for Andy's hips, but stopped before she touched the black jeans.

She wanted more. She wanted the heat of Andy's skin. She wanted…

Blood rushed to her face again.

"Delicious," she said, looking at her feet on the worn combat boots. "What is it?"

"Raw beef, strawberries, and tomatoes in a blender. I added some thyme. I find it helps to take the edge off."

"Uggh."

A soft smile, a cocked eyebrow. "Be glad you didn't have to make it."

"I am. I like the thyme."

"Thanks. Can you get up?" Andy asked again.

Isabelle moved closer to the edge of the bed and shifted her feet to the concrete floor. "I think so."

It was amazing how much better she felt after the previous times she'd dreamed. Better yet was the realization that Andy knew and understood what had happened. In fact, it almost felt as if she respected the dream.

Her.

"How do you… Do you know about the dreams?" she asked as she stood up from the bed, her body flush against Andy's, still slightly off balance.

"We'll talk about that in a minute. First we have to get you out of here."

"They'll never let us out."

"Oh, I think they will."

"How do you know that?"

Andy sighed. The sound reverberated through her tall body. Isabelle had the urge to drop her head on Andy's shoulder, to taste her skin, to bite into her shoulder as she moved against…

She fell back down on the bed again, fighting the need that felt so primitive and raw. Ancient. She rolled her eyes at her own thoughts. *Right.*

Andy crouched next to her. "Are you okay?" Her voice was low, concerned.

The steel door that trapped them in the concrete room opened. An older, tall woman, bearing a striking resemblance to Andy, walked in. She crossed her arms over a tight blue top, a multitude of golden bracelets dangling from her arms. She smiled, and for a moment Isabelle could see what it would look like if Andy really smiled—broad, reassuring, begging you to trust her completely and without question.

But she didn't trust the smile. Not on this woman. She wore it callously.

Isabelle struggled to her feet, resting her hand on Andy's arm to keep her balance. Andy waited until she was steady, then turned to the older woman. "I'll take her through this dream, but then I'm leaving."

"All of it. Start to finish?" asked the older woman. Her eyes were as black as night as they weighed Andy, Isabelle.

"Yes."

"Okay." She stepped toward Isabelle, reaching out to shake her hand. "My name is Kate. I'm sorry about all of this, but I really had no other choice."

Isabelle recognized the older voice from the intercom. She unmoored from Andy, pulled back her fist, and smashed it into Kate's face.

CHAPTER ELEVEN

Bloody hell," muttered Claire as she dabbed the wet towel against Kate's face.

Isabelle was asleep somewhere, exhausted from her ordeal over the last few days. She shouldn't dream again until later. Whether that was tonight or a few nights from now, nobody knew.

"You could have stopped her," Claire admonished Andy.

"Why?" Andy shot back. "Kate deserved it. She grabbed Isabelle without even trying to explain why. Took me from London without my consent. I'm just as pissed off." Her anger mounted with every word. "We're talking abduction here. A federal crime. And what she's going to do now is even worse. She's going to force someone—a complete rookie at this—to put themselves in danger for the sake of some murky, outdated ideal."

Kate batted the towel away and touched her nose gingerly. "Stop talking like I'm not in the room." She stared at Andy. "It's not a murky, outdated ideal. Your lack of faith doesn't make it any less real than it was thousands of years ago."

"Spare me the politics. It's like everything in this world. It starts out all nice and idealistic, but in the end, it's all about power and money. Surprise, surprise."

"How could you even say—"

Kate placed her hand on top of Claire's, stopping her midsentence.

Kate shook her head. "You don't have to believe. I can live with that. But you do have to keep Isabelle Templeton safe." She looked Andy up and down. "You're a bit softer than you used to be. Won't hurt you both to get some training." She gently patted her nose again. "Woman's got a mule kick in that left hook."

"I know." Andy sounded pleased and she knew it.

She still couldn't believe that Kate would bring her here against her will, especially after everything that happened.

Kate inspected her face in the mirror. Andy looked out the window. At least she finally knew exactly where she was. A nondescript five-story building in Brooklyn, one of the many buildings that belonged to Ma Soeur. My Sister. A registered nonprofit organization with offices in thirty-three countries dedicated to uplifting women.

Kate swung around on her black, red-soled heels. Christian Louboutin's. She always liked the expensive stuff. Andy looked down at her own boots and ripped jeans, surprised at the skin showing through the material. Sure didn't start out that way. She must have fought like crazy on the way here.

She couldn't remember anything though beyond the Taser in the Black Sheep.

Kate turned from the sink. "You and Isabelle can take the unit in the southwest corner," she said. "Third floor."

"Two units." Andy wasn't sharing a bed with a dreamer ever again. Besides, there was no way she would ever force herself into Isabelle Templeton's life. The woman deserved better.

"Nice try, but no. You said you'd look after her. You share a room like the rest of the teams. I don't want her disappearing on us."

"What if she doesn't want to play your little game? You can't force her to become part of Ma Soeur."

"Then you better welcome her to the family. Warm her up a bit. Or can't you seduce a woman anymore? She's beautiful, smart. Would it be such a misery to sleep with her?"

Andy gritted her teeth. "You can't keep her here against her will."

"Maybe she'd want to stay after we explained to her who we are. What she is. What she is capable of doing. Ever considered that? Moving from wondering what the hell is going on to a sense of magnificent purpose? Using your gift for the greater good?"

Andy squared her shoulders. "The problem comes in when you interpret this so-called greater good for something that suits your own little power plays."

"Despite what you may think of me, I don't play games. If we don't even out the world's power structures, if we don't create a far better balance between men and women in power, then we are going to be extinct as a species within a few generations. In fact, it won't be more than two generations. If someone presses that little red button, we're all screwed and you know it."

Andy had heard this a thousand times before. It was the justification for everything that went wrong in her mother's world. "Say you."

"Say thousands of years of Ma Soeur. The ancient texts. The prophecies. We serve a purpose. We strive for balance. We—"

"Spare me the detail."

"What happened to you—"

"Stop it." Claire shook her head at both of them. "There's no time for this. Isabelle had a dream and we need to know what that dream was. We're only guessing that she can dream four days in advance. We're not certain. Maybe today's dream happens within the next twenty-four hours, like we're used to."

Kate contemplated her words. She looked from Claire to Andy. "You're right. Let's get going. We can talk to her in the comm center."

Andy shook her head in disbelief. "No way. If I'm doing this I'm talking to her privately in our…in the room. Whatever. Just Isabelle and me. That's it. No watching, no controlling. She needs a safe space and she needs someone to trust. Give her a key to the door and give us some peace. She's twenty. That's very young."

"You started when you were sixteen."

"I was raised to do this. She's a novice with no idea what she's about to get into. How on earth did you miss her? How did the network not pick her up at school already?"

"I don't know." Kate seemed angry at the oversight. "She was a foster kid. That's all we know. Believe me. I also want to find out where the hell she comes from."

Next to Kate, Claire stirred impatiently. "Can we please stop arguing now? We're wasting time." She looked at Andy. "We can put her in the unit alone with you, and with a key to the room, but with no access through the front and back doors. What if she escaped?"

"I'm sure you've got the building on lockdown," said Andy.

"Yes. But you know this place like the back of your hand. You know exactly how to get out of here."

"I said I'll do this. Don't you trust me?"

"I trust you about as much as you trust us," Claire said.

"Then think of us as enemies working toward the same goal—for me to get out of here as soon as possible and for Isabelle to decide, for herself, what she wants to do with the rest of her life."

"Stop it, you two." Kate held the bridge of her nose between her fingers, as if attempting to calm the pain. "I'm trying to think."

"There's nothing to think about," Andy retorted. "You'll afford Isabelle Templeton the same courtesy you give the other dreamers. The same level of safety. The same protection. The same privacy. Otherwise I'm out of here." She looked from Claire to Kate. "And there will be no cameras and no microphones in the unit. Ever."

Kate mulled it over for a few long seconds.

"Okay," she agreed. "But you better tell us everything about this dream, and fast. You have two hours and then I want to see both of you in the comm center so we can work through the dream."

As Kate and Claire turned to leave the bathroom, Andy called Kate back.

"How did you find Isabelle? You never said."

"Interested?"

"Just answer the question."

"We keep tabs on psychiatrists who specialize in dreaming and hypnosis. She went to see one once, three months ago. She said she wondered whether she could dream the future. He didn't believe her. We did."

CHAPTER TWELVE

Isabelle woke in a room that felt strangely familiar. She turned and snuggled deeper into the bedding, then sat up, ignoring the steady beat of a headache behind her eyes. She was in a strange room, but the duvet was her own. Next to the bed, under a lamp, a few of her books rested in a neat pile.

She sat up. More were stacked in a long bookcase that ran across the length of the wall above the bed. Some of them were hers, others not. Whoever they belonged to loved history, jazz, and philosophy.

She glanced around. She was in a big room with a bay window, the blinds drawn against the outside world. In the dim light she could see there was a closet on her left and, at the end of the bed, a comfortable leather couch. And was that a TV and small kitchen on the other side of the room? Yes. The kitchen even had a breakfast nook that could seat three people. A laptop sat on the granite counter, the screen black.

The apartment's colors were earthy, browns and deep reds, designed to calm.

She looked around again and quickly found what she'd been looking for—a door leading to what must be the bathroom. She looked through the closet. Her clothes hung next to a stranger's clothes. A woman's clothes. Jeans, a few neat shirts, functional underwear, T-shirts, shorts, and running shoes.

She leaned in and smelled the nearest black cotton shirt. It was familiar, comforting. Cedarwood and lemon. The woman from the concrete room with the green door. Andy.

She fingered the soft material and waited for the door to open, smiling at the memory.

Behind her the door creaked. She swung around.

Andy stood in the doorway. "You're up," she stated the obvious.

Isabelle closed the closet door, walked to the window, and pushed two fingers through the blinds. The window overlooked a park dressed in the muted shades of winter. People wrapped in coats and scarfs hurried by on the sidewalk below. She guessed they were on the third or fourth floor of a building somewhere in New York. The skyline visible through the buildings looked familiar. Manhattan was to the northeast, at quite a distance. She would guess that she was in Brooklyn somewhere.

She turned back to Andy. "I was looking around." She pointed to the closet, the bed. "My stuff is in there. And that's my duvet." She took a big breath and again asked the questions that had been burning inside her for days. "Who are you? And your mother? These people? This place?"

She tried to remain calm. If she wanted to survive this place she would have to keep her wits about her.

Andy looked at her watch. "I need to shower and you probably should too."

"I think you owe me some answers first. And I have to call some people. I need to tell them that I'm safe." Isabelle's hands stopped midflight. She locked them in front of her, suddenly aware that she was dressed in her pajamas, which were nothing more than skimpy shorts and a T-shirt. She had no recollection of changing.

"*Am* I safe?" she asked.

Andy held up her hands. "You are. One hundred percent. And I promise to keep you as safe as I possibly can."

"That's a pretty vague promise."

"It's the only one I can offer you right now. But I'll do my utmost to keep it."

Isabelle held her breath. "No promise that I can go home then?"

"No."

"Why not?"

"Let's get cleaned up and then I'll explain everything as best I can."

❖

They sat on the couch. Andy had turned it to face the window, as if she needed a horizon to look at. Her hair was wet, slicked back from her face. Despite the shower she looked tired, her face drawn.

"We don't have a lot of time, so forgive me for providing you with only the highlights." Andy glanced at her watch. "If we don't do this quickly, someone else will come in here and talk to you and I don't want that to happen."

Isabelle pulled her legs to her chin. She wore jeans and a white T-shirt, her feet bare and her skin on fire from the hot shower she'd taken. She smiled nervously. "Better hurry up then."

She liked Andy, perhaps even trusted her—at least, more than she trusted anyone else in this place.

"Ma Soeur means My Sister," said Andy. "The organization is thousands of years old. Joan of Arc was a part of it. Victoria. Elizabeth I. The head office is here, in Brooklyn. A nice, five-story stucco building. It manages to look like a nonprofit because it really is one. Digging wells in India, campaigning against female circumcision, making small, interest-free loans to women-owned businesses, you name it. Ma Soeur is basically a group of women all over the world trying to push the female agenda. We…they also try to boost women into power positions in order to create balance. The belief is that more women in power would mean fewer wars, less violence, and greater ecological awareness. In short, it would ensure the prosperity and survival of the human race."

Isabelle digested the thought. Decided to ignore the "we" that had become "they." "Okay. Sounds feasible, I suppose."

"The organization has been struggling the last few years. The advent of technology has meant that physical power plays less of a role in daily life. Things have started to change for the better. These days women can do a lot of what used to be male jobs. You don't need to plow with oxen anymore, you have tractors. Anyone can drive a truck because of power steering. Anyone can use a gun. Fly a drone. Write code. You get my drift."

Isabelle nodded.

Andy continued. "However, this technological advance—something Ma Soeur has been pushing for generations—has also meant that the frequency of dreamers has lessened quite dramatically. Nobody knows why."

"Dreamers?"

Andy looked at her pointedly.

"What?"

"People like you."

"People like…like me?" Isabelle turned on the couch to face her, sitting cross-legged. She stared at Andy, who was dressed in a black T-shirt and black jeans fraying over her bare feet.

"Yes. Ma Soeur operates in two-person teams. One is a dreamer and the other is what we call a keeper. One dreams, like you, what will happen in the near future, and the keeper guards the dreamer, and then tries to prevent the event in the dream from happening. The dreams are often about episodes of violence, when somebody's soul departs the body, or when they are badly injured. Nobody knows how it works, or why the ability was given to certain people."

"Wait, back up a bit. Violence?"

"Yes." Andy seemed hesitant to continue.

"Explain, please."

"Often it is a murder. Or murders. Or an accidental death or deaths. Things like that. So, the team would work to identify and locate the person in the dream and save their life."

"How would they—you, we, whatever—do that?"

"There are various options available to the team. Depending on the threat you can take the person concerned to a different location or you can find the intended killer." Andy shrugged. "Mostly the team, and here I actually mean the keeper, are able to step in just in time to stop it from happening. The problem is to do that without showing ourselves. No one is to know about our existence."

Isabelle shook her head, then turned away from Andy again. She leaned forward, arms crossed over her stomach. The headache from earlier had returned to hammer against her temples in a persistent, angry beat.

"Dream the future?" she whispered. Was she stuck in some twilight zone? An alternative reality?

"Yes." Andy's voice was gentle. "What happens to you…you are dreaming the future. I know it sounds preposterous, but it's not. It's real and I can only imagine how scary it is."

Isabelle blinked through the sudden tears. Andy reached out and rubbed her back in a smoothing, circular motion.

So, this was what it was all about? This? The dreaming? Could it be?

Isabelle sat back on the couch, pushing her hair out of her face. "So…" She swallowed, then exhaled slowly. "So, I'm not mad? This is…the dreams are not…they are real? Will be real?"

"Yes."

Isabelle stared at her for two, three minutes, then a new realization dawned on her. "It's horrible. To dream about death all the time."

"Yes. It takes someone awfully strong to manage it. And the intensity…That's why you lose your balance when it happens. Why your body retreats into itself when the dream is over. It is also part of the keeper's job to watch over you while you dream. To bring you back safely."

"And that's you?"

"Yes."

"One dreamer, one keeper?"

"Yes."

Isabelle considered Andy's story. Prevent the dream's events. "Which is the more dangerous job? Being a keeper, or dreamer?"

Andy smiled wanly. "I won't lie to you. A lot of keepers have died over the years. And two or three dreamers. What also happens, however, is that some dreamers have…"

Her words dried up. She looked out the window and crossed her arms over the T-shirt, her biceps becoming tight and angry. Long, strong muscles stirred in her forearms as she closed her hands into fists and opened them again.

Isabelle put her hand on Andy's arm. She needed an answer, for herself, her own sanity.

Andy relaxed her arms, her jaw. She rested her hands on her thighs. "It differs from person to person. Some dreamers go on until they die of old age. The dreaming does get less frequent the older they become, even if not less intense necessarily. Other dreamers seem to retreat inside their minds as they grow older, almost as if they've seen enough."

"Madness." Isabelle could believe that. Could understand it. How many times had she been right there, at the edge, wondering if she should jump in?

"Perhaps. Or maybe there is peace and safety in solitude." Andy sounded wistful, sad.

Isabelle squeezed her hand. Andy looked at her watch. Isabelle ignored the unspoken signal to hurry up.

"You said two-person team. Not women. I've only seen women around here," she added.

"There are men. Quite a lot actually. A lot of men share Ma Soeur's vision. There are male dreamers, female dreamers. Same goes for the keepers. And the combination differs. Two men, mixed, two women." Andy looked her in the eye. "Do you prefer a male keeper? Just because my mother forced me on you, doesn't mean you have to accept it."

Isabelle didn't answer. Instead she asked, "What I don't understand is why your mother locked you in that room with me. You made it sound like she abducted you too. Why would she need to do that?" A realization hit her. "Was it all a ploy for me to trust you?" She inched away from Andy.

"No, not at all. I can promise you that," Andy said quickly. "I walked away from Ma Soeur three years ago. Things happened."

"So why bring you back?"

"Kate came to London asking me to return to Ma Soeur to become your keeper. I wasn't quite as willing as she hoped I'd be. She wanted someone with experience and no one else was available. It takes a certain amount of training to look after a dreamer, especially a new dreamer. A certain understanding. It also requires a certain skill set to prevent a dream from happening." She looked Isabelle square in the eye. "I'm not here to deceive you. I can promise you that. I'm simply here to keep you safe and to see what we can do about this dream you had earlier."

Isabelle decided to believe her, to believe what she had witnessed with her own eyes. Felt inside.

She smiled faintly. "Okay. Then the answer is no. I don't want another keeper. Not at all."

"Are you sure? It is a pretty intimate arrangement at times. If you are uncomfortable with me, it is best we get you a male keeper."

"Why? Do dreamers and keepers sleep together?" Isabelle pointed at the bed, the closet. "I noticed that both of us will be staying here."

Andy cleared her throat. "It's believed that sex can enhance the dreaming and rush the repair process when you wake, but that's not always the case."

Isabelle stared at the bed, a jumble of images in her mind. The most prominent was one where she was screaming with pleasure as she came, Andy inside her, on top of her. She crossed her arms over her breasts where she knew her thoughts had become visible.

"I'm not interested in you. I mean in sex. With you," Andy said quickly. "I'll sleep on the couch. I'm only here to guide you through this one dream, as a…call it a favor…and then I'm leaving. Think of me as a personal trainer. My job is to get you into shape and then you can decide whether you want to stay or not."

Isabelle frowned. That didn't sound right. And it was not what she'd expected. "So you want to hand me off to someone else when…?"

"When we've analyzed the dream you had earlier and decided what to do about it."

"Oh. Okay."

Isabelle felt disappointed. Probably looked it too as Andy scrambled to say, "This relationship should be your choice. You should choose your keeper. It shouldn't ever be this contrived." She took a deep breath, as if trying to calm herself. "That's if you want to stay. If you want to leave right now, I'll help you get away."

Andy shook her head, seemingly frustrated with her inability to find the right words.

"If?" Isabelle asked. "Do you mean your mother will let me go if I want to leave right now?"

"Maybe. Maybe not. But I'll help you anyway. What she did…she shouldn't have taken you like that. She's one of the many reasons I left Ma Soeur in the first place."

Isabelle remembered what had happened earlier, in the concrete room, the conversation between Andy and her mother over the intercom. "Why do you hate her so much?"

Andy glanced at her watch again. "That will have to be a story for another time. I have negotiated a two-hour window for us to talk through your dream. If we don't show some results soon we'll have to go to the comm center and do this in front of a bunch of people who are going to gawk at you like you're crazy."

"Why? In here I'm normal, right?"

"Not quite. Normal dreamers can only see about twenty-four hours into the future. I hear you can see four days, from the little Ma Soeur knows about you. They've not seen such a powerful dreamer since the 1400s."

CHAPTER THIRTEEN

"Tell me about the apartment in your dream." Andy's voice was calm and relaxed.

"It's a normal apartment. Big. I'd guess someone with money lives there. Everything seems high-end." Isabelle's eyes were closed. She was lying on the couch. Andy sat on the floor with a pen and notepad, the laptop from the breakfast nook open next to her.

"Is there a number on the door?" she asked.

"Yes. Forty-five."

"Great."

Isabelle could hear pen scribbling on paper.

"Is there something on the door? Blood? Is the lock broken? Tell me what you see."

Isabelle's eyes flew open. "How many times have you done this before?"

Andy didn't meet her gaze. "I know what I'm doing, if that's what you're asking."

"It's not. It's more that you seem sad. Yes. Sad. I think that's the word."

"Nope. Not sad." Andy smiled and pointed at her watch. "We have forty-three minutes. Better get going. Close your eyes."

Isabelle obliged.

"Is the lock—"

"No," Isabelle said. "The lock is not broken and there is no blood on the door."

"But the door is not locked."

"No." More scribbling on paper.

"Describe what you do next in the dream."

"I go inside the apartment. I walk down a short hallway."

"Wait. What do you see once you are inside? Is it light or dark outside? Are the curtains drawn? Is it day or night?"

"Wow. You think of everything."

"Focus, Isabelle. We're trying to save a woman's life here."

Andy regretted the words as soon as she'd said them. Less than twenty-four hours and she was already sucked back into a world she'd sworn she'd left behind.

"Sorry. I didn't mean to snap."

It was the responsibility Ma Soeur dumped on you that got you in the end. That ate you alive. The massive weight of someone else's life in your hands.

The guilt when you failed. She hoped Isabelle would be spared that, at least for this dream.

Isabelle reached out her hand. "It's okay."

Andy tapped her fingers with the pen in a silent admonishment. "Close your eyes. Concentrate."

Isabelle obliged.

"Tell me the time of day."

A moment's silence. "There is low, unnatural light through the window. Evening. I think. Wait. The clock in the kitchen says it's 2:59 p.m. But it's dark outside. Strange."

"You can read the time? Good. That's very good. Can you also see what day it is? Perhaps it's also visible on the clock? Or what about a nearby phone? Or a calendar or newspaper?"

"Hmm," said Isabelle, pleased with herself. "There is a calendar against the fridge. All the days are marked off as if someone was counting down to something. The last day crossed out is the twenty-first of November. So maybe it's the twenty-second?"

"What's the season?"

"Must be winter. It's snowing. Rather heavily. That's why it's so dark outside. And the heat is on inside the apartment."

"Okay. Look around you. How many people live in the apartment?"

"How would I know that?"

"Dishes, glasses. Clothes. Shoes on the floor. Photos."

"No photos."

"Nothing?"

"No," Isabelle said. "But there are two wine glasses on a round dining room table. One with lipstick."

"That's good."

"The wine is French. Looks expensive."

"Food?"

"Two empty dishes next to the sink."

"Did somebody cook or was it a delivery?"

"Looks like it was a delivery. There are no dishes anywhere, unless someone cleared it before the other person came."

"Looking at everything as you stand there now, do you think it was a romantic encounter?" asked Andy.

"Hmm," Isabelle considered. "I don't know. Impossible to tell. I can't see any candles or anything."

"Is the victim dressed?"

A moment's silence. "She seems fully clothed."

"Expensive clothes?"

"Yes."

"And the apartment is upmarket?"

"Yes," Isabelle said. "The place is huge. And it's got leather couches, a big fridge, and a crazy expensive Mac laptop on the coffee table. You can see it from the hallway."

"Let's go to the window in front of you. What do you see?"

"What do you mean, what do I see?"

"Buildings. Landmarks. Things like that. Are you in New York? Paris? London? On what floor are you if you were to guess?"

Isabelle was silent for a while.

"I think I'm in New York. Yes. I can see…it's dark, but I'm sure I can see the Metropolitan Museum of Art through the snow. "

"Great. Fantastic."

"And I think I'm rather high up. I'm looking down on the museum. Maybe the fifth or sixth floor? Wouldn't forty-five mean we're on the fourth floor?"

"Not necessarily. Are there any other buildings in your line of sight?"

"Not that I can see. Only the museum right in front of me."

Andy jotted down the info. "You're doing fantastic, Isabelle."

She nodded.

"Are you ready to look at the crime scene now?" Andy asked. "At the woman?"

Isabelle bit her bottom lip. Andy reached out and squeezed her hand.

"This is the most difficult part. If you want to take a few moments first we can do so."

Isabelle shook her head. "No. I can do it. And as you say, we don't know how much time we have."

Andy nodded. "Okay. Describe the woman to me."

"She's next to the coffee table. She's in her forties, I think. Really beautiful. Long thick, curly blond hair. But it's all tousled around her head. Scrunched up. And her face is surprised, shocked. Blue eyes, I think. Light blue. There is a pool of blood under her. It looks…" Isabelle swallowed audibly. "It looks as if she was shot in the back, as if she was running away. I count three gunshot wounds. They're so tiny…"

Again, Andy squeezed her hand, but this time she didn't let go. "Try to remember that she's still alive. This is just a dream. A projection. It hasn't happened yet."

Isabelle nodded mutely.

"Is there anything around the woman? In her hand?"

"No."

"Near her?"

"There's an access card on the couch. It says…Lily? Can't see the surname. The company…no. It's a consulate. The Norwegian consulate."

Andy wrote down everything Isabelle had said. "You mentioned a laptop on the coffee table? Is the laptop open?"

"No."

"Is there a handbag nearby?"

Isabelle was quiet as she mentally darted through the room. "Yes. Next to the couch. On the floor. Fancy. Louis Vuitton."

"Can you see anything inside?"

"No."

"Anything else in your line of sight?"

"No." Isabelle sighed in frustration. "But maybe I'm just not remembering. Maybe there is more and I'm too stupid to see it."

"You're planning a master's degree in artificial intelligence and mathematical forecasting. You're anything but stupid."

Isabelle's eyes flew open. "How do you know that?"

"It was in your file."

"My file. The one Kate compiled?"

"Her minions, more likely."

"So, she's the big boss?"

"Yep, so she keeps on telling me."

"And she's your mother?"

Andy smiled. "Again, that's what she says."

CHAPTER FOURTEEN

"Are you sure you're okay?" Andy asked.

"I am."

They were walking to the comm center to try to locate the apartment and woman in Isabelle's dream.

Andy trudged behind Isabelle, lead in her shoes. She hadn't seen these people in ages. She'd opted to just walk away. And now she was back for round two. What price would she pay this time around? Isabelle was a rookie. To be a rookie dreamer at twenty, and powerful at that, was looking for trouble. It could get both of them killed in an instant.

She didn't think—no, she *knew* that Isabelle was unaware of the danger they would face over the next few days. But she had promised her that she would keep her safe and she was committed to doing exactly that, no matter the cost. Kate would not ruin another life, especially not one that seemed so innocent.

Isabelle came to a stop. "It will be okay, you know."

Andy nodded.

"I'm okay. I promise. I'm not scared and I'm not going to flake out on you. I want to see this through. I want to see who I am. Who you are."

Andy's stomach tightened. "Who I am? I don't know if that is such a good thing."

"Nobody is going to judge you. Least of all me."

Isabelle smiled gently and turned around before Andy could see the expression on her face. She continued down the hall and turned left to the elevators.

"Wait."

Andy's breathing hitched as the realization hit her. As Isabelle's words finally registered. The comm center was on the fifth floor. Isabelle had led them through a maze of hallways on the third floor straight to the elevators, Andy lost in thought.

And she wasn't lying about not being scared. She'd been abducted, held against her will, drugged, told outrageous stories, and she hadn't been nearly as scared as would have been expected.

Andy shot past Isabelle and came to a stop in front of her. "You've seen all of this before. You've seen me."

Isabelle stood completely still. Andy could trace the curve of her body through the white T-shirt, spot the expectant exhalation of someone caught in the act, bracing for the backlash.

Isabelle looked at her feet as she spoke. "If I'm the most powerful dreamer Ma Soeur has seen since the 1400s, do you really think I've not dreamt all of this before? That I haven't dreamt about your mother? Claire? The abduction? This moment?" She leaned in, touching Andy's arm, her fingers sliding down her hot skin, into her hand. "You?"

❖

Andy was angry and it showed. "I don't get it. Why let yourself be taken? Why end up here?"

Isabelle shook her head, then headed to the fire escape next to the twin elevators. She shouldered the door open and walked through, then stopped as the door closed behind them. The stairwell smelled faintly of water and dust. A naked lightbulb dangled above their heads, throwing grotesque, exaggerated shadows against the concrete walls.

"I was desperate for some answers. Any answers." She pointed to her head. "I had to know if the dreams meant something or if I was simply going crazy."

"So, you allowed Ma Soeur to take you?"

It was clear that Andy could not comprehend such surrender.

"Don't talk to me as if you know what it's like to be me," Isabelle snapped. "You know nothing about what it's like to live with these images in your head. Night after night. The violence. The blood. I was going mad trying to figure out what was going on. Who in their right mind keeps on dreaming about stuff like that? And then, with Horace, the dreams came closer. It was someone I knew and cared for. And then I dreamed about you and your mother and this place and I knew I could find the answers to what was happening to me here."

Isabelle lowered her voice. "I had to see if it was real or just some trick my mind was playing on me. I had to trust myself. Take a crazy, blind leap of faith." She blew out a slow breath. "It was that or some institution, and I really, really didn't want to do that."

She moved closer to Andy. She could sense the tension and the anger, the trepidation and the fear, even though Andy would never admit to those feelings.

She counted to ten in her head and placed a hand on Andy's shoulder. "I'm here because I want to be here. I'm here because everything I dreamt said I could trust you. That you are a decent, honorable person underneath everything you are feeling right now."

Andy eyes fluttered wide in surprise. She stepped back as if Isabelle's hand was burning her skin. "Did you…Have you dreamt anything else about this place? Me?"

"No," Isabelle lied.

Andy stood anchored to the floor, hands on her hips.

Strong hands. She'd always imagined that she liked strong hands.

All of this was new to her. This woman. What could happen. Would happen. She'd only dated a few times. First, there were boys, then men, and then only recently had she agreed to blind dates with women. The first one had turned out to be an awkward evening, with her date, a law major, leaving as soon as politely possible. The second and last woman she couldn't even really remember, only the uncomfortable fumbling in the back of an old pickup truck somewhere outside the city.

Isabelle had felt out of place—even more so than usual. In fact, everything about dating had felt wrong until the dream about this woman. Andrea Feraud Bouchard.

The silence lingered.

Andy rubbed her hands down the sides of her jeans, then balled them into fists. "Whatever you do, don't tell anyone about the earlier dreams. The dreams about me and Kate that got you here. It will keep you safe. What was that? Three, four days ago?"

"Seven."

"Fuck. If my mother knew that she would use it to her advantage, and that could be dangerous for you."

Isabelle nodded. "Don't worry. I won't say anything."

Andy scrubbed through her hair. "You have to be careful. Don't trust anyone, not even me. These people will make you buy into something that isn't real. Nothing can change the future. It's just backpedaling against the tide. A useless exercise in treading water until we all eventually drown anyway."

Isabelle didn't want to argue with Andy, not now. "The future is never what we want it to be. That I know. I can write you a very simple algorithm to prove that concept."

Andy smiled wryly. "I don't need an algorithm to know that." She walked the two steps to the fire escape door, then turned. "Just tell me one thing. How could you dream about me if there was no violence involved?" She hesitated. "Or was it some other type of event?"

Isabelle looked at her sneakers. Andy had said that dreamers had visions of highly emotional and traumatic events. Hers had been of herself, moving under Andy, groaning frantically as she sought release, biting into Andy's shoulder as she came.

She blushed, wiped at her chin. "It was…I can't remember exactly. I just know you were there. That's all."

Andy nodded, not convinced. "Okay. Let's go. But remember, don't tell anyone what you told me. For both our sakes."

CHAPTER FIFTEEN

The communications center at Ma Soeur housed around twenty people. Kate met Isabelle and Andy at the door, secured with handprint and iris recognition, and guided Isabelle and Andy through the maze of computers and people to one of the desks at the front.

A familiar face was sitting there, feet on the table, staring at a huge screen showing images of New York. She swiveled in her chair as she heard them approach and dumped a can of Red Bull into the trash as she jumped to her feet.

It was Jam, her neighbor. Isabelle had wondered how Kate's team had known when to grab her. Funny how her dreams had shown the Ma Soeur building, but revealed nothing about Jam.

"Jam," she said evenly. "If that's even your real name."

"Yeah, sorry about that," Jam said. "Had a job to do. Real name is Johanna, but shit if anyone's ever going to call me that." Jam ran a hand through her purple and black bangs, her head shaved on the left side.

Isabelle managed a smile.

Kate invited her and Andy to sit in a half circle of chairs behind Jam. There was almost no sign of the left hook Isabelle had delivered earlier, bar slight bruising below her eyes.

Kate turned to Andy. "Okay. Tell us what you've got. Maybe we can identify this woman before she's murdered."

The room quieted as Andy gave them the breakdown of Isabelle's dream, everyone fixated on her. Every now and then Isabelle would interrupt, adding new detail to the events and surroundings.

As Andy continued, the silence gave way to murmured disbelief.

Jam stopped typing. "You could see the woman's ID tag for the Norwegian consulate? And the museum? Through the window? All of that?"

"Yes."

"Really?"

"Jam," Andy shot angrily. "You'll show Isabelle the same respect you do any dreamer. You won't question her. She's not here because she wants to be here. She's here because Kate abducted her, so I don't want bullshit from anyone. Got it?" She turned around, glaring at the men and women at the workstations behind her.

"There's no need to be aggressive," Kate said in a soothing tone, her hand on Andy's arm. "None of these people did anything to Isabelle or you. As you said, it was my decision to bring her here, and mine alone."

Kate turned to Isabelle. "But yes, perhaps I've never apologized for my behavior. Please accept my sincerest thanks for being here. I hope you have come to understand the reason for our unorthodox behavior. Hopefully, Andy has explained everything to you?"

Isabelle wondered if Kate's words even counted as an apology. "She has. And I'm willing to see where all of this leads, *if* you keep on talking to me. No more pushing me into corners." She locked eyes with Kate. "By the way, I'm convinced I would have listened to you if you simply walked up to me and explained yourself. I was desperate enough to come here willingly."

From the corner of her eye, Isabelle caught Andy's fleeting smile.

Kate lifted an eyebrow. "Well, yes, of course," she said in a cold voice. "As I say. My apologies for that."

Jam cleared her throat. "Sorry too. It just…there's so much detail. It's rare."

"No problem," Isabelle said to Jam. "I'm equally surprised I could see everything in such detail. And remember it all."

Jam turned back to her computer. "Okay. Let's get cracking. I know Kate said you can see four days into the future, but I normally work with a few hours, a day-and-a-half max. I think it's safer if we don't make any assumptions about the time frame here and work as quickly as we can."

They waited in silence as Jam opened several windows on her computer.

Finally, after about ten minutes, she gave a satisfied grunt. "Okay. That's better. Now we're getting somewhere."

She called up a satellite map on the big screen at the front of the room. "I think I can narrow it down to the corner of Fifth Avenue and East Eighty-Second Street. The buildings here overlook the Met. It's also the same type of neo-federal townhome of the 1920s you described." She pointed to one of the roofs on the map. "The fourth floor of this building has a two-bedroom apartment registered to Arlene Hampton. She often goes by the name Lily, it seems. And her photo matches your description."

Jam pointed to one of the three computer screens in front of her. She swiped the picture on the middle one to the large screen at the front of the room. "What do you think?"

Isabelle looked at the woman. "Looks like her, yes."

The next photo showed an upmarket building.

Isabelle nodded. "Could be it, yes."

"Okay, everyone." Jam got up, stood on her toes to add a bit of height to her five foot three. "Drop what you're doing and find out if Arlene Hampton is still alive. Surveillance footage, cabs, trains, credit card transactions, the works."

Isabelle heard the room come alive as fingers dashed across keyboards. Kate sat, legs crossed, her eyes locked on the big screen, her face unreadable. Claire showed even less emotion.

"You okay?" Andy asked.

"Yes," she said, her voice a whisper.

"Hampton used her credit card at the UN's coffee shop this morning at nine nineteen," a blond man to her left said suddenly.

"Anyone can steal a credit card," Jam said. "Get me CCTV."

"On it."

A minute later, a curvy brunette called from the back of the room. "Here you go."

An image of a blond woman appeared on the big screen. They all turned to look. Arlene Hampton was elegant, dressed in a camel colored coat and blue dress. She strode across the foyer of the United Nations building, coffee to go in her hand.

"That's her," the brunette said. "Facial recognition says there is a ninety-seven percent probability it's her."

"Corroborate," Jam called. She brushed the purple bangs to behind her ear, rubbing the shaved side of her head as if a headache lurked there.

"City's cameras got her as she steps into a cab outside. Ninety-nine percent," shouted an unseen baritone.

"Great work." Jam turned to Andy and Isabelle, a lopsided grin on her face. "She's still breathing. That's our job done for now. Go forth and make merry. Happy hunting."

Isabelle turned to Andy.

"Now we try to find Arlene Hampton before anything happens to her," Andy translated. "Without revealing ourselves."

"Sounds easy enough."

Andy shook her head. "It always does."

Andy looked to Kate who remained seated, her eyes still locked on the screen.

Jam cleared her throat noisily.

Kate finally stirred, nodding stiffly in Andy's direction. "Good luck."

Claire rose. "David and Iona will be your backup. They have been briefed about your circumstances."

"Okay," said Andy. She started to move to the door, gesturing for Isabelle to follow.

"Make sure you leave no stone unturned in saving this woman," Kate called to her. "She's clearly a high-profile target."

"I will."

"And don't let your personal feelings toward me or Ma Soeur get in the way."

"I won't."

Kate mumbled something, her mouth grim.

Isabelle wondered about the pressure on Kate to be right. Right about taking her, bringing her here against her will.

As they were about to walk out, Jam came running up to them. "Sorry about earlier, Andy."

"No problem."

Jam stared at Isabelle with something akin to wonder.

"What?"

"You were right."

Andy frowned. "What do you mean?"

Jam ignored her. "You said you saw snow in your dream?"

"Yes."

"It's November. Weather patterns don't normally see a lot of snow this time of year, but then, what's normal weather these days."

"Okay," Isabelle acknowledged, somewhat defeated.

"But there is a forecast for snow on Friday the twenty-first."

"That's three days from now," Andy said. "And we think Arlene Hampton dies on the night of the twenty-first, considering the calendar."

Jam nodded, her eyes bright. "I know. Quite impressive." She gave a slight bow in Isabelle's direction. "May the force be with you."

Chapter Sixteen

Andy was tired. No, she was beyond that. Exhaustion nipped at her heels like a yapping lapdog. She needed to sleep and so did Isabelle. At this rate they were going to make mistakes—big mistakes that were going to cost them dearly.

She wasn't going to lose another dreamer, especially one this young. Fucking Kate Bouchard.

"How are we going to get into Arlene Hampton's building?" Isabelle asked. "A place like that has security everywhere. At the very least there would be a doorman. Perhaps even surveillance cameras."

"Don't know," Andy muttered.

They were sitting in a coffee shop across from Hampton's building, weighing their options. Andy knocked back her second espresso, then glanced up to see a look on Isabelle's face that suggested she might kill her.

"Why can't I drink coffee?"

"The caffeine is bad for you," she said. "It upsets your dream cycle and increases the violence. Your experience of it."

"Oh. And we don't want that now do we."

The sarcasm was not lost on Andy. She picked up her cell phone, did a Google search, and made a few calls. Isabelle sipped her tea and continued to page through the *New York Times*.

Andy slipped her phone back in the pocket of the long black coat slung over the chair next to her. It was late in the day, and harried commuters were straggling home in the wintry evening air.

Isabelle closed the newspaper and looked at her.

"Yes?"

"Tell me what you would usually do in a situation like this." She filled her cup from the tea pot.

"What do you mean?"

"Tell me how you would normally go about solving these dreams."

Andy thought about it for a second. "It's much the same as you see now. There is a dream, Jam and her team finds the person, and we keep an eye on them to prevent the attack or accident from happening. In your case we have more time. That's quite a luxury."

"That easy?"

Andy shrugged. "No. It can be difficult to locate the person. Or it can be impossible to get to them. We once had a dream about a four-star general. That proved almost impossible to stop. Remember, there is no way we are ever allowed to show ourselves. That remains one of the most important rules."

Isabelle mulled her answer. "And the dream? How does that happen? How did I get to dream about Arlene Hampton?"

Andy blew out a soft breath. "You tell me, but history shows that you perhaps touched her, or somebody in the recent past connected to her. It could be on the subway, in a shop, on the street, or in Starbucks. Anything as random as that." Andy reconsidered. "With you, though, it may even be more random. Maybe you saw her photo in the paper. Who knows."

"Okay, but I still don't—"

"It will never make sense if you keep looking for a rational answer." She stood. "It's best to just jump in. Trust me. We have an appointment to look at an apartment in Arlene Hampton's building tomorrow afternoon. It's for rent. That's the only way to get closer to the point of attack." She scrutinized Isabelle's face. "I also want to see if we can run into this woman so you can touch her. It will intensify your visions, maybe give us some clue about her attacker. Are you up for it?"

"Why not just drink some coffee?"

"Ar-ar," Andy imitated a laugh.

Isabelle held the teacup in front of her mouth. "Exactly how intense will it be?"

"It will be bad. It's okay if you don't want to."

Isabelle thought about it. "No, no, I can manage. If it saves her life, it has to be okay."

Andy nodded, put on her gloves, and held out her hand to help Isabelle down from the barstool at the window. She watched as Isabelle bundled herself up in a white parka that had seen better days. "Shall we go get some sleep? Another team—David and Iona—will sit on Hampton until our appointment tomorrow."

Isabelle tied her scarf around her neck. "I need some stuff from my apartment. Can we go there first, please?"

"Of course."

❖

Andy stood inside the cramped space of Isabelle's apartment, looking at the scribbled formulas and yellow Post-it notes on the walls. She peered inside the fridge. It was empty, apart from a handful of bruised, overripe tomatoes, tomato juice, and milk that was way past its due date.

The small kitchen nook was stacked high with books and papers, balanced next to an open laptop.

"What will happen with your exams?" she called to Isabelle, who was in the bedroom packing.

"I'm done with exams for now. I have to hand in assignments. I have a project due in a few days. I emailed my professor while we—you—drank coffee. Seems like I can hand in the next assignment at the end of the month. He's not worried."

"That smart, eh?" Andy paged through the books. *A Course in Mathematical Cryptography. Conceptual Mathematics.*

"Yup."

"And not shy about it," Andy muttered under her breath.

"I didn't imagine you'd want me to fake anything," Isabelle spoke behind her.

Andy jumped. "Nothing wrong with your hearing either."

"Nope." Isabelle stood in the doorway with a single small suitcase.

"It that all you're taking?"

"I don't have much else of value. I'll take the laptop and some of the books as well, if you don't mind. You look strong enough to carry them." She smiled, and a dimple creased her right cheek.

It was the first time Andy saw her smile. It was beautiful.

Isabelle was beautiful.

And young. And naive about Ma Soeur and what was going to happen in the next few days. Andy knew she couldn't afford to mess this up. She had to keep her distance. Her job was to keep Isabelle safe. That was it. Nothing more and nothing less.

"I'll manage," she said as she snapped the laptop closed and stuffed it into a protective sleeve lying next to the kettle. "What books do you want to take?"

Isabelle selected four from the pile and Andy placed them on top of the computer.

"Can we stop at a few shops on the way as well, please? I need a new coat." Isabelle pointed at the white parka and a tear that ran down from under her left arm.

"Of course. Ma Soeur will pay." Andy contemplated the battered suitcase, the old laptop, wondering what else she could add to Kate's bill.

"That's not what I meant. I don't want your money. I can buy my own clothes. I've already sold a part of my predictive algorithm to a telecoms company. I just never get around to doing any shopping. I don't have anything to run around in in this weather."

"Oh, it's not my money," Andy said. "It's Kate's and I'm very happy to spend it."

❖

"What about this one?" Isabelle stepped out of the dressing room in a new pair of tight, faded blue jeans.

"Nice."

Andy's eyes said it was more than nice.

"And the top?"

"Oh. Great. Too. You know."

Andy ogled the olive green sweater that hugged Isabelle's body. She glanced away quickly to stare at her boots. Isabelle turned, careful to hide her smile from Andy. She was right. Andy couldn't keep her eyes off her breasts. And her butt too, if what she saw in the dressing room mirror was true.

Good to know.

"Boots and jacket?" Andy cleared her throat as she rose from the wicker chair at the entrance to the change rooms.

The salesperson, barely out of her teens, looked up at her with something between awe and fear. Andy was dressed in black from head to toe, from her boots to the long-sleeved T-shirt and military watch wrapped around her wrist.

"I got both already," Isabelle said. She closed the dressing room curtain and changed back into her own jeans.

"Did you make sure it's something you can run in?"

"I took something with a bit of a heel, but I also got some sneakers, yes. You're a pain in the neck, you know? I can't look up at you like that the whole time."

Andy didn't laugh. "Are they warm enough?"

"Yes, they are. Promise."

Isabelle opened the curtain.

"Here you go," the salesperson said, pushing a dress and some underwear into Isabelle's hands. "Black, in your size."

"Thanks." She turned her attention toward Andy. "Do we have time for me to quickly try these on? It's been a while since I ventured outside the apartment, and when I had to pack today I realized I had nothing suitable for…" What was this? "Work?"

Andy's eyes fixed on the lacy underwear in her hands. "Sure. No problem. Work. We have time. I'll just go look at something. Call me when you're done."

"Sure? You're welcome to stay. I can use a second opinion."

"No, no, it's okay. I'm sure Luciana here can help you." She pointed to the salesperson before disappearing into a throng of Japanese tourists moving through the department store.

Luciana looked perplexed. "Doesn't she want to see what it looks like on you?"

"It's a surprise," Isabelle said. "For later."

She retreated back into the cubicle. She had to guess Andy's favorite color and style of lingerie, but she was one hundred percent sure it was not something light and frilly.

The look in Andy's eyes suggested she'd made the right choice.

As she changed, her grandmother's words echoed in her mind. *You don't seduce strength with weakness. Your mother doesn't get that and she never will.*

Her grandmother had looked after her while her mother worked her minimum wage job, always looking for that special man who would take care of her for the rest of her life. Gran died when she was fifteen. A week later, her mom dropped her off at social services, fed up with the dreams and numbers.

Isabelle knew it would take a very particular, special set of circumstances and skills to get Andy Bouchard into her bed, the woman she'd been dreaming about for almost a year already, even though she could never admit that to anyone.

She didn't know if she would manage it, but she was damn well going to try.

Chapter Seventeen

The apartment where Andy and Isabelle slept looked small all of a sudden. Andy stared at the queen-sized bed. Under any other circumstances she would have been happy to jump in there with a woman as beautiful and smart as Isabelle, but this was a completely different ball game.

Besides, there was nothing to say Isabelle was remotely attracted to her, or that she was interested anyway.

"You can take the bed," she offered. "I'll take the couch." She had to be here in case Isabelle crashed again. "How often do you dream?"

Isabelle sat on the white duvet. She looked drained. The last few days had been long and hard. "Twice a week, on average." She laughed dryly. "Is that a good or bad thing?"

"It's quite frequent, I have to admit. And it may increase as we work this case."

Isabelle looked over at the couch. "You'll never fit on there."

"I will. Just go finish up in the bathroom and get in bed."

"Sleep next to me. I promise not to bite." Isabelle kicked off her sneakers.

"It's better not to."

"For who?"

"Both of us."

"Do you always decide what's best for other people?" Isabelle cocked her head to one side, the long red hair a curtain over her face.

"Is everything always an argument with you?"

"This isn't an argument. It's a discussion."

"Then we're done discussing the issue."

Isabelle got up. She closed the space between them and tapped Andy on the chest with a neatly trimmed fingernail. "Let's get this straight. You're not the general and I'm not some stupid little trooper you can command as you please."

Andy raised one eyebrow. The woman had guts, she had to admit. "Okay. Got it."

Isabelle walked to the bathroom, blindly jabbing a thumb in Andy's direction. "Sleep on the bed."

"Thanks, but I'll take the couch." Andy picked up Isabelle's shoes and put them in the closet.

She couldn't think if everything wasn't in its proper place.

❖

Andy woke early, her back in a spasm. She'd been forced to sleep with her legs dangling over the end of the couch, putting strain on her lower back. She glanced at the illuminated hands of her watch. Four eleven. She'd probably managed three hours of fitful sleep.

She might as well get up and go do some exercise. She struggled to her feet, groaning as she stretched from left to right. She slipped past the bed on her way to the bathroom, unable to resist staring at the peaceful figure sprawled on the bed, arms outstretched.

"Sleep on the bed. Yeah, right. Where exactly?" she muttered.

Isabelle had slept soundly throughout the night. No dreams, no sound, except for steady, rhythmic breathing.

Andy nearly bumped into the half-closed bathroom door. What was Isabelle wearing anyway? Those weren't even shorts. What was shorter than a pair of shorts?

Her legs were long and smooth, her hips round, with a sensual curve that invited you to put your hands around them, to pull them toward you. The white T-shirt she slept in was see-through thin, enough so Andy could make out the full—

Stop. Just stop, Andy berated herself. This was what her mother had wanted from the start. She wasn't going to get suckered back into this place and all of its promises. Not in a million years.

❖

The sound of loud punching almost made Andy turn around as she approached the gym. She wanted to be alone, to get rid of some of the restless energy inside her without anyone watching. She contemplated going back to the apartment for a moment, but then pushed the door open. Anything would be better than to face a sleeping Isabelle again.

She immediately recognized the only other person in the gym. René Allandale was a few inches shorter than Andy but bulkier. She didn't have the predictable, acceptable muscle lines developed for photo ops and social media apps, carved out in one-hour poolside gym sessions with personal trainers. Her defined body was the result of being Ma Soeur's drill sergeant and a former mixed martial arts champion. She was the woman who looked after all the keepers and their dreamers, who made sure they were fit and ready for fieldwork.

Her coppery brown hair was short, soaked through from her workout, but still she went at the kicking bag as if she wanted to kill it.

She dropped her fighting stance when she saw Andy and placed her gloved hands on her hips, panting heavily.

"I heard you were back, but I didn't believe it."

Something like regret tugged at Andy's conscience. She didn't exactly leave Ma Soeur in the best way possible. "I'm not back. I'm just here for a few days."

René padded over on her bare feet, appraising Andy.

"Gotten a bit soft, I see." She nudged a glove into Andy's midriff.

"Bull. Still got a six-pack."

"You used to have a ten-pack, Bouchard." Rene smiled and deep lines formed next to her mouth.

She must be in her mid forties by now, Andy thought, but still rock hard. Twenty years in the army would probably do that to you.

"Okay, maybe," she acknowledged. "But why should I? There's no need to chase the dragon anymore."

Dragons were what she and other keepers called the dreams. The elusive, mythological vision that could spit fire in your face quicker than you could possibly imagine.

"How have you been?" René asked. She took off her gloves, grabbed a towel from the floor, and wiped the sweat from her face. "Are you okay?"

"I'm fine."

"You left in a hurry. Didn't even say good-bye," René said in her usual shorthand.

There was an accusatory tone in her voice.

"Yes. Sorry about that. I just had to get away."

René shrugged. "Sorry about what happened. You got a pretty raw deal there."

Andy dropped her bag to the floor and pointed with her chin to the boxing ring. "I'm here to get that ten-pack back. You up for it? Or are you scared I'll kick your butt as always?"

Chapter Eighteen

Isabelle stood at the gym door, watching as Andy and an unknown muscular woman in black exercise gear circled each other in a boxing ring. John Coltrane's "Out of this World" was playing on the speakers.

Isabelle loved his music. At times it was soothing and other times intrusive, noisy, and messy.

She'd woken to an empty room. She'd searched through the closet to find Andy's exercise gear and trainers gone and hoped she would find her here.

Andy feigned a left hook, then went in with a right jab, which too was fake. Instead she lifted her right leg and kicked the other woman against her right side.

"Fuck. Every time," the muscled woman groaned as she doubled over. "Faking it twice. So not nice."

Andy kicked her again, but this time the woman caught her leg, dipped her backward and slammed her to the ground.

The breath oozed out of Andy in a soft, painful hiss. She locked her legs around the other woman's midriff, the muscles straining as she applied pressure. She pummeled her opponent with short jabs as the woman pushed her elbow against Andy's throat.

"Yield," demanded the other woman.

"Hi," Isabelle called, hoping to win Andy some reprieve.

The other woman didn't look away. "Yield. No way your girlfriend's going to distract me."

Andy tapped the floor of the ring.

The other woman jumped up, offering her hand to Andy. "Not bad, Bouchard. But you're rusty. You better come in twice a day if you don't want to get killed out here." She turned to Isabelle. "You too. Heard you've never done this before."

Isabelle couldn't stop staring at Andy, wearing only boxing shorts and an exercise top. Her body was slick with sweat, her hair tied back in a ponytail that exposed her broad shoulders. Hers abs were defined, strong, just like the rest of her body. She turned to wipe off her face with a towel in the corner of the ring and Isabelle got another view of a gorgeous muscled ass. And a jagged scar on Andy's right side, three inches long.

She blushed as the woman caught her admiring Andy. Two fingers in training gloves prompted her closer. "Do you know how to defend yourself?"

"I'm Isabelle."

"René. But that's not what I asked."

"Yes," Isabelle said slowly, slightly irritated. "I've taken boxing classes since I was eighteen."

"With?"

"Horace Gibson."

"Horace the Menace? Excellent. Heard he died. Big loss."

She nodded, pursing her lips.

René wiped the sweat from her brow with her forearm. "What's your best defense?"

"Blocking."

Behind René, Andy was shaking her head vigorously, indicating something with two wiggling fingers.

What?

"Wrong," snapped René. "Stop it, Bouchard," she said without turning around. "Don't think I don't know what you're doing."

Andy smiled cheekily, more broadly than Isabelle had ever seen.

"Try again," René said to Isabelle.

Isabelle looked at Andy's fingers, still puzzled. "Dancing around?"

"Nope." René turned, rolling her eyes like a teenager. "Bouchard, you've always been shit at charades. Running away. The best defense is to get away as quickly as you can. The fancy stuff only starts when you're trapped and your attacker is right on top of you. If you can, you leave everything and everyone behind. Even this lazy ass," she pointed over her shoulder to Andy, "probably can't even do a mile sub four-forty anymore."

Andy said nothing.

"You up for a bit of sparring?" René asked Isabelle.

She nodded. "Just give me a few minutes to warm up."

❖

Ten minutes later, Isabelle stood in the ring across from Andy. René stood outside, leaning on the ropes, towel slung over her shoulder.

"Go easy on the old lady," she told Isabelle.

"I'm not even thirty yet," Andy shot back.

"Might as well be sixty the way you're moving."

Andy dropped her hands and looked at René. Isabelle slammed her fist into Andy's side, causing her breath to escape in a loud whoosh.

René laughed. "I see she's got a firm grasp on the first rule of attack. Do the unexpected." She looked at Andy. "I like her."

"Yeah, yeah," Andy said, not taking her eyes off Isabelle.

With her hair tied back, fists lifted to protect her head, Isabelle seemed smaller than usual. But damn, those fists packed a mean punch.

Andy moved forward, feigning a right kick to Isabelle's side. Isabelle moved left so quickly Andy had trouble tracking her.

"Man, she's fast," muttered Rene. "What you gonna do, Bouchard?"

Andy advanced with two long strides toward Isabelle. She feigned a slow left, hiding her right coming out of nowhere and hitting Isabelle against the shoulder.

Isabelle stumbled back, surprise in her eye.

"That wasn't even half-strength, Bouchard."

"I'm not going to hurt—"

Isabelle danced in under Andy's fists and pummeled her ribs in quick succession.

Fuck, she *was* fast. And it sure didn't feel like she was holding back.

Andy slipped forward, grabbing Isabelle around the waist, absorbing the blows. She lifted Isabelle with ease and slammed her as gently as she could to the floor. She pulled back her fist and stopped an inch from Isabelle's surprised face.

"This isn't a real boxing ring," she said. "There's no right or wrong. You have to defend yourself with everything you got."

Isabelle gave a slight smile and nodded slowly. She threw her head back and pushed her right leg between Andy's legs, searching for her core, moving her hips as if she was arching against her. She leaned into Andy's neck, groaning like she was on the brink of an orgasm.

Andy jerked back.

Isabelle slipped out from under her and scrambled on top of Andy's back and secured her head in a chokehold.

"Fucking hell, Bouchard. Really? A little bit of dirty and you lose it like a rookie?" René bellowed, a smile threatening on her face.

She climbed into the ring and motioned for Andy to stay down. "Let me show this woman of yours how to do a proper chokehold."

CHAPTER NINETEEN

Isabelle glared at the coffee in Andy's hand. She missed the jolt of caffeine. The sharp, swift kick that first espresso delivered at breakfast. She sipped her tea, following it up with a mouthful of scrambled egg on rye.

Jam strode into the briefing room, followed by Kate and Claire. Seemed like Kate and Andy both favored black when it came to their choice of clothing. Claire wore a blue pantsuit and white blouse, while Kate was dressed in black slacks and a midnight sweater. She looked drawn, her eyes heavy with worry. The bruising from the punch Isabelle had given her yesterday had disappeared.

Isabelle didn't know how anyone could figure out what Claire was thinking, not with that cool stare that kept everyone at a distance. Probably not a bad trait for the person who acted as Kate's gatekeeper.

Jam looked like she was up all night, exhaustion evident in every tired, slow movement.

Andy put her cup down and pushed it in Isabelle's direction. Isabelle looked at her questioningly, then drank the last bit of coffee before Andy could change her mind. Andy was still smarting from what had happened in the ring this morning. She lost twice today, to her and René. She didn't think that happened a lot to six foot of muscle and attitude.

Isabelle licked the taste of coffee from her lips. Damn, it tasted nice. Strong, black, and bitter, but oh so good. Maybe it would help ease the headache that had been chasing her all morning.

Kate gave a curt nod to Jam, who got up, switched on the laptop in front of her, and pointed to a screen, an image of Arlene Hampton filling the frame.

"Hampton is the co-owner of a personal security company. Fortress looks after blue-chip company CEOs, pop stars, and other celebrities, as well as visiting foreign dignitaries. They're an approved contractor to the Departments of State and Defense."

Isabelle looked at the photo of the Fortress head office. It was nondescript, elegant, the building set in an immaculate, orderly English garden with rows of white roses in full bloom.

"Hampton is forty-six, a Harvard graduate, lots of connections, and I'm guessing she has a history with the CIA. Some of the details are fuzzy, but she spent a few years at the Turkish and Greek embassies as some vague kind of attaché before going out on her own."

"In other words, there may be a shit storm if she gets killed," Andy guessed.

"Maybe," said Jam, gently tugging on her left ear where three silver rings pierced the flesh. "Or maybe not. Depends on how she left the company. And I have to say, Hampton and her business partner, Phillipe Lautrec, both keep a pretty low profile."

The next image on the screen was one of Hampton standing next to a man in his sixties. He had a hard, tight body, military style gray hair, and a ramrod bearing that said he was used to giving orders.

"The details are bit sketchy on Lautrec," Jam said. "He was French military, but a New Yorker for the last twelve years where he's been slumming it somewhere in Upper Manhattan. Poor guy."

"Are Phillipe and Arlene sleeping together?" Isabelle asked.

"Nope. No bumping uglies from what I can see. No sexting, no sharing of GPS locations. No shared holiday snaps. Could be hush-hush, but I don't think so," Jam said.

"Gay?" Kate suggested in a cool tone.

"Could be, but then they're very discreet. There's no relationship info on Hampton. Lautrec seems to favor high-end strip clubs of the female variety. Both their phones are synced with their work computers, and I got an easy in through an appointment request from a high-profile CEO they now expect to meet next month."

Jam stood in silence as she waited for further questions. When there were none she turned back to the screen and clicked to the next photo. It showed Hampton and Lautrec at the UN complex, then inside a plush room, next to a pale, unknown middle-aged man with clear blue eyes.

"This is the Norwegian consul general. Johan Berg," Jam said.

Kate rapped her fingers impatiently across the table surface. "Did you pick up any red flags? Any reason why Arlene Hampton would be killed?"

"Only one that I could see," Jam said. "Hence this photo. The Norwegian prime minister is on her way to the US, Siv Sandberg. She is the leader of the Labor Party and will deliver a speech at the UN on the twenty-second. She's leading a bloc of countries to push for a far more comprehensive climate deal. And I mean comprehensive. She is working on a deal that could severely limit the business operations, including sales, of companies from non-signatory governments in any of the countries that signed the deal. It's a miracle she even got on the agenda. From what I could glean from radical dark web forums, it seems like she's got some juicy info on the Russian president that she's using to strong-arm him into siding with her on the vote." Jam suppressed a yawn. "With Russia on her side she can maybe also get China on board, leaving the US out in the cold. Fortress is providing Sandberg protection for the duration of her stay. Sandberg and Hampton go way back. It seems Sandberg spent a year or two teaching macro economics at Harvard, where she somehow bumped into Hampton." She glanced at Kate. "Apparently, you also know Sandberg?"

Kate nodded. "Yes, but not well. Ma Soeur helped with her election campaign in Norway."

"Did you find anything interesting on Hampton's phone?" Andy asked.

"Nope. Everything on there is mostly work-related, so I'm hoping she has a private phone that she uses under a different identity, or that is paid through some shell company or something."

Kate lifted a silent, accusatory eyebrow. "So, you haven't found this phone yet?"

"Not yet, but I will, if it exists, which I'm starting to doubt." Jam rubbed the earrings again, then scrunched up her mouth.

Andy recognized the gesture immediately. Jam was tired and irritated—perhaps just as tired and irritated as Kate.

Kate motioned for Jam to continue.

"There have been five death threats against Sandberg in recent weeks, promising to kill her in all sorts of creative ways. Doesn't help that she's bringing her wife along on her visit either. One guy is pretty focused on the fact that she is an 'abomination to family values.'"

"So, we have a starting point?" Kate said.

"Yes."

"Great." Kate stood. Claire followed. "Then get going. Time's a wasting. And keep a team on Arlene Hampton at all times. Just in case we got the timing of her death wrong." Kate stopped at the door and stared at Andy. "Are you up for this?"

Andy nodded. "Yes."

"If not, we can send in another primary team. This is big. I don't want to waste time on people who are not committed to Arlene Hampton's safety."

"We'll do our best," Andy assured her. "You know that."

"You better. I don't want to lose this one."

❖

"I'll map the threats made against Hampton and try to track down her personal phone—if she has one—while you keep an eye on her. Maybe you guys should try to organize a touch event to trigger another dream we can use," Jam said as they exited the conference room.

"I'm looking into it," Andy said.

Jam pressed the button for the fifth floor. She glanced at Kate and Claire as they disappeared down the corridor, then looked at Andy and Isabelle as if she had something to say but didn't quite know where to start.

"Don't worry about me," Isabelle said. "I know to keep my mouth shut."

They got into the elevator. Jam shook her head. "It's not that. It's…well. Kate has a lot riding on this. I heard Ma Soeur's council initially voted against the way she brought you and Andy here, but she eventually convinced them otherwise."

She turned her gaze to Andy. "You know she's up for election this year. She's been running this place for so long some people have forgotten that she has to be reelected every seven years. If this whole thing with Arlene Hampton blows up in her face, I'm pretty sure she won't make it at the polls. This is a biggie." Jam ran a hand through her hair. "You guys should have gone for something smaller for your first dream. This? Where the hell did you get this? It's a complete mess."

Andy gave a wry smile. "We didn't have much of a choice, eh. Isabelle has no control of the process. You know that."

"Yeah, yeah. But, man, I don't envy you."

The elevator spat them out in front of the glass doors leading to the comm center.

"Is anyone running against Kate?" Isabelle asked.

"René."

"René Allandale? Our René?" Andy asked.

"Yep. And she's got a lot of support. Lots of people believe Kate is abusing her power. That she's running around unchecked. René is popular, steady."

"Not to sound ignorant, but isn't René a trainer?" Isabelle said. "Not that it matters, but just in case I'm missing something."

Jam stopped before they entered the comm center. "René was an army colonel. She served in Japan, did tours in Iraq and Afghanistan. People respect her. She's smart, efficient, and she cares about everyone, from the dreamers to the cleaners. And yes, she is a trainer, but she often goes into the field as backup to the teams, which means she knows what it's like to get her hands dirty. It's been way too long since Kate even sat down to have dinner with any of the teams."

"When you say lots of people believe Kate's abusing her power, does that include you?" Andy wanted to know.

She heard something in Jam's voice when she spoke about René. Something akin to awe. Or was it love? Both René and Jam were single. She couldn't remember Jam ever connecting with anyone, but she was still young. Probably only in her mid-twenties.

Jam laughed. "Nice try, but I'm not saying anything. I do what the boss tells me to do. It makes for a lot less stress. I have enough to worry about chasing after you lot."

❖

"Here you go." Jam offered Isabelle a thin, flat silver bracelet.

Andy slipped hers on her right wrist, next to her watch. "It has a small device that will keep tabs on you," she explained. "It will measure your heart rate and tell Jam and her team where you are. You'll get calls through an in-ear phone system that can also keep track of you, but your phone is normally the first thing the bad guys take when you're in trouble."

Isabelle fidgeted with the bangle and pointed at the array of computers in the comm center. "It seems almost primitive compared with your other technology."

Jam lifted a lazy eyebrow in Andy's direction. "That's because your charming partner here doesn't want an implant again. She says she's leaving as soon as this is over. And she didn't want you to get one either, until you've decided whether you want to stay at Ma Soeur."

"Oh. Okay. I suppose it makes sense then," Isabelle said, staring at her feet.

No use correcting either Andy or Jam, even if she did know—had hopes—for a different outcome. Nothing was bulletproof, dreams included.

"No time for a first aid course," Jam said as she checked their bracelets on her computer, nodding when they both pinged their location correctly. "We'll do that after the Hampton case. But we'll see if we can fit in a short course on self-defense and firearms training."

"First aid?"

"In case you need to patch up General Pissed-Off here." Jam glanced at Andy.

"I can take care of myself," Andy retorted. "No need to worry about me."

CHAPTER TWENTY

The Greenwich café was busy. Small and intimate, Thirteen Forks probably seated around thirty people. It was just off Perry Street, two empty tables with blue-and-white tablecloths hugging the front window. An empty mug said someone had recently braced the chill to sit under the clear blue sky.

People hurried by, the frigid weather an ominous warning of the snow expected at the end of the week.

Andy took off her gloves and stuffed them in her coat pockets, then looked at her watch. It was Wednesday, November nineteenth. Two days until Arlene Hampton's murder, if the scant indicators they had were to be trusted.

She stepped aside so that Isabelle could walk into the warmth of the café first. She glanced at David and Iona poring over a city map on the corner like lost tourists before she followed. She'd always liked them. They were a strong, competent team to have as backup.

Somewhere close by there should also be a white van they would have parked out of sight on their way here.

Thirteen Forks served breakfast and dinner. Bookshelves lined the wall opposite them, reaching up to a white steel-pressed ceiling. The hardwood floors were slightly scuffed from countless feet walking to the cake and takeout coffee counter.

"Lovely," Isabelle exhaled.

Inside, the restaurant smelled of freshly ground coffee, hot bread, and fried bacon, despite the clock on the wall saying it was already twelve fifty-three. Arlene Hampton had a lunch appointment here.

According to her diary, she was to meet an EKW at one. Jam said she always used initials, or some kind of code, to mark appointments in her online diary.

Hampton hadn't arrived yet, and Andy and Isabelle were shown to their table. They sat down, Andy with her back to the wall, Isabelle to her left.

Andy knew she had to be on the lookout for Hampton, but it was difficult not to stare at Isabelle as she took off her coat. White certainly suited her. The tight white skirt showed off her glowing skin, punctuated with the odd freckle. Her red hair tumbled over her shoulders in a thick, wavy mass.

"You okay?" Isabelle asked without looking up from her menu.

"Huh? Sure. Why do you ask?"

"You're staring."

"Oh. Sorry." Andy scrambled to find a reason for having had her eyes latched on Isabelle. "I was just wondering if you're okay, that's all. It's been a tough few days."

Isabelle smiled without looking up. "I am. Don't worry. And I'll be okay if things get nasty. I'll run away, just like René said I should do."

"Liar."

"I'm an important asset, remember." Isabelle winked at Andy. "You're just a piece of meat. An attractive piece of meat, but still."

The compliment silenced Andy. Pleased her too, but she tried not to show it. Or think about why exactly it pleased her.

The café door opened. Two heavyset men in dark jeans and black bomber jackets walked in. One had biceps the size of Andy's thighs and a beard in desperate need of trimming. The other was bordering on obese, cleanshaven, with ears that suggested some sport that required a helmet through a large part of his life. His left ear was mangled into a mess of skin and cartilage.

Could be football. Could be a whole lot of dirty work and getting your ass kicked on a regular basis.

Andy looked at the men's shoes. They always told you a lot about a person. These guys were wearing heavy, black boots. Worker boots. Steel-tipped and in need of a shine. Her eyes traveled upward. Belts that have recently loosened a notch. Barrel chests. Skittish eyes that went looking…for a guy in a suit in the corner opposite Andy. He was in his thirties with floppy bangs and short sides. Neat suit. Expensive, bespoke in an elegant genteel light gray.

He was sipping tea from a fine white china cup while reading a Kindle.

"Are you looking at the man drinking tea?" Isabelle interrupted Andy's thoughts.

To her credit she didn't look at the man, but instead kept on staring at the menu.

"Yes. And the two big guys with black jackets who just walked in. Do you recognize any of them?"

"From my dreams?"

"Yes."

"No. That man in the corner just felt strange. Out of place somehow."

Excellent instincts, Andy thought.

The Black Jackets sat down near the entrance.

Andy wanted to leave, to take Isabelle somewhere safe, but knew it would be a fool's errand. Someone's life was at stake. And besides, it was possible that none of these men had any connection to Arlene Hampton.

She gave a wry smile at the notion. Experience had taught her that coincidence tended to work against her. She certainly wasn't a favorite among the fates.

She ordered a meatball sandwich and double espresso. Never knew when you were going to get the chance to eat again. Isabelle ordered tea and a Thai beef salad.

The door opened and an elegant blonde walked in, a camel-colored leather handbag slung over her left forearm. She waved a greeting to the elderly women behind the counter and walked to a table against the wall that sported a "reserved" sign. She sat down, moved the chair next to her closer, and placed her handbag on it and flicked it open. She pushed up her sunglasses and removed her leather gloves, then placed them on the table.

Andy realized she was doing everything with her left hand, keeping her right hand free to reach for the gun she probably had hidden inside her handbag.

It meant she didn't trust her environment, even though the greeting had suggested Thirteen Forks was a familiar lunch spot. But was this habit, or did something about this particular lunch meeting make her nervous?

The guy drinking tea and reading his Kindle had looked up when she walked in.

The Black Jackets were trying not to stare, but they were definitely interested.

Nobody had registered Andy or Isabelle yet.

Hampton ordered from the server. He returned two minutes later with the *New York Times*, and four minutes later with tea, also served in fine white china.

The clock hit 1:04. Hampton looked at her watch. Whoever she was waiting for could show at any time. Time to push Isabelle into play.

"Think you could go select a slice of cake and inadvertently touch her?"

Isabelle nodded, tension a tiny nervous tic on the left side of mouth. "Skin?"

"Preferably, your people tell me."

"Okay."

She made her way through the tables in front of her. Stumbled as if she'd misstepped, sucking in her breath in mock shock. She grabbed hold of Hampton's shoulders. Hampton reached out to steady her without thinking, her protective instincts well developed.

"Oh, I'm so sorry," Isabelle gushed. "Thanks very much." She held on to Hampton's hand, squeezing her gratitude before letting go.

"No problem," Hampton smiled. "You okay?"

"Yes." Isabelle rolled her ankle tentatively.

"Careful on those pumps." Hampton eyed them with envy.

"Thanks. They're new. Don't know what I was thinking wearing them in this weather."

"Beauty always metes out some form of punishment," Hampton said with a practiced wink, slipping an appreciative glance over Isabelle's body.

Isabelle laughed. "I bet that chocolate cake will also make me pay." She pointed to a decadent mousse cake sitting at the front of the display.

Hampton turned to look at the array of confectionary. "No doubt. But it might just be worth it. Excellent choice, by the way. I'd recommend it."

Isabelle laughed again and walked to the server behind the display. She ordered a slice of cake to go and walked back to their table.

The Black Jackets couldn't stop staring at Isabelle. They'd ordered hot chocolate, a fifty lying on the table, as if they wanted to clear out quickly if they were forced to do so. Tea Guy still didn't look up from the Kindle he was reading.

Weird. Almost everyone in Thirteen Forks had looked up when Isabelle had stumbled.

Their food arrived, followed by the slice of cake in a takeout box. Andy bit into the sandwich. Heaven, just like the coffee. She slipped out her phone and surreptitiously took photos of Black Jackets and Tea Guy to see if Jam could identify them.

Hampton looked at her watch. It was 1:11. She signaled the server for the bill.

"Not a very a patient woman, is she?" Isabelle noted.

She was right. Hampton hadn't looked at her phone once, so nobody had notified her that they had better things to do on this Wednesday afternoon.

"She's here for the show," Andy said slowly, as the realization hit. "But why? For those guys?" She pointed to the Black Jackets, then to Tea Guy who was settling his bill.

"Could be," Isabelle said.

Andy had to make a quick decision as Hampton got up and walked out. "I'm going to follow Tea Guy when he leaves and see where he goes. You stay here and have lunch."

"Will you be okay?" Isabelle asked, a worried tone in her voice.

"Yes. And David and Iona are on standby outside. And you'll be able to follow everything on your earpiece."

"Okay." Isabelle nodded. "I'll see you later. Please be careful. And remember, we have that meeting at Arlene's apartment building at three."

"I'll be there. And if I'm not, don't worry." She pointed to her bracelet. "Jam will know where to find me."

❖

Tea Guy walked with quick, long strides, but it was easy enough for Andy to keep up with him. He dodged errant sidewalk trash and pedestrians glued to their phones with the ease of a born New Yorker, hands dug into his coat pockets.

His shoes were black and pointy. Shiny to a fault. He wiped his bangs out of his face. His hair was somewhere between light brown and dark blond. He was older than Andy had first thought, more in his forties than his thirties. He had a lean and sinewy build, and his chin was as sharp as his cheekbones.

Andy was lucky he was walking and not taking a cab. That would complicate things, even though David and Iona were standing by to pick her up should that happen. They saw her leave Thirteen Forks. And Jam would be tracking her.

Her phone was in her pocket and the earpiece where it should be. Holding the number nine turned her phone into a multi-channel encrypted radio system.

"Heading southeast," she said as Tea Guy kept going in a straight line. She kept fifteen paces back, to his left as he hurried through the crowded streets.

"Got you," Iona said in her crisp English accent. "David is on foot trailing you. He's about a minute back."

"Got you too," said Jam from the head office.

Iona spoke up again. "Isabelle said to tell you that the guys in black jackets left shortly after your guy. She's having trouble with her phone."

"Okay. Thanks," Andy said.

They walked for another minute or two. Then Tea Guy abruptly turned left, disappearing down an alley.

Andy's heart rate picked up.

Her earpiece buzzed.

"You okay? Your heart rate has jumped," Jam asked.

"Yes. No problem."

She didn't know if she should follow Tea Guy, but then did it anyway. Time wasn't on their side, and hurrying things along was sometimes the only solution to preventing an impending murder.

She exhaled sharply as she turned the corner.

"Scratch that," she said as she came to a halt. "Send in the troops."

She removed her hands from her coat pockets. In front of her, Tea Guy stood waiting. She waved, smiled, and moved left, as if to pass him. He gave one long stride into her space, her body bouncing off his.

"Hi, buddy, what's your problem?" she asked as she again hinted to move left.

He again stepped to block her. She jabbed him in the throat with a quick fist. He'd dodged right with lightning quick reflexes, but she still managed to make him gag. She rushed forward, lifting her knee to his groin. Followed it up by slamming his face down on her knee.

She grimaced at the crack of bone. She was lucky. She'd had the element of surprise on her side.

Behind her she heard footsteps. She spun around. David?

No. One of the Black Jackets threw a right at her. She ducked and his fist cut a hole through the air above her. She punched him in the stomach and got a slight whoosh out of him through the layers of fat and muscle.

Where is the second Blac—

Pain exploded between her shoulders.

She rammed her body back, slamming the block of flesh behind her into the alley wall. She lifted her right leg, punching the heel of her own steel toe boot backward and down on the man's knee behind her. She heard a snap. A groan. The body sinking to the ground. Something heavy hitting the asphalt.

The sound of running feet turned her head.

A white van stopped, its doors already open. David and Iona stormed out of the van, followed by René.

The other Black Jacket was nowhere to be seen. Same for Tea Guy.

She groaned in frustration. He was the one she'd wanted. It felt like he was the one who could have told them what was going on.

CHAPTER TWENTY-ONE

Arlene Hampton's building was a five-story structure with fifteen apartments. The top floor was a penthouse. Hampton and three other owners or tenants were on the level just below that.

The apartment they—Hannah and Wren, a young couple moving here from Washington—were interested in was on the third floor. Number thirty-four.

Gerri Hope was eager to make the sale. Andy was impressed that she insisted on showing off her calf muscles despite the weather. They said she biked a lot. The rest of her body betrayed that she was a gym fanatic. Couldn't sell upmarket real estate if you didn't look good and smile, her entire body, brimming with energy, screamed as she bounced to the elevator in stilettos, security tag in hand.

There was no way Andy could determine her age. Thirty, forty, fifty? Not one muscle north of her lips moved when she smiled, and there were no frown lines in sight.

Getting inside the lobby required a small gray security tag and getting into the elevator a second tag.

The owners were considering a number of biometric options, Hope explained.

A security guard was stationed in the lobby, keeping an eye on an array of screens that suggested there should be about fifteen cameras dotted throughout the building.

"Would you mind if I take a few photos?" Isabelle asked as she dug around in her handbag. "My mom is curious about the places we're looking at."

"Of course, please go ahead," Hope said.

Andy wondered whether Isabelle was still miffed at her. She hadn't had time to fully explain what had happened in the alley, but it had been clear that Isabelle wasn't impressed about being left in the restaurant. Not to mention being cut off from the comm network when Andy walked into trouble. Jam would never allow a rookie dreamer to distract a keeper.

Hope pointed to the left as they walked into the building. "There is CCTV in the lobby and the elevators, but not in the hallways. The residents like their privacy." She beckoned them into the elevator, which looked like a gilded, mirrored cage. "May I ask what it is you're looking for specifically?"

It was clear she'd not yet determined who carried the purse between Hannah and Wren, so the question hung in the air, not directed at either of them in particular.

Andy knew she'd been vague on the phone, and deliberately so. She rolled her shoulders in an attempt to soothe the ache between her shoulder blades. It hurt like hell. That damn Black Jacket in the alley had made a solid connection with a baton of some kind. René had said nothing was broken, then asked why she hadn't heard him coming.

Andy felt a hand slipping into hers. She watched as Isabelle held a protective hand over her stomach. "We're pregnant and we're looking for a safe, secure place to rent until we decide on where we want to buy," Isabelle explained. "Wren travels a lot for her job. She's in the defense industry."

"Ah." Hope's eyes gained a sparkle, as if she'd just heard a delicious story. "Then you're at the right place. This building has got excellent security, and a really open-minded homeowners association. The penthouse is owned by Fabricio Bernardo. The fashion guru from TV? Real drama queen, but nice, I hear."

She frowned as her phone rang and muted it quickly. She shot Andy an appreciative glance. "You must be doing well for yourself to afford a place such as this at your age. If you don't mind me saying."

"Not at all," Isabelle answered. "Wren is really driven. I can't get her to sit down for anything. Not even a hot meal."

"Ah. One of those." It almost looked as if Hope wanted to add something, but then she resorted to flashing the practiced smile of someone who had spent years in the sales industry.

Andy squeezed Isabelle's hand, motioning with her eyes. *Keep going*. She could almost feel Hope quickly warming to Isabelle and her story.

They stepped out of the elevator.

Isabelle kept her hand in Andy's, as if it belonged there. They walked past two doors to number thirty-four. Again, Isabelle took some photos.

"Here you go," Hope said. She unlocked the door. "The apartment is really spacious. Lots of room for a little one to run around. And Central Park is close by, as you probably know."

"Won't it upset the neighbors, though? Having a baby around?" Isabelle asked, hand still on a nonexistent baby bump.

"Oh no. Don't worry. The apartments are almost soundproof. And the tenants include one other couple with a baby, and as far as I know nobody has ever complained about the noise."

Isabelle nodded, as if relieved. To Andy it meant only one thing. Nobody would hear Arlene Hampton scream when the shooter entered her apartment two days from now.

Isabelle walked to the kitchen and opened a cabinet or two. She nodded as if impressed by their size. She snapped a few aimless pics. "What about the other tenants? And the owners? Are they nice people?"

"From what I hear, absolutely."

"That's good news." Isabelle peered down the hallway, then walked down to take an obligatory look.

"Bedrooms," Hope noted as she followed. "A big main bedroom with an en suite and a cozy second bedroom."

Andy walked to the large window overlooking Central Park as Isabelle and Hope explored the apartment. As Isabelle had explained in her dream, this should almost be the same view as the one from Hampton's place.

She turned when she heard the sound of heels and looked past Hope to Isabelle. "What do you think, darling?" she asked, pointing to the Met, slipping her hand around Isabelle's waist and inhaling her particular scent: freshly turned soil and wildflowers.

Isabelle stiffened at first, then scrutinized the picture in front of her. "I think it's just about right." She turned to Hope. "We'll take it."

"But you haven't even seen the rooms?" Hope asked Andy, the surprise causing the slightest of creases between her eyes.

"No need," Andy said. "I trust Hannah completely. When do you think we can move in?"

❖

As they left Hampton's building for Ma Soeur, Andy called Jam.

"Her name is Gerri Hope. Do you see her?"

"Yeah. We got eyes on her. Silver BMW across the road."

"You need a security tag to get into the building, and another to get into the elevator. I suspect the same tag will also get you into the fire escape. Isabelle took some photos of the tags and of Hope. I'll send them to you now. We need you to lift the tags from Hope's handbag and replace them, if possible. We can only move in in three days' time and that may be too late."

"We'll do our best."

"Better be quick. I'm getting nervous." Andy looked up at the weather. It was eerily silent in the city. The air was cold and unexpectedly humid. She could almost smell the coming snow.

CHAPTER TWENTY-TWO

Jam stood waiting for them when they returned to Ma Soeur, tablet in hand. "The big guy in the alley is Marat Sharapov. He's forty-one. Priors for assault. Seems like he's a low-class enforcer for the Russian mafia."

"Russian mafia?" Isabelle kicked off her heels, showing some leg as she pulled up the tight skirt. "Does that mean he is connected to the UN vote? The Norwegian prime minister forcing that vote on Russia?"

"Could be," Jam ventured. She rubbed her eyes, her neck, then combed through her hair in a tired, slow motion. "But he's not talking." She looked from Isabelle to Andy. "Kate wants Isabelle to talk to him. To touch him. Maybe she can establish some connection to Arlene Hampton."

"We're talking to the bad guys now?"

"Don't shoot the messenger." Jam shrugged. "Can we? Take Isabelle in to see Sharapov?"

Andy wanted to say no, that it had been enough for one day, but she couldn't speak on Isabelle's behalf. She turned to face her. Isabelle was wearing a wry smile and the same exhaustion Jam had on her face, her high heels dangling from her fingers.

"My, my, imagine this. Somebody finally asking me what I want to do," she mocked them.

Andy ignored the sarcasm. "You can rest first. Sharapov can wait." She looked at her watch. "It's almost six. Have a cup of tea, eat something, and sleep an hour or two, if you want."

Isabelle contemplated the suggestion, realizing that she feared falling asleep. She'd touched Arlene Hampton. Tonight's dream would probably be similar to the one before, but far worse. More intense.

Best to do it all in one go.

She reached out to Andy. "I can talk to Sharapov. You'll be there?"

Andy took her hand. "If that's what you want, yes."

❖

Sharapov looked even bigger than what Isabelle remembered. Hulking, with an unkept beard, he was chewing on the inside of his mouth in what seemed a nervous gesture. Every now and then, he moved in his chair, trying to get more comfortable, groaning as he bumped his injured knee against the table. His arms were clasped around his body, a slight blueish tinge to his face. His black jacket had disappeared, the only protection against the cold his black trousers and a long-sleeved black T-shirt.

Round face, round fingers. Hands that could crush a watermelon. Feet the size of rowing boats.

Isabelle peered at him through the two-way mirror. They were in the basement of Ma Soeur, three floors below ground floor. It was cold, the thermostat on a ridiculous number. Isabelle had to squint to make sure she was reading it correctly.

"Bunt likes it that way," Andy said. "Gave him a broken chair too. Apparently, there's some loose screw sticking up Sharapov's ass. And he refused to give him pain meds for his knee."

Marc Bunt seemed to be Ma Soeur's interrogator. He and René worked in tandem, Jam had explained on the way down here.

Marc was of average height and weight. A normal man who looked as if he should have a wife and 2.2 kids at home playing ball with a golden retriever. Raised by a single mother, he'd been with government in some form or the other since he was eighteen, Jam had explained vaguely. That is, up until the time he was taken hostage in Iran and left to die. Didn't like government much when he came back.

Marc had greeted Andy as if he'd missed her. René had asked about Andy's back.

Isabelle shifted her gaze to Andy. She knew now was not the time to argue but promised herself that there was no way she would ever again be left sitting in a restaurant when Andy went after the bad guys.

"You ready? I'll go in with you," Andy said.

"What happens if it doesn't work?"

"Then it doesn't matter."

"Maybe none of this works. Touching Arlene, him. Maybe I'm a fraud. A wannabe."

"You don't believe that."

Isabelle didn't respond.

Andy placed her hand on Isabelle's arm. "What you do is not an exact science. It isn't math. And we all know and appreciate that."

Isabelle gave a half-hearted laugh. "I would kill for a math exam right now. A nice, clean sheet of paper with only one possible correct answer."

She looked up at Andy, still swathed in her black coat. "How accurate are the dreams? On average. Give me a number."

"Eighty percent?"

She bit her bottom lip, then laughed. "Did you just pluck that out of the sky, Miss Bouchard?"

"Never."

❖

Isabelle's breath spilled from her mouth in a white cloud and billowed into the gray interrogation room as if she were smoking. Gray walls, gray table, gray chairs.

Marat Sharapov looked up, surprise on his face. He didn't expect her. Not a woman. And certainly not one of the women from the Greenwich café. The hint of hope on his face vanished when Andy followed Isabelle inside the musty room.

As Isabelle sat down, Andy went to stand behind Sharapov, leaning against the wall, an ominous presence that forced him to look over his shoulder to plot her exact position.

Isabelle shook her head slightly and indicated the door. Andy frowned, shrugged, and then did as she was told.

It felt good that she trusted her. Isabelle liked that.

"Marat. My name is Isabelle." She reached across the table, as if to shake his hand.

He didn't oblige.

"We are worried about Arlene Hampton, Marat. The woman you were following in Greenwich."

His eyes narrowed at the mention of Arlene's name.

"Why were you following her?" she asked.

Silence.

"You can tell me or you can tell them." She gestured to Andy. The mirror behind her. "I think it would be considerably easier to talk to me."

He crossed his arms and snorted. "Are you the good cop?"

His accent was less Russian than she expected, the guttural edges worn smooth by years spent underfoot another language. She would guess he'd been in the States for some time already.

"I'm not a cop." She pointed to Andy. "She's not a cop. None of us are cops."

"Then why am I here?" He planted a huge fist on the table and pushed himself upward. "I'm leaving."

He looked at the door. At Andy smiling at him. It was a dead, cold smile that gave Isabelle a chill. She could feel the warmth leave her body, the room's deep-freeze temperature seeping into her feet, her bones. Her parka provided no protection to her feet, still clad in heels.

"Tell me why you want Arlene Hampton dead," she asked. "Is it because of the vote she is trying to push through the United Nations?" She stood up as well, unclenching her hands that dreaded touching him. Dreaming him.

She walked around the table. Stopped. Then gave two steps forward. She heard Andy inch closer. She reached out and touched Marat's arm, his black shirt thin under her fingers, his skin goose pimpled. She stared into his face, urging whatever lurked there closer to the surface, close enough to touch it through his skin. She wasn't looking for information. She was looking for emotion, boiling to the surface unchecked.

"Why Arlene, of all people?" she said in a calm voice. "She's a woman. Innocent. Powerless."

He stared at her, as if mesmerized. She slipped her hand past his wrist, to the surprisingly soft, warm skin of his palm, her fingers lingering there.

He stumbled back, staring at her.

She took a step back. Another. She held on to the table.

Marat's touch was different from Arlene's earlier today. With him the promise of violence bubbled just below the surface, brooding in his blood.

"Who are you?" he called. He looked at Andy, something like fear on his face. "I'm not talking. Not to this woman. Not ever. Get her out of here."

Andy stepped around Sharapov toward Isabelle. Isabelle steadied herself against the broad shoulders, resting her head against the thick black coat. She slipped her hands to the hips in front of her and exhaled slowly.

She heard Andy say, "You don't have to talk to any of us. You've already told her everything she wanted to know."

❖

As they left, Jam pushed two access tags into her hand. "As requested."

Andy looked at the two circular gray tags and hoped there was no biometric security they hadn't spotted at Hampton's building. "Thanks. Was it a pickpocket or a mugging?"

"A good, quiet lift. David's fingers are still the best, especially for such a big guy. Hopefully, Gerri Hope will think she lost them somewhere. We need a little bit of time before she lets security know they're gone, in case they cancel them." Jam suppressed a yawn.

Andy squeezed her shoulder. "Go get some sleep. I'll phone you when something happens."

CHAPTER TWENTY-THREE

Night came.

It was inevitable, Isabelle considered as she stood at the window of her and Andy's small apartment. It was time to sleep. She was exhausted, but she dreaded the beast that would get into bed with her. That would wake as soon as she closed her eyes.

At least Andy would be here.

The thought gave her some degree of comfort.

In the bathroom the shower was running. She imagined Andy there, standing as Isabelle had done earlier. The warm water running over her body, exhaustion from the day eating away at her.

No. Andy would use cold water. She had no idea how she'd known that to be the case, but she did.

Maybe she was wrong.

Maybe not.

She groaned in frustration. Andy was adding complexity to an already maddening situation. Previously, she only had to cope with the dreams and their aftermath. Now she had to be right, like a jury or a priest.

Right. What a word. One hundred percent. No gray areas.

She walked to the small kitchen. Andy had made her dinner and tea, but it had grown cold since she'd finished getting ready for bed. The pasta was simple. Mushrooms and a bit of grilled chicken. She sat down, pushing the plate to the side. The thought of food made her stomach churn.

She tasted the tea, then swallowed it in a few gulps.

The shower stopped. The door opened, followed by sounds of someone getting dressed. Isabelle looked at the bowl of pasta and felt like she wanted to gag. What she really wanted was far more appetizing. She craved Andy's touch. Andy's skin setting her own on fire, scorching her until she came again and again and there was nothing left but ashes and the silence she so desperately craved.

She caught the sound of desire in her throat and exhaled it in a soft murmur she failed to control as the bathroom door closed.

"My food that bad?" Andy was dressed in black sweatpants and an old Notre Dame T-shirt. She dumped her dirty clothes in the laundry basket in the corner.

"No, it's nice. I'm not hungry. But I drank the tea, thanks."

"No problem."

Andy busied herself with grabbing a pillow and a blanket from the bed and making up the couch. She did everything but look at Isabelle.

Of course, Isabelle realized. She'd been here before. Isabelle wasn't her first dreamer. And what did she say when they'd spoken about this? Sex intensified the dreams? Perhaps what Andy had neglected to say was that dreamers craved sex before dreaming. That it settled the body. The mind. Emptied it before the dreams arrived.

Fuck Andy for not wanting to give her that. Would it be that hard? That difficult? Was she that ugly that Andy couldn't just fuck her like a woman she picked up in a bar? Who said she had to care?

Isabelle stood up from the breakfast nook. She was too restless too sleep. She wanted to go running. She looked for her gear. Andy wandered to the kitchen and switched on the kettle, then started picking at Isabelle's pasta.

Isabelle grabbed her running shoes and pulled them on.

"Whoa. Where are you going?" Andy dropped the fork and gave three long strides to suddenly stand next to her.

"Running."

Andy glanced at her watch. "It's late. And it's been a long day and you must be exhausted."

Damn woman still wasn't looking at her. Isabelle stood up, stripping her top as she rose. She was naked underneath.

She could hear the catch in Andy's breath. She turned and faced Andy, her nipples erect and aching. She moved into Andy's space, running a finger down the front of her T-shirt, slipping it underneath and scratching her nails across the tight stomach.

"Or *you* can give me what I need."

"Okay, I…I can go running with you."

Isabelle slipped her hand lower, rubbing it down Andy's thigh, inching closer to the V between her legs. "I had something else in mind and you know it."

Andy grabbed Isabelle's hand. "I can't."

Isabelle burned with anger. She knew she was being rash and impatient, but she couldn't stop herself. She'd always been that way. It was her biggest enemy. She could never wait for something to come to her. She always had to go and fetch it.

"Won't," she said as she pushed herself to her full height. "Don't be a coward. Say it. Won't, not can't."

"Isabelle, I was very clear from the start about our situation."

"Situation? Oh, don't patronize me. Just say you don't like me. That I'm not your type. That I don't turn you on. That you don't care. Whatever." Isabelle turned back to the closet. "Forget the running. I'm going out." She kicked off her shoes and grabbed a dress, anger and resentment burning exhaustion to the ground. "I can't breathe in here."

❖

When Isabelle emerged from the bathroom Andy stood ready, all dressed in black. Tight jeans, boots, button-down shirt, and leather jacket.

"Where are you going?" Isabelle asked.

"With you. To make sure you're okay." Andy held up her hands. "I'll drive you to wherever you want to go and make sure you get back okay." She pointed to the door. "They won't let you go out on your own. In fact, we may just have to beg Jam to let us leave."

"So, I'm a prisoner after all?"

Andy didn't answer, but at least she looked her in the eye. She seemed sad and a little bit angry.

Isabelle would love to see a lot of anger. A lot of anything. Not that stoic face that kept on insisting that everything was fine. Just okay and all right and *fine*.

She grabbed her coat. "Let's go then, James."

Chapter Twenty-four

Where do you want to go?" asked Andy.

"She Bar."

That certainly dispelled all notions Andy might have had that Isabelle was straight and just hoping to use her for release. "You're not serious?"

"Where else do you think I'm going to get laid tonight?"

Andy blanched at the crass words and the unspoken accusation in her voice. She glanced in the rearview mirror, gritting her teeth at Isabelle and the headlights of the black truck following them.

Jam had snuck them out, urged on by a promise that René would follow them in a second vehicle. Everybody was hoping and praying Kate and Claire wouldn't find out about tonight.

Andy glanced at her watch. Eleven. "It's early for a club. You may not find what you're looking for."

"Clearly you know the place." Isabelle's voice was mocking, angry.

"I've been there a few times."

"For what? Anonymous sex with women who don't expect anything from you?"

Isabelle crossed her legs. She wore a soft black dress that flowed to her ankles. Black stilettos that made her walk with a sway to her hips that made Andy's throat go dry. Her hair hung loose and wild down her back, down an expanse of smooth, creamy skin the dress didn't bother to cover. Didn't cover too much at the front either.

It was a fuck-me dress and fuck-me shoes and Isabelle knew it.

Andy cleared her throat. "I gather you've been to the She Bar before as well."

"No."

"Any other similar bar or clubs?"

"You mean gay clubs? Once or twice."

The realization hit Andy, followed by relief. "You're not twenty-one. They're not going to allow you in."

"They will."

"How? Do you have a fake ID? We can't afford to have you arrested."

"Will you please just keep quiet and drive? You made it clear that you are not interested in me."

"It's not that."

"What is it then? Is there someone else?"

"No," said Andy.

"Am I not experienced enough for you? We can fix that tonight, you know."

"No. Just drop it."

"Are you able to have sex? To climax? Or are you into kinky stuff? We can fix that too, you know. I don't mind being tied down. And strap-ons are completely fine. I'm a quick study."

"Will you…For fuck sakes. Let's just get there."

Andy wanted to thump the steering wheel. She had a bad feeling about tonight. A really, really bad feeling.

René slipped into the empty seat next to Andy. Andy was sipping on an ice-cold vodka, her gaze locked on the bartender in front of her. She wasn't in the mood for sharing how she felt, and René had never succeeded at faking idle chitchat.

The bartender had a mop of curly brown hair and tits that she kept on pushing in Andy's direction, offering a view of red lace every time she bent over.

Anything was better than looking at the woman flirting with Isabelle in the corner booth.

"If you drink one more vodka I'm going to have to drive Isabelle back," René said.

"Fuck." Andy slammed down the glass. "Sorry. You're right." She signaled the bartender. "Water, please?"

The woman frowned.

Andy shrugged. "I'm driving."

The bartender shot a smile at her, then at René. René smiled back, ordered a beer, and slung her arm over Andy's back. She was wearing her trademark low-slung jeans and white hoodie.

"What's eating you, Bouchard? Your woman getting under your skin?"

"Girl. She's twenty." Damn bouncer didn't even ask. Didn't even bother to check her ID.

René turned to look at the booth. "No way."

"Yeah."

"Okay, but twenty is not the same for everyone."

"Hmm," Andy grunted.

She Bar was filling up, the noise levels increasing, along with interest in the newcomer in the black dress. Andy remembered the bar as a local hangout, but it had picked up in popularity since she'd been here three years ago.

The dance floor was small, the music picking up to an almost frenetic beat as the night progressed. It was Wednesday, the distant promise of weekend lingering in the air like something sweet and addictive.

"You can't keep hanging on to her, you know," René said without looking at her.

"Who?" She regretted the response immediately.

"Victoria."

"Don't. She's gone."

"No, she isn't. You just don't want to face up to it, otherwise you may have to go see her and admit that your mother isn't the only one to blame here. Vic made her own choices. And you did the same."

"Shut up, René. You're sticking your nose where it doesn't belong."

The bartender placed a bottle of water in front of Andy and a frosted beer glass filled to the brim in front of René.

Andy pushed the bottle to the side and ordered another vodka. The bartender looked surprised but didn't say anything. "Why are you taking Kate's side all of a sudden? I hear you're challenging her in next month's election?"

"Hey, whoa. I'm not choosing sides here. And what happened with you and Vic has nothing to do with me thinking things could be done more ethically at Ma Soeur. What happened to you was by the book. Painful and incredibly unfortunate, yes, but by the book. This here tonight is about you opening your eyes to reality."

"What reality? Vic's to blame? I'm to blame?"

"Maybe, yes. And what about the fact that you just up and left without saying good-bye? That hurt, man. I thought we were friends. Good friends." René gestured over her shoulder. "And it's also about her. Isabelle. I like her. Really like her. She's got something special. Grit. Guts. And I think you could like her too, if you just allow yourself to feel something again. I mean look at her. She's gorgeous. And damn smart. She's watching and learning at an amazing rate. And you'd be stupid not to notice that she likes you. She can't stop watching you."

René drank her beer to the halfway mark. "And sometimes your mother knows what she's doing. Not in the way she brought Isabelle here. In other ways. Like bringing you in to partner with Isabelle. You're the only one with enough experience to work with her. And have you ever considered that Kate maybe knows something about you that you are not willing to acknowledge yet?"

Andy took a swig from the vodka. "There is nothing to know. Isabelle is too young."

"You were young too, or have you forgotten that?"

They both watched as a woman with short, black hair, shirt sleeves rolled up to show wiry tattooed forearms, put her arm around Isabelle. She leaned in to whisper something in her ear. Isabelle laughed, a red blush traveling up her neck. She looked up and her gaze met Andy's. Her eyes were an angry, calculated green.

The woman got up and held out a hand to Isabelle. Isabelle smiled at Andy, took the woman's hand, and followed her down a dark hallway.

CHAPTER TWENTY-FIVE

The woman had Isabelle backed up against a wall, standing underneath the soft glow of a pink heart-shaped neon light. Her kisses were urgent and deep. She smelled of tobacco and beer.

Isabelle turned her face away. She didn't want to be kissed. She wanted release, anything to calm the raging monster inside her. She opened her legs, guided the woman's eager right hand to the slit in her dress. The hand slipped in underneath the thin, silk-like material. She folded her palm around Isabelle's sex, then ran one finger teasingly along the edge of her underwear.

Isabelle closed her eyes, arching her back, urging the woman to enter her. Could someone just please understand the need in her? Andy was just as stubborn…

Andy.

She froze, recoiling from the woman. Then she opened her eyes in surprise as the weight of the body against her disappeared.

"Hey, what the fuck?" the woman shouted, Andy holding her by the scruff of her shirt. She turned and kicked at Andy but missed as Andy held her at arm's length.

Andy pulled her closer, wrestling her into a wrist lock. She made her kneel in submission. "Not your night. Not your girl. Sorry."

"You can't just barge in here!" Isabelle shouted, pulling her dress down. She walked up to Andy and slapped her against the arm. In the face.

Andy stood still, blinking rapidly, exhaling an angry puff of air. "You shouldn't be here," she said. "And this…sex like this. It's not you."

"How would you know?"

"You're twenty, for fuck's sake."

Isabelle looked at her watch. "Twenty-one."

Andy frowned and let the squirming woman on the floor go. She looked at her own watch. It was three minutes past midnight.

"It's your birthday?"

"Yes," Isabelle hissed. "What? You all looked at my file like I'm some valuable commodity and nobody noticed that little detail?"

The woman with the short black hair looked from Andy to Isabelle. She seemed to measure Andy's size and the glare on her face and then scrambled down the hall, back to the music.

Good decision.

Isabelle stared at the disappearing woman, then turned back to Andy. "Looks like I've just become your problem. And this time you better deliver."

❖

Andy pulled Isabelle through the throng of people, back to the bar. René's seat was empty. Her phone rang. It was Jam. No one was wearing their earpieces, in an effort to give Isabelle some privacy tonight.

"Your pulse is through the roof. It's like you want to murder someone. Are you okay? And Isabelle? Kate's going to kill me if something goes wrong tonight."

"Yeah, yeah, don't worry. We're all fine."

"Okay then, bu—"

Andy stepped around a woman in a wedding dress. "What about Isabelle's?"

"Isabelle's what?"

"Heart rate."

"Let me see." A moment's silence. "Steady as the dead."

"And earlier?"

"Bit higher. Nothing spectacular, though."

"Okay."

Andy terminated the call without thinking why she'd wanted that particular bit of information. She paid the bartender, who looked sad to see her go. She left her a generous tip and shoved the rest of the bills back into her wallet.

She froze as she looked to her left. Two people had just walked in. Young and heady with love, they were clinging to each other, the shorter one's head buried in her partner's neck. There was snow on their coats. Heavy flakes, enough to have survived the twenty yards or so from the front door to the bar counter.

She looked at her watch. Quarter past one. Couldn't be. The time was wrong. The snow. The date.

Unless…unless they fucked up by taking the Russian hostage earlier today. Did something to mess up the timeline.

"What's wrong?" Isabelle asked as she hurriedly put on her coat.

"Snow. It's snowing." Andy looked at Isabelle. At the dress, the heels. There was no time to drop her off first. "We need to go. And we need to be quick."

❖

Andy raced the midnight blue SUV to Arlene Hampton's building. Isabelle sat with her phone on her lap, speakerphone on, waiting for Jam to report back on Hampton's whereabouts.

"Nothing. There's nothing," Jam said. "Iona and David say they haven't noticed anyone out of the ordinary entering or leaving the building, but there has been a delivery truck obscuring their view for about four minutes. We've got eyes on the back, front, and the basement. Hampton's phone says she's inside the building, at home. Probably asleep, like we should all be."

Iona and David were in their early thirties. Iona was a petite flax-blond former British triple jump Olympian with a lean physique and David a grumpy bearded German surveillance specialist, a bulky and hairy alpha man, like a teddy bear with attitude. They were an excellent team, their trust implicit and unquestioning.

"Did you try calling her?" Andy asked.

"Yes, even though we risk revealing ourselves, as you know, but there was no answer." Jam took a deep breath. "Maybe you're overreacting. So, the snow is early. Big deal. It doesn't have to mean anything."

"I don't like it." Andy glanced in the mirror. René's black truck was keeping pace behind them.

"You're not the one who's not supposed to 'like' it," Jam said testily. "If you'd allowed Isabelle to dream we could have had something concrete to work with tonight."

"It was my idea to go out," Isabelle interrupted her.

"It doesn't matter," Andy declared. "It happened. All that matters right now is that I have a really bad feeling about this."

"Okay," Jam agreed reluctantly. "As long as you know Kate is going to eat us for breakfast. Better wear your big girl pants when you see her."

The call ended abruptly. Andy turned left, right, jumping a yellow light as she accelerated. Isabelle rested her hand on Andy's leg, the anger and frustration from earlier forgotten. "Tell me why you're worried."

"The snow. It's a small thing, but it's enough." And the last time she didn't listen to her gut, the dragon ended up devouring everything she'd held dear.

It was as if Isabelle could sense she was holding back, but then let it go. "Okay. Let's go see if Arlene Hampton is okay."

CHAPTER TWENTY-SIX

The SUV skidded to a halt in front of Arlene Hampton's building, René's truck a few yards behind. The streets were empty. The unease sat in Andy's stomach like a swarm of restless, trapped butterflies.

"Stay here," she told Isabelle. "Keep in touch with Jam. I'll call you if we run into trouble. You can listen in on your earpiece."

"Like last time?"

Andy blanched. "Hopefully, that's been fixed by now."

"Why can't I help? What's the use of just sitting here?"

Andy gave her a grim look. "You're not trained yet, and I'm not going to get you killed."

"I don't like this," Isabelle said, an unhappy frown on her face.

"You don't have to like it, but you're still staying." Andy grabbed her phone, popped in her earpiece, and jumped out. She collected her bulletproof vest from the back and slipped it on.

"Be careful," Isabelle called after her.

René followed Andy across the road. The snow was heavy, falling at a pace that promised to bury the roads within the hour.

Everything was wrong. All wrong. Weather was fucked up. Being back in New York was fucked up. Andy shrugged up the collar of her coat, then felt under the leather jacket for the array of seven throwing knives hiding to the right in a special leather sheath tied around her stomach, and the Sig P226 in the small of her back. She'd always favored the P226. Fifteen rounds made a difference.

She could shoot right, throw left. A multitalented killing machine by age seventeen thanks to Kate Bouchard.

Isabelle had to outrun. She had to outgun.

"Big girl pants, my ass," she murmured as she remembered Jam's words. "That's all I've damn well got in my closet."

"Going bonkers already, Bouchard?" René mocked her as she fell into step with her. "Mother Superior up your ass?"

"Like a borrowed swimsuit."

They stepped up on the pavement. Andy swiped one of Gerri's security tags and heard the soft beep as the thick glass door slid open. The security guard behind the desk looked up and froze. He didn't know them and chances where he knew everyone who lived here.

At least it was a different guard from the one on duty this afternoon.

Andy unzipped her jacket, relaxing her shoulders and softening the hasty tread of her boots. She put a sway in her hips as she swept the hair from her face and mock shivered from the cold.

"Hi there," she said, smiling broadly. She leaned with her arms on the guard's high desk hiding an array of screens from the surveillance system keeping an eye on the building, making sure not to touch anything.

René remained at the door to keep an eye on the street.

"We're looking for Ms. Arlene Hampton. Number forty-five?" Andy said. "We're part of her security detail and we haven't heard from her in quite a while. We're worried something may have happened to her."

The guard, a gray, tall man with bad teeth and fingernails bitten to the quick, frowned.

"Don't know about any security detail."

"It's a new thing. She got a couple of fresh death threats last week."

"Oh." The guard stood up from his chair and clipped a radio onto his belt. He was close to sixty-five and still in pretty good shape. "It's one in the morning. What do you want me to do?"

"Could you buzz her, please? Just to see if she's okay."

"Why not use your keys? Or phone her?"

"She's not answering and we don't have keys. We can only get to her front door." Andy held the security tags aloft. She thought about Hampton's private phone which Jam had not yet been able to track—if it even existed in the first place. "You know she has serious issues about her privacy."

"Which is exactly why I'm not going to buzz her."

"Okay. Then we'll have to go upstairs and knock on her door. And hope we don't disturb her."

The guard remained unmoved. He pointed to the screens in front of him. "I'll keep an eye on you to make sure you're okay." He scowled at them as if he didn't trust them.

René walked to the elevator, calling it with the sleeve of her bomber jacket tucked over her fingers. No one wanted to leave any fingerprints.

Andy followed, then turned back to the guard. "Did she have any visitors tonight?"

"Shouldn't you know that?" The guard stood up, suspicion oozing from his voice.

"New shift," she said and tapped on her chest. "And I'm new. Left the Twenty-third last week to take this job. Much better pay even though the hours aren't great."

"Twenty-third?" His voice eased into something like grudging respect. "Rough neighborhood to be a cop."

"Tell me about it."

"Used to be an EMT in Queens."

She counted on him being retired from a job related to law-enforcement. Emergency services was close enough.

He weighed her and finally said, "There were two guys here, about ten minutes ago. Nicely dressed."

The unease in Andy ratcheted up to bare-knuckle tension. She thought of this afternoon in the alley. "One of them look like a bouncer?"

"Black suit and gym muscles? Yeah. But that's not strange for Ms. Hampton. Lots of people like you around all hours of the day and night."

"Have the men left already?"

"Don't know. Can't even tell you if she's still in the building."

Andy thought about what Jam had said earlier about Hampton's work phone being in her apartment. "But her car is still here," she guessed.

"Yes, but sometimes the residents leave through the basement. And they often take their guests with them. The exit pops out on the east side. Saves you five minutes' walk to the subway. Ms. Hampton often leaves that way. Didn't your people tell you that?"

"Nope. Sorry. Ms. Hampton is not exactly cooperating. Her business partner suggested she get a security detail. Mr. Lautrec. Real asshole."

His distrust seeped away some more.

She considered her options. "Are there no cameras in the basement?"

"Been on the blink since yesterday."

"Just my luck." She shrugged, smiling wanly.

The guard looked at her, weighing his options. "I'll buzz her if you want."

"Nah. Don't worry. We'll go check. Probably a good idea anyway. But thanks. Appreciate it."

Andy walked to the elevator and stepped in. She swiped the security tag to the elevator and pushed the number four, her hand also tucked in her sleeve, out of sight from the security guard.

As the doors closed, her breath escaped in a puff of frustration. "That took forever."

"I know," René said. "Come on, come on," she urged the elevator to the fourth floor.

She looked at Andy, at the camera staring at them in the elevator. They couldn't pull their guns, not with the guard downstairs keeping an eye on them.

"Jam?" Andy said.

"Yeah?"

"The building's surveillance system. Crash it as quickly as you can. We've got problems."

"Doing that will erase info we might need."

"That's not important right now."

"Okay. Will do."

Andy heard a sharp intake of breath on the line and guessed it was Isabelle. She couldn't worry about that now.

The elevator announced their arrival on the fourth floor. The doors opened and they stepped out.

The hallway was quiet. Andy looked at the numbers on the nearest door and pointed to the right. They moved down the hallway, Andy keeping to the left-hand side of the carpeted space and René sticking to the right.

They stopped in front of number forty-five. They waited. Listened.

"Done," Jam spoke in her ear. "Building is yours."

Andy pulled the Sig, the cold metal providing her with some much-needed comfort. How long had it been since she'd found herself in a situation like this? Had the peace and quiet in London really only lasted three years? She hoped Jimmy was taking good care of the Black Sheep. She wanted her life back when this was done. All of it. Even the hooligan football supporters.

She steadied her breathing and looked to her right where René stood against the other wall.

Andy nodded, then knocked on the door, making sure to stay out of the firing line. "Ms. Hampton? Maintenance. There's a gas leak on your floor."

René pointed to her ear with her left hand, the Walther PPQ M2 she favored in her other. Andy heard the sound as well. Footsteps. Scrambling footsteps.

She reached out again and knocked. "Ms. Hamp—"

Wood splintered as a volley of gunshots rang through the door. Andy ducked, hurrying back down the hallway as Hampton's front door flew open. Someone next door screamed.

More shots. Heavy feet running at them.

Andy fired at the black suit coming her way, hitting his arm. It didn't stop his momentum, though. She felt herself lifted off her feet and slammed into the wall, gun falling from her hand in a sharp exhalation of breath.

She hit the man in his face as he again slammed her into the wall.

Fucker was huge, heavy, and muscled. And familiar. It was Marat Sharapov's buddy. The one from the alley.

He dropped her and ran to the fire escape, gripping his arm in his left hand. She looked for her gun. Too far. Her attacker would be gone before she could reach it.

She pulled a knife from her back and threw it at the disappearing figure. She hit his side. She threw another one.

Missed.

He opened the door with a tag.

Fucker got a security tag?

Her third knife flew to the left as a boot connected with her head.

She fought the sudden darkness, reaching for the shoe as it stomped past her. She felt a crush as it came down on her fingers. She shot forward, on hands and knees, tackling the passing figure, crawling on top of him.

He squirmed under her and groaned as her fists connected with the back of his head, his neck.

He turned slightly, a gunbarrel pointing out from under his torso. He fired. Andy dodged left, but still the bullet hit, the air escaping her lungs in a sharp, short sound.

CHAPTER TWENTY-SEVEN

Andy leaned back on her knees and thumped her chest gratefully. Bulletproof vest caught the bullet. Day two and already she'd been shot and assaulted with a baton. Lovely.

Where was René?

There. Lying on the ground.

"René!" she called as she stumbled to her. "You better be okay, you useless piece of shit. Still got to teach me that left—"

René coughed.

Andy turned her onto her back. From the blood covering her left eye and the wall, it seemed like someone had slammed her face into it.

"Shut up, Bouchard. I'm okay. Don't go all soft on me now. What happened to chasing down the bad guys?"

"Your job. I've got to check on Hampton."

René stumbled to her feet, wiping the blood away with her sleeve. She called Jam as she leaned against the wall, getting her bearings. She described the men to David and Iona who were standing by downstairs.

"Cops are three minutes out," Jam said in their ears.

René nodded at Andy who was still waiting to see if she was okay. "Go. I'm all right. Check on Hampton and leave. And police your brass." She pointed to the bullet casings. "And your knives. Be quick."

"Will do. Be careful," Andy said.

"No problem." René inhaled sharply as if in pain, and then started jogging to the stairway door, Gerri Hope's security tags in hand.

❖

Andy donned plastic gloves and quickly collected the two knives that had missed her target, hoping René would get the other if Black Jacket pulled it from his side on the fire escape. She picked up the casings and rushed inside Hampton's apartment to check on her, the wailing sirens growing louder.

She could hear the neighbor's front door inch open carefully.

Arlene Hampton lay on the carpet, sprawled between a set of oxblood leather couches. She was facing the window, her hand outstretched, as if reaching out to the soft, distant scattering of city lights in front of her.

Andy felt for a pulse and found one.

"Fuck it."

She turned the woman over. That was unexpected. While she was grateful Hampton was alive, it also complicated matters. Andy rushed to the sink to collect a handful of kitchen towels. She applied pressure to the bullet wounds while she spoke to Jam.

"Get the ambulance," she said. "Hampton's alive."

"Shit."

A minute's silence. The elevator behind her pinged.

"And tell Isabelle to leave. Tell her to take the car and go to Ma Soeur right now."

She knew Jam had again cut Isabelle from all comms on this operation when the bullets started flying. No doubt she was going to be livid.

"Will do," Jam said. "Legal?"

"Yeah. Get Caroline down here."

The apartment door burst open.

"Hands in the air," a gruff, testosterone voice bellowed.

"Applying pressure to a bullet wound here," she said evenly.

"Hands where I can see them!" the voice was nervous. Angry.

"I can't—"

"Put your fucking hands up! Lock them behind your head."

More feet, more people arriving.

Andy lifted her hands in the air.

CHAPTER TWENTY-EIGHT

Detective Jane Wright eased out of her car, identified herself to the officer on duty, and picked her way through the throng of flashing lights, curious onlookers, and uniforms. It'd been three months since she'd joined the new team in the Major Case Squad tasked to investigate crime against prominent people in the city. Who'd have known she'd be this busy?

She hadn't even wrapped up Horace Gibson's murder yet and here she was, at a new crime scene. And this one promised to be even bigger than the Gibson case.

Arlene Hampton was close friends with the mayor and the commissioner—close enough for Jane to get a phone call kicking her out of bed, telling her to get her ass down here immediately.

She hoisted her collar up against the snow and quickened her step to the welcoming door across the road. Inside Hampton's apartment building it was warm, the precinct detective probably the middle-aged guy with dirty shoes who looked like he'd been boozing it up until he got called to the scene.

"Micky Fulsom," he said in an unexpected Southern drawl.

From close by she could see flecks of sour milk on his jacket. Not boozing then. More likely had a little one at home struggling to sleep.

Fulsom's eyes trailed hers. "Twins."

She pulled a face signaling sympathy. "Better run me through it, then you can get home."

He laughed. "Think I'd prefer sleeping in a holding cell right now."

"That can be arranged."

They walked to a quiet corner. "Arlene Hampton is in apartment number forty-five." He pointed to a security guard giving his statement to a uniform. "Guard there saw two men go up to her apartment. Invited guests it seemed. Hampton buzzed them up. Few minutes later, two women showed up. Claimed they were Hampton's personal security detail and that she wasn't answering her phone. They had security access for the door and elevator so they went up."

Fulsom raised his eyebrows, hitting his notepad with a cheap yellow pen. "This is where it gets weird. CCTV of the lobby and elevators died two minutes later. Just like that. Guard heard shots. Neighbors too. We got five nine-one-one calls. Two, three minutes later, more shots in the basement. Basement's got CCTV, but that's been down since yesterday. Whoever shot up the basement, may have taken the fight to the street, it seemed. We have broken auto glass about four hundred yards down the street. Two parked cars streaked with black paint. No luck with CCTV outside the building yet."

Fulsom gestured to a glass encased room behind him and the two women sitting there. It seemed like a small kitchen and bathroom, probably for use by the building's security guards. "Unis showed up at number forty-five. Caught this chick administering CPR. Guard says she's one of the two women who said they were on Hampton's security detail. Other one is in the wind."

"And let me guess, she's not talking, right?" Wright pointed to the tall, athletic woman with the black hair and neutral, calm face.

"How did you know it was her?" Fulsom smirked.

"Oh, I have a nose for troublemakers," Wright said.

"Okay. Two out of two. Now strike me out and tell me what's funny about the woman in black?"

"Apart from the fact that's she's like six two?"

"Yeah?"

Wright contemplated her. "Nah. Don't know. Tell me."

"Clean as a whistle. Perfect record. Not even a parking ticket to her name. Saved Hampton's life only for her to check out in the ambulance. DOA at the hospital."

"Shit." Jane wiped at her mouth. She wished she still smoked. She stared at Fulsom who looked like he was holding something back. Something juicy. "Yeah? And?"

"Our girl here policed her brass. Picked it all up before she went into the apartment."

"Only hers?"

"Yes."

Wright turned on her heels. She stared at the woman with the dark eyes looking right at her. "Now why the hell would you do that unless you had something to hide?"

❖

Isabelle stood on the sidewalk, hidden between a handful of diehard onlookers watching as the cops finally opened the street to traffic. It was after four in the morning and her feet were freezing in her heels. She was exhausted beyond belief, but she couldn't leave. Jam had told her to go back to Ma Soeur, but she didn't want to leave Andy here alone. Jam had assured her that Andy was fine and in good hands, but she wanted to see it with her own eyes. She got her into this predicament—she and her messed up dreams.

Isabelle waited as the uniforms packed up and disappeared, the only crime scene tape remaining the one blocking the entrance to Arlene Hampton's building. Arlene, whose murder she supposedly saw, but did not predict for tonight. And not like this, with Andy here.

She wrapped her arms around her body swaddled in a long black coat. She felt like a fraud. A liar. The most powerful dreamer since the 1400s? Bullshit. All of it. She belonged in an institution. Maybe it was time to face the truth.

She trudged back to the SUV as the curious crowd thinned out. She ignored Jam's repeated calls. If they wanted to cut her off when the bad stuff happened, she would cut them off too.

She'd wait here for Andy to make sure she was okay and then go back to Ma Soeur to pack her bags and leave.

CHAPTER TWENTY-NINE

How long is this woman going to make us wait?" Caroline Diaz glanced at her watch.

Andy shrugged and yawned. "She's probably going to look at the crime scene before she does the interview."

They'd both watched as the woman with the black pantsuit, comfortable shoes, and thick curly hair, the color of ripe wheat, stood talking to the detective who had herded them into the small kitchen. She had a coffee cup in her hand, drinking from it as if she was dying of thirst. When she'd drained it, they walked toward the elevator and got in.

Caroline made a noise in the back of her throat. "Waste of time." She turned to Andy. "We're clear on what's going to happen here?"

"Yes. Don't worry. I know what to do."

Caroline regarded her with cool blue eyes under dark blond hair that hung halfway down her back. Her skirt and jacket screamed money and power, as did the thick golden earrings and the matching chain around her neck. She looked magnificently put together, as always.

Caroline was a born professional. One hundred percent so. You didn't get to be Ma Soeur's legal counsel without the balls and fortitude to deal with the absurd and farfetched as an everyday occurrence.

It did help that Caroline's father and mother were a Ma Soeur unit before they retired three years ago.

Caroline's job was to hide Ma Soeur. To block and obscure and redirect.

Caroline jutted her chin out. "You left without saying good-bye." Her firm, low-pitched voice sounded as if she was indicting Andy for murder.

Andy stared at her boots, guilt rising in her throat like bile. René, Caroline. She'd left good people behind without saying a word. "Sorry about that. Really."

"I just woke up and you were gone. I had to go talk to Kate to figure out what had happened, just to find out that she had no idea where you were either."

"I'm…I just couldn't anymore. I just couldn't breathe."

"I never thought of you as a coward. Not for a single moment did I ever imagine that you would act that way."

Andy hung her head in shame, only to find herself trapped looking at the trim legs that once straddled her, the Blahniks that Caroline favored, especially when being taken leaning over a kitchen counter wearing nothing else.

"We were good together," Caroline said.

"I know. I'm really sorry. I was a coward. You're right."

"Victoria. You could have gone to her and fixed it." Caroline sighed. "Returned home."

"I am back, even if not of my own free will. No one told you?" Andy feigned a smile as she straightened her back.

Caroline hefted her briefcase onto the seat next to her. "I heard. The redhead. The little girl your mother thought she'd push into your bed."

"She's not in my bed."

"Won't be long."

Andy breathed out slowly. She deserved Caroline's anger. They got together just after Victoria. It was quick, but Caroline was invested. Saw a future for them. Andy was bruised and hurting, but that was no excuse for the way she'd behaved.

"I'm sorry. I'm really sorry for the way I treated you."

Caroline smirked. "Save your apologies and put on your game face." She pointed to the elevator door as it opened. "It's time to play stupid."

❖

Jane looked at the tall woman in front of her, the gorgeous lawyer next to her. She tried to stem the sudden tide of attraction she felt for the blonde with the elegant bone structure. And those furious blue eyes that bored into hers.

Hell, she needed to get over herself. And Amy. Amy the cheating bitch.

"I told you Ms. Bouchard has no comment on her relationship with the victim beyond the fact that she was her bodyguard."

"And I'm asking if there is any documentation that will prove this." Jane's icy tone matched that of Caroline Diaz. "You can see that I would find this rather strange—a bodyguard guarding the owner of a security firm."

Diaz sighed irritably. "Ms. Bouchard didn't interrogate Ms. Hampton on why she would need her services. Maybe she didn't trust her own people. And Ms. Bouchard favors oral contracts. Her clients are high-powered individuals who do not want to leave a paper trail."

"So, no, in other words."

Diaz said nothing.

"And the woman who was with her when she entered the building to go check on Ms. Hampton? Is she also a bodyguard?"

"What woman? Ms. Bouchard was alone."

"That's not what the security guard says." Jane's eyes swiveled to Bouchard. Ice-cold black eyes stared at her as if she was a piece of meat. Dead meat. This woman would scare the shit out of you on a dark, stormy night.

"He must be lying," Diaz declared. "CCTV will show that she was alone."

Ah. There it was. "CCTV's gone. Apparently, the entire system crashed just after your client stepped off the elevator. Everything has to be rebooted."

Diaz shrugged underneath her expensive suit. Must be Gucci or Armani. Woman must charge a fortune. Jane didn't know how Andy Bouchard could afford her. Bouchard's black clothes were nondescript, not the slightest sheen of money on her.

Jane narrowed her eyes as she looked at the women in front of her. She couldn't shake the feeling that there was something between these two. Something unexpected. Something angry and sexual. She'd always been good at reading people—not a bad trait if you dealt with criminals for a living; not so good if you wanted to share your bed with someone every now and then.

Jane gathered there was not going to be any confession forthcoming about the surveillance system.

"Tell me about the Sig," she asked instead.

"My client has a permit," Diaz said. "Concealed carry. And your forensics team is welcome to try to match her gun to the weapon that killed Ms. Hampton. They won't find anything. Ms. Bouchard attempted to save Ms. Hampton's life, as she was paid to do."

"And the knives?"

Diaz didn't bat an eyelid at the stash of throwing knives her client had carried. "Surely you can appreciate that they are necessary in her line of work."

Jane looked at Bouchard. She hadn't said a word since they'd started the interview. She looked happy to let the lawyer bat away every question. They were like a well-oiled team. How many times had they done this before?

Even more interesting was that the lawyer had shown up without Andrea Bouchard making a single phone call. The uniforms had emptied her pockets when she was detained. Everything was lying on the table in a clear plastic bag—everything except for one thing.

"Where are the tags you used to get into the building, Ms. Bouchard?"

"She lost them," Diaz answered. "Must have been in the rush of being arrested by your colleagues."

Convenient. "You know those tags are null and void now? In case your client wanted to use them again at some point. The system reboot means everything has to be reprogrammed."

Which also meant that Jane couldn't see who had entered the building at what time.

"Why would she want to come back?" Diaz asked, frowning slightly. "Ms. Hampton is dead."

Jane bit back the swear word and tried a new angle. "Tell me about the bullet casings. "Your client picked them up. Messed up the crime scene. She'll be arrested for tampering with a crime scene."

"She only picked up hers. Old habit. And she apologizes profusely. Really. You are welcome to charge her, but you know we'll have her out on bail tomorrow. She tried to save Ms. Hampton's life. Your officers can attest to that fact. She was knee-deep in blood when they arrested her. In fact, Ms. Hampton might still be alive if your officers didn't prevent her from continuing to administer CPR. We also have some questions about why you didn't immediately pursue the two men she pointed out to you. The two men who attacked her in the hallway as she attempted to enter Ms. Hampton's apartment."

Yeah. Great. Jane had wondered how long it would be before Caroline Diaz raised that particular point.

It took two minutes or so to secure Bouchard and for the first uniform to attempt resuscitation. Could it have saved Hampton? Probably not. But that's not what the media was going to claim.

Sometimes she hated her job.

"Anything else?" Diaz placed her hand on Bouchard's knee in an intimate gesture, then realized what she'd done and moved her hand away.

Bouchard shifted uncomfortably in her seat. It was the first time she'd shown any emotion.

"Yes." Jane moved in quickly. "We'd like Ms. Bouchard to provide a DNA sample for exclusion purposes."

"Certainly."

No hesitation. Jane blinked in surprise and tugged at her right earlobe. She realized she was revealing her tell, just like in those poker games she kept on losing the last few weeks. She pushed her hands back into her lap. Bouchard had been wearing latex gloves when she was administering CPR, but carrying those was apparently also part of her job.

But gloves wouldn't necessarily stop a perp's DNA from entering a crime scene when they killed someone violently. And Hampton was killed violently. Four shots to the back as she was running away.

"We can do it now, if you want?" Caroline smiled. It was a wonderfully fake smile, practiced and professional. "My client and I are tired and would like to get this over with."

Jane swore. Maybe the Bouchard woman was right. Maybe they should be looking for two men in their thirties dressed in black. One big, one lean and wiry. Sounded like every second guy in the city.

"And her phone? Can she unlock that for us too?"

"Sure. We are happy to help in any way."

Too easy. Again.

Jane fished Bouchard's phone from the plastic bag and handed it to Diaz. Diaz showed it to Bouchard, who pressed her thumbprint on the screen.

Diaz handed it back to Jane.

Jane scrolled through it. Nothing. There were only two numbers programmed on it, one of which was Hampton's. Nothing else, no call records, no email, nothing.

She dialed the number she didn't know. No one answered.

"Is this really your phone, Ms. Bouchard?"

"Of course," Diaz said. "You are welcome to check with her service provider. It has been for about six months, if I understand my client correctly."

Fuck. They were smooth.

To her right, standing outside the glass encased kitchen, her partner, Russo, was trying to get her attention. She walked to the exit.

"Unis at the tape says we got a girl here. Says she's your perp's partner. As in between the sheets, not the office."

"Bouchard's?"

"Yes."

"Who?"

"Dunno. Unis says she's insisting on seeing Bouchard. What are you going to do? Arrest Bouchard?"

Jane thought about the men in black. The casings. She could get Bouchard for the casings, but she didn't want to. Not yet. She wanted her to think she was off the hook. She wanted to know more about her. And her lawyer.

"No. Tell her to come and collect Bouchard. In fact, give me two minutes and then tell her to come in. Bouchard isn't giving me anything. Maybe seeing her partner will shake her up a bit."

Jane was especially eager for the woman to show, as she had placed the lawyer in Bouchard's bed. At this point she'd take any reading she could get from Bouchard.

"I'll tell them to bring her through." Russo pointed upstairs. "I'm going to wrap up the crime scene."

Jane sighed. It was almost five already. "Thanks. Grab some sleep when you're done and meet me at One PP at ten."

CHAPTER THIRTY

So we can go?" Caroline said. "About bloody time."

She got to her feet, her anger masking a tiny bit of relief, Jane imagined. "Just don't go anywhere," she warned. "And I mean, don't even go smell the air outside the city. Understood?"

"My client knows to stay put," Diaz said.

Jane looked at Andy, waiting for an answer.

"I won't. Promise," she said.

The door opened. Jane didn't turn, locking her eyes on Bouchard instead.

A woman rushed in. Out of the corner of her eye, Jane saw a flash of red hair and heard a vaguely familiar voice.

"Andy! Are you okay?"

The woman rushed to Andy's side, her voice filled with concern, her hands doing a quick body check to see if her lover was okay.

Diaz froze, her eyes turning ice cold. Jane's jaw dropped. It was the woman. The young woman who two weeks ago told them that she'd dreamed about Horace Gibson's murder before it had happened. The crazy redhead with the beautiful eyes.

Jane watched as Andy got up and enveloped the woman in her arms. She looked surprised, pleased, but also slightly angry.

"I told you to go home," she said in a low tone.

The woman—Isabelle, that's right—now Jane remembered—shrugged. "I couldn't leave you here. I had to make sure you're okay."

It was clear she wanted to say more, but turned, suddenly aware of the stranger in the room.

She stiffened when she saw Jane.

"Miss Templeton." Jane gave a slight bow. "How nice to see you again."

Finally, Jane got what she'd been looking for the entire night. She turned her gaze to see Andy Bouchard looking worried. Very, very worried.

❖

Isabelle hadn't been able to face the car anymore, the concern about Andy eating away at her, so she'd gone to Arlene's building to see if the police were done interviewing her. Maybe Jam was lying to her. Maybe Andy had been injured and nobody had the guts to tell her that she was in the hospital. Or dead. Ma Soeur didn't exactly have a great track record when it came to being honest with her.

The uniforms outside had made her wait, then let her in, much to her surprise. She hadn't imagined getting beyond the front door.

And now this. Her mind searched for the policewoman's name. Jane. Jane…Wright. Detective. Major Case Squad.

Andy was angry at her for being here, bordering on furious. The hand that gripped hers was strong, fierce, hurting her as Andy stared at Detective Wright.

"Andy, my hand," she whispered.

Andy looked down at her, their intertwined hands. The white-knuckle grip she had on Isabelle's fingers.

"Sorry. I'm sorry." She let go and smoothed over Isabelle's hands in an apology.

Detective Wright looked at them with open curiosity.

The blond woman next to Andy suddenly swung into action, ushering them toward the door. "You can kiss and make up later. Let's get going."

Isabelle looked at her. She looked like a tougher version of Arlene Hampton. Smooth, groomed to a T. Angry.

The blonde pushed them toward the door.

Detective Wright stood up. "Wait just a moment. Is nobody in this room interested in how I know Ms. Templeton?"

"No," said the blonde. "It's late. My client is tired. Her girlfriend is tired. We're all eager to get home."

Detective Wright moved to the door and stood, arms crossed.

"Come on, Detective, you said we could go," the blonde argued, clearly upset.

Detective Wright pointed to Isabelle. "Allow me one more question." She turned to Isabelle. "Have you dreamed about any murders lately, Ms. Templeton? Perhaps like the one of Ms. Hampton tonight?"

CHAPTER THIRTY-ONE

Andy rushed to the door, dragging Isabelle behind her. "I won't leave the city. Contact me through Ms. Diaz any time you want."

The detective didn't budge. She stood firm, hands in her pockets, blocking their exit. "I asked you a question, Ms. Templeton."

Isabelle found her voice as she let go of Andy's hand. "I was stressed and tired that night. I made a mistake. We all make mistakes. I didn't dream anything. My studies…they took their toll." Isabelle tucked a few errant strands of hair behind her ear and bit down on her bottom lip.

"You were convinced you'd dreamed about Horace Gibson's death before it happened."

Isabelle let go of Andy's hand and walked up to Wright, feigning irritation. "You didn't believe me back then, so why worry about it now?"

She wanted to get out of here and she wanted Andy with her, away from the blond woman who looked as if she wanted to eat her alive.

Detective Wright stood her ground, looking at each of them, a fresh curiosity flaring up in her eyes. "Who exactly are you people? There's something going on here. Something more than personal protection. Much more than what you're telling me."

Isabelle shook her head. "Now you are the one who is delusional, Detective. Dreaming up things that don't exist."

❖

"What the hell were you thinking walking in there?" the blonde snapped once they were inside Andy's car.

"I was worried about Andy."

"And you thought it would be okay to just go and find her?"

Isabelle turned to face the woman in the back seat, placing her hand on Andy's leg as she did, feeling the flinch of muscles under her fingertips. Screw this woman who obviously carried some torch for Andy.

"If I understand this correctly, Andy and I are partners." Her voice was calm, controlled, anger crowding out the exhaustion. "We are supposed to look out for each other, so stop screaming at me. I don't work for you. In fact, I don't work for any of you, so stop ordering me around. My only debt is to Andy. Do we understand each other?"

The blonde sat back, surprise on her face. "I'm sure Kate will love your answer." She dug around in her handbag and took out her phone. "Tell me how you met Detective Wright. I need to be prepared the next time she corners us. Because there is no way she is going to let go now."

CHAPTER THIRTY-TWO

Isabelle stood at the side of the bed as Andy kicked off her boots and dropped her coat on the couch.

"Are you mad at me?" Isabelle said, her voice a whisper.

"Yes." Andy sighed as she realized she was lying. Maybe the drive here and the cool night air had helped to clear her head. "No. We cut you off from all communications and then expect you to just be okay. To trust us. I probably would have done the same. I just wished you'd told us earlier about the thing with Horace Gibson and the police."

"And when exactly should I have done this?"

Andy gave a wry smile. "Yeah. I suppose you're right."

"No hard feelings?" Isabelle asked.

"No." Andy tilted her head. "I'm not sure Caroline feels the same, but I'll deal with her."

Isabelle bristled at the mention of Caroline's name but said nothing. "So, if you're not mad at me, sleep with me," she said, her voice gaining a sultry lilt. "Here. In our bed."

Andy rubbed her chest where the bullets had hit the bulletproof vest. "I'm okay on the couch."

"I'm not okay with you there. You made me run around the city to make sure I dream and now you want to run away from your responsibility." Isabelle smoothed down the white bedding. "Besides. It's my birthday, remember? And I'm pretty sure you didn't get me anything."

Andy couldn't help but smile. "*That* you had every opportunity to mention."

"And ruin the emotional blackmail? This beautiful moment?"

The smile turned into a laugh. Andy untucked her shirt. The cops took her gun and knives. She would need to go to the quartermaster to get new weapons in the morning. She glanced at her watch. Later today. It was six already. Kate had demanded to speak to her and Isabelle, but she'd flatly refused. They needed to sleep. Jam and Caroline could fill her in until they were ready to surface.

Arlene Hampton was dead. They failed to save her life. She locked eyes with Isabelle. Her green eyes were already murky with sleep, with the dream that would undoubtedly haunt her as soon as she closed her eyes, perhaps of Marat Sharapov this time.

"Are you okay?" she asked. Losing Hampton must have impacted Isabelle more than anyone else on the team.

"No," Isabelle said.

She stood up, stripped her black dress from her body, and stood next to the bed in heels and a garter belt and black lace that made Andy's heart rate pick up a notch, despite the exhaustion. Then she remembered. Isabelle would probably still carry the scent of the woman from the club.

"I messed up," Isabelle said in a clipped tone. "If I stayed here last night we could have maybe saved Arlene."

"If we stayed here we would have slept right through the snow and only woken up this morning." Andy closed the gap between them. She wanted to tell her that it was okay. That dreaming wasn't a science. It was a hope. A dark road you traveled down with the vague ambition that you could prevent a catastrophe Fate had every intention of carrying out.

Isabelle looked at Andy, her eyes shiny. "Perhaps it's better if I leave. This is obviously a mistake. I'm not what your mother imagined I'd be."

"Nobody made a mistake. I'm absolutely certain about that." Andy stepped closer and took Isabelle in her arms. "And you can't leave now. We need to see this through. And I sure as hell can't do it without you. I want to know who murdered Arlene. I need to know."

Andy knew it would be better for Isabelle to leave, but only in a physical sense, as it would keep her safe. Emotionally and intellectually, she would suffer major harm. If she packed her bags now, she'd end up with some doctor dosing her up to her eyeballs with drugs she didn't need. Great if you required it, but Isabelle didn't. It would be a life lost, and it would be Andy's fault.

Isabelle needed to understand her skill. Trust it. Then make a decision about her future.

Then you better help her, a tiny voice inside her chimed in. *Help her like you mean it.*

"Take a shower," Andy said, Isabelle warm against her body, her hair smelling of the ocean and the gentle hint of smoke and musk. "And go to bed. I'll be right behind you."

When Andy emerged from the bathroom, Isabelle was fast asleep. Andy watched as she breathed deeply, numbed by the day's exhaustion. She leaned down and kissed her in the gentle slope below her ear, the elegant, taut muscle of her neck so much less stubborn in sleep.

"What am I going to do with you, Isabelle Templeton," she murmured. "What on earth am I going to do with you?"

CHAPTER THIRTY-THREE

Isabelle didn't fall asleep as much as crash into it. The darkness enveloped her, pitch-black and dense, lifting only to slip in the dream like a dagger—silent and deadly.

The steady stream of images was unexpected. Andy was running down a dimly lit street. She was angry, her face contorted with rage. She charged into a front door and across a noisy space, fighting against a stream of panicked people rushing to escape.

It was a…restaurant. No, a diner.

Andy's breath was hurried, as if she'd been running for a while. Her boots hit the floor like gunshots. She had her weapon in her hand.

Isabelle's heart thrashed in her chest.

Not Andy. No, no, no.

Andy stopped abruptly. In front of her, on the ground, was a body. It was a woman. She was lying on her stomach, face turned away, arms outstretched, a gun inches from her hands, as if she had been crawling toward it when she was shot in the back, just as had been the case with Arlene Hampton.

Andy bent down next to the woman and turned her over.

It was Detective Jane Wright. Andy placed her gun on the floor and called for help, but there was nobody left in the diner to come to her aid. She bent down to listen if Detective Wright was still breathing.

Behind her, from another booth, a shadow emerged.

The figure stealthily approached Andy.

Oh no…

Andy turned on her heels.

No, no, no…

The shadow lifted a gun and pulled the trigger.

Isabelle screamed, trying to warn Andy, but she couldn't get the words out. They stuck to the roof of her mouth, like birds clawing at closed windows.

Then the mud came. The thick, black mud sucking her in. Covering her feet, her hands, her eyes, her mouth.

❖

Andy held on as Isabelle's body bucked like a wild horse against her own. She kept on whispering soothing words as Isabelle struggled to escape the dream, her breathing erratic and her body increasingly panic-stricken as she tried to find her way back to the Brooklyn apartment.

They'd slept six hours before Isabelle's screams had woken her.

"I got you," she murmured. "Come back to me. I got you. All is well here. Come back."

But the fear remained. In fact, it ratcheted up a notch, emerging from Isabelle's mouth in a high-pitched scream. Andy stopped thinking and kissed her, capturing the terror in her mouth, breathing it in.

Isabelle's body froze, then melded to hers. Her arms, battling unseen foes, slipped around Andy's neck, pulling her closer. Desperate, hungry, she clung to Andy, slipping her tongue into her mouth.

Andy tasted a strange mix of blood and peppermint, then groaned with the unexpected pleasure of Isabelle moving against her, opening her legs, inviting Andy in. She forgot about the constant dull ache in her upper body and flipped Isabelle on her back, her mouth in the crook of Isabelle's neck, moving down to her clavicle, pushing aside the white T-shirt to taste the sweet expanse of skin that lay hidden beneath. She explored one full, heavy breast, the nipple rock hard in the palm of her hand.

She pushed her leg into Isabelle's core. The pressure made Isabelle gasp and groan as she moved against it, her hips riding a sharp wave of arousal.

Retract.

Isabelle was in no state to know what was happening to her. Yesterday's flirtation was not this morning's consent. She retreated even further, opening her eyes and staring down at Isabelle's forest green gaze.

"Sorry," she whispered. "I'm so sorry."

Isabelle gave a strained smile. "I'm not. Why did you stop?"

Isabelle immediately closed her eyes again, grabbing her head as if it was going to explode. She leaned over the edge of the bed, giving a dry heave.

Andy rubbed her back in slow circles. "I'm going to make you something to take the edge off. Just hang on a minute."

❖

"And you're sure it was me?"

"Yes. Absolutely." Isabelle ate the last bite of the beef sandwich hungrily, then washed it down with a mixture of strawberry and tomato juice. She sat up in bed, resting her back against the wall, the bedding a white pool around her waist.

Andy sat next to her, contemplating the dream Isabelle had told her about. She sipped her coffee, trying not to stare at the white T-shirt and what lay underneath the thin white cotton.

"Is there any link to the Hampton case?" she asked. "Did you see anything that may point to Arlene Hampton?"

"No. The only possible link would be Detective Wright."

"And Marat Sharapov? Was he anywhere in your dream? You touched him yesterday."

"Not that I could see, no."

"Any idea of time and date?"

"No. I got the sense it was night, but I can't even promise you that." Isabelle reached out, cradling Andy's hand in hers, stroking it softly. "We have to stop the dream. You can't…you can't die. Please. You have to make sure you don't walk into any diners in the next week or so."

Andy smiled wryly. "It's never that easy."

Isabelle's hand stopped, then gripped Andy's tightly. "You've been here before."

"Where?"

"Someone dreamed about you. About you dying."

Andy put down her coffee next to the bed. She didn't want to answer.

"Tell me about Victoria."

"How do you know about Vic?"

Isabelle shrugged. "I overheard René talking to someone."

"What did she say?"

Isabelle shrugged. "She's surprised that you're back—glad, because you should be able to temper your mother's ambition, and because she's happy to see you. It seems you left without saying good-bye?"

Andy was torn between talking and running away.

When did running away become such a knee-jerk reaction?

"Vic was my previous dreamer," she said. "The how and when are not important. She dreamt one night that I was going to be killed along with sixty-seven other people in a terrorist bombing in the subway." Andy swept her hair from her face and touched the scar under her eye. "It was going to be later that day. Evening rush hour. She could spot it from the newspaper a businessman was reading on the platform. And his watch gave the time. Anyway. I went in. Kate sent me in. I decided to go. It's irrelevant how I got there."

Andy looked at her hands. "Vic deceived me. We had a good-bye drink and she put something in my vodka. She timed it perfectly. I passed out fifteen minutes later. I only woke up hours later when the EMTs carried me from the subway rubble. I had made it as far as the stairs before I collapsed."

Andy took a deep breath. "Ninety-three people died, much more than the sixty-seven Vic had dreamt about. I was so angry. Kate was livid. Vic couldn't understand…Dreamers and keepers are not allowed to stop their own deaths unless they are the focal point of a dream. The domino effect may be too big, the price too tremendous to comprehend." She pulled her hand from Isabelle's grip. "Vic betrayed me. What we were trained to do. And yet…"

Isabelle rubbed her arm gently. "You're glad that you are alive?"

Andy hung her head in shame. "Yes."

Isabelle moved closer to her, putting her arms around Andy. She could fully understand Victoria's motivations, although she was careful not to say it. Clearly, Andy had a great sense of duty. But what was it like to know your mother was willing to send you to your death?

"What happened to Victoria?" she asked.

"From what I heard she went mad. I have no other explanation. She saw the stories of the people who died. The parents. The eleven children. She retreated into her head." Andy cleared her throat as if looking for the words. "I wasn't here to see it. I had moved in with Caroline Diaz."

"The blonde from yesterday?"

"Yes. Messed that one up too. Royally."

Isabelle didn't offer any hollow words of consolation. "And now you are here again, with someone who's dreamed of your death."

For a minute or two, Andy didn't move. Then she inhaled and exhaled deeply. "Yes, but there are a few differences. I'm the focal point of your dream, along with Wright. And this time around, everything won't happen on the same day as the dream. We have time. We can prevent it."

"Like we prevented Arlene Hampton's murder?"

Andy didn't want Isabelle to go there. "That's a different matter altogether and I hope to prove that to you later today."

❖

Isabelle walked to their small kitchen and made tea for her and coffee for Andy. The smell of coffee made her crave caffeine, but she resisted the temptation. She searched the handful of cabinets until she found a pan, then scoured the fridge for eggs, locating a dozen in the fresh compartment. Somebody had stocked the apartment before they'd moved in.

She turned to Andy, fork in hand. "I can do fried or scrambled."

Andy looked at her like she was a lifesaver. "Two scrambled eggs on wheat toast would make my day."

"Doesn't take much to please you, does it?"

"Apparently not."

Andy smiled at her, then returned her attention to the computer on her lap. It seemed she was searching for something—what exactly, she'd refused to tell Isabelle yet.

Isabelle watched as she typed, frowned, then rubbed her mouth as if she was considering her options. She turned to switch on the kettle, the kiss from this morning a sudden, vivid memory. It had carried the same intensity Andy seemed to do with everything. The same absolute, complete focus, but coupled with something else. Something unexpected. Something hinting at a kind of release. Of letting go.

Finally.

She flushed as she broke the eggs into the frying pan, the butter already sizzling.

"Why did you stop?" she asked, her eyes fixed on the stove top.

"Hmm?" Andy asked from the couch.

"Why did you stop? The kiss, earlier?" Isabelle stirred the eggs, too scared of what she might see on Andy's face. "Did I do something you didn't like?"

"No," Andy said quickly. "I just…you know. You weren't…back yet," she fumbled. "I didn't mean to force you into anything. It was a mistake. The moment. We're not in a space of trust where it can just happen naturally. You know?"

This conversation wasn't going the way Isabelle had wanted. A mistake? "I liked it. Very much. I wanted you to continue." She swallowed, the apprehension turning her mouth dry. "And I trust you completely. Maybe next time—"

A knock on the door stopped her mid-sentence.

Andy turned to open it with something like relief on her face.

Isabelle cursed inwardly.

René stood on the threshold. "Kate wants to see you. No excuses this time. Her words, not mine." She looked past Andy to Isabelle. "Smells divine. Got any bacon with that?"

Isabelle waved her in. "Come sit. There's enough for the three of us."

Andy placed a hand against René's chest, glancing over her shoulder. "Maybe just let Isabelle change first."

Isabelle looked down at her shorts and T-shirt, then at Andy. She didn't imagine that she was dressed in anything more revealing than the clothes she wore to the gym, but she liked what she saw in Andy's eyes.

She put down the spatula and moved the pan from the heat. "Just give me a moment to put on some sweats. Andy can make you some coffee while I'm busy."

❖

"So?" René asked as she leaned against the counter next to Andy. "What happened last night? This morning. Whatever."

"Another dream," Andy said as she handed René a cup of coffee. She looked at her watch. Past noon. The day was slipping away from them.

"And?"

"Nothing."

"Nothing? Don't mess with me, Bouchard. Your girl dreamed something significant. You're all tensed up. Otherwise why hide her from my prying eyes?" René popped two slices of bread into the toaster, then turned, a teasing smile on her face. "Unless you're jealous. Because I am interested if she's up for grabs, you know."

Andy switched on the kettle for a fresh cup of tea for Isabelle. "Back off. Things are complicated enough."

"Exactly how complicated?"

Andy sighed with relief as the bathroom door opened and Isabelle stepped out in a pair of white sweatpants and a green T-shirt.

Damn woman would look good in anything.

"Complicated?" Isabelle asked.

Thinking fast, Andy pointed to the eggs, then to René. "Making breakfast for René. She eats about six eggs a day to keep up muscle weight. To the big disappointment of her cardiologist."

Isabelle squeezed past them and switched on the stovetop again. "Don't worry, we have enough to feed you. But remember this act of kindness when I get into the boxing ring with you again."

René smiled, then looked at her with concerned eyes. "You okay about last night? About Hampton?"

Isabelle bit her bottom lip, stared at her feet. "I'm okay. Sort of."

"Sometimes we lose someone. It happens. It's part of the deal."

Andy held out her hand, and Isabelle reached out to take it. Isabelle wasn't okay. Far from it. But hopefully, Andy knew how to fix it.

CHAPTER THIRTY-FOUR

It was a simple dream—simpler than the one of Arlene," Isabelle insisted as Kate continued to interrogate her. She sat on the edge of one of two sofas in Kate's office, a brooding Andy next to her. "Detective Jane Wright was shot by a woman. She was in a diner and I think it was night. I don't know the date or any more particulars. The same woman shot Andy. I couldn't see who she was or what she looked like."

"Are you sure there was no window, newspaper, or clock around? Even a computer or phone screen will do."

"Nothing." Isabelle rubbed her hands together, looking at Andy surreptitiously.

Andy's face held the same unreadable expression as Claire's. Claire sat on the back of Kate's couch, watching Isabelle's every move. Kate was angry, her eyes red from a lack of sleep, her body language uneven and off-kilter; choppy and harsh, so different from the elegant blue and white dress she was wearing.

Did all keepers employ this stoicism as a survival method? Did they hide their feelings until they finally died due to personal neglect? How did anyone survive this job?

Isabelle sucked in a breath. She had to do better. "Maybe if I went back to bed I'd be able to dream again."

"Maybe Arlene Hampton would still be alive if you hadn't messed around at the She Bar last night." Kate's fury, carefully controlled since they'd walked into the door, finally exploded. She pointed to Andy. "I should have put a better team on this."

Claire put her hand on Kate's shoulder. "Honey, you can't say that."

Andy shook her head, her anger matching her mother's. "You wouldn't have had the dream in the first place if it hadn't been for Isabelle."

"Isabelle would have stayed home and had another dream if you made the effort to fuck her," Kate hissed. "Jam handed in her report this morning." She sat back in the plush black sofa, turning her gaze to Isabelle. "Going to clubs to look for sex because Andy here didn't want to look after you. What bullshit is that?"

Isabelle could feel the heat rising on her cheeks as she shot up. "My sex life has nothing to do with you or anyone else."

Kate jumped up as well. "It does if it gets people killed."

"Kate!" Claire attempted to intervene again, moving around the set of couches and reaching for Kate's arm.

Andy got to her feet and positioned herself between Kate and Isabelle. "You will not talk to Isabelle this way. It was…is her twenty-first birthday. She had every right to go out and celebrate. So, sit down."

Andy's voice was even and controlled, but Isabelle could hear the effort she made to restrain her white-hot anger. She watched as Kate and Andy stared at each other, then she slipped her hands around Andy's waist. "It's okay."

No response. The body under her hands was tense, coiled, ready to strike. "Andy. It's okay," she said again. She nuzzled her head into Andy's back. "Please. It's okay. Let it go." She slipped her hands under Andy's T-shirt, soothing the tight back muscles, the taut stomach. "Please sit down. You're scaring me."

Andy blew out a puff of breath. She shot her fingers from her balled fists a couple of times, then turned to Isabelle. "Are you okay? Don't listen to her. You know you didn't have anything to do with Arlene Hampton's death."

Isabelle shrugged, attempted to smile. "That I don't know, but I know that it's done and that we have to look after you now. And Detective Wright." She looked from Andy to Kate. "Isn't that right? Can we just take a deep breath here and focus on the new problem at hand?"

She sat down, crossing her legs in her new, tight jeans. Who would have thought she'd end up being the grown-up in the room?

❖

Isabelle shook her head in disbelief. "That's it? That's the plan? We put a team on Andy and wait to see what happens?" She paced Kate's office irritably, wringing her hands through her hair.

"Did your dream show you who killed Andy and Detective Wright?"

"No."

"What more do you want to do then? Stop everything and cower in the corner?" Kate said. She stood behind her desk, arms crossed. "René knows what she's doing, and Andy will have you, Iona, David, and Jam to help her. More people than that will only attract attention. And remember, you also dreamed about Detective Jane Wright's death, which means she's involved in this mess somehow and we certainly can't put a team on her. At least not until things get desperate. It's clear we've piqued her interest and we can't afford the police showing up and digging around in our business. That's happened before and it got pretty nasty really quickly. So, we'll work with Andy and we'll try and stop it all from happening."

Isabelle marched up to her desk. "And if you fail? If she gets killed? If your daughter gets shot?"

Kate's mouth became a thin, angry line. Her eyes narrowed. "Don't play that bullshit card with me. You don't understand what's at stake."

"I know that you dragged me here against my will, made me share a connection with someone, all but forcing me into her bed, and now you expect me not to care?"

Kate leaned forward, her index finger digging into her desk's leather-covered surface. "You want to help? Sleep with Andy. Have sex with her. Dream a proper, intense dream. One we can use to save her and Detective Wright's lives and to—" She stopped, blinking back the unexpected emotion. "To find Arlene Hampton's murderer. If Wright was in last night's dream, then these cases must be linked somehow. As it stands, we have nothing solid. None of the death threats leveled against Arlene Hampton have delivered a possible suspect."

Claire rose from the sofa and walked to Kate. She put her arm around her. "We'll make sure Andy is okay," she told her. "Don't worry." She turned, locking eyes with Isabelle. "It would help you know. Sex."

Isabelle backed away, the anger inside her cooling. She avoided Andy's eyes. Andy didn't want her. Not yet. Maybe never.

All she needed was for Andy to survive this and then she had to disappear. She wanted to get back to her studies and the certainty of mathematics. She'd find a way to deal with the dreams. Screw the future she'd seen with Andy. Her dreams were futile. Useless. They didn't help anyone.

Andy rose from her seat. "I'll go along with Kate's plan." She nodded in the direction of her mother. "René and I will work something out. We'll hunt down Hampton's murderer. Kate's right. Doing that has the potential to stop any potential knock-on event."

"I don't know if we can just assume that the two events are related," Isabelle argued.

"If Detective Wright catches Hampton's killer it severs the link between me and her," Andy said.

"Not necessarily. There is no certainty in that theory. You don't know what other problems solving the murder will create. It's simple chaos theory. If a butterfly flaps its wings here…"

"I know, I know." Andy smiled. "Who knows what other actions it sets in motion? But we have to start somewhere. "

Kate nodded. "Glad you agree. I'll put Marc on Sharapov. If it was indeed his black-suited friend in Arlene Hampton's building it means he's been holding out on us."

"Just don't kill him," Andy said.

Isabelle looked at Kate as if she would deny being capable of such a thing, but she said nothing as she waved them out the door.

❖

Back in their apartment, Andy jumped in the shower. It was as if she wanted to wash Kate and her accusations from her body. She couldn't believe Kate had all but demanded that she sleep with Isabelle.

Isabelle hadn't seemed too perturbed by the idea, though. But then again, she'd said that she needed sex, and judging by last night she wasn't too discerning about who she invited into her bed. She didn't know the extent of Isabelle's sexual appetite. Maybe she was willing to do quick rolls in the hay, even though she'd never have imagined that to be the case.

The thought of another woman having sex with Isabelle made her angry, just like last night, and she didn't want to think about why it bothered her so much.

When she walked out of the bathroom, dressed in jeans and a sports bra, Isabelle sat cross-legged on the couch, working on her computer. A rip in her jeans gave a tantalizing peek of smooth, white skin.

Let it go, Andy scolded herself. Arlene Hampton was dead, and apparently, she was about to die too. If that wasn't sufficient motivation to focus on the task at hand, nothing was.

"What are you doing?" she asked as she dug around in the dresser for socks. She was growing tired of dressing in the bathroom. She kept forgetting stuff in the bedroom.

"I'm working on an algorithm that predicts human behavior. I have been for about a year. Jam gave me some detail about Detective Wright, so I'm trying to input the parameters." She looked up. "Seems Jane Wright is as gay as they come."

"Okay. Wouldn't have guessed that necessarily. I've seen lots of straight policewomen do the no-nonsense, tough guy routine."

Andy sat on the bed, putting on her boots. She realized the room had gone quiet.

"What?"

"Your back. Was that the alley or the gunshot?"

Andy touched the bruise on her chest the bullets had punched through her vest. Luckily, it didn't crack a rib or any other bones. Bats were okay. Guns scared her. "Some kind of baton or club in the alley," she said as she turned to look at it in the mirror. "Sharapov's buddy. The one I saw in Hampton's building."

"Ah. Does that happen a lot? The injuries?"

"Now and then." Andy didn't want to lie.

The silence lingered. Andy pulled on a T-shirt and sat back down on the bed to tie her laces.

Isabelle cleared her throat. "Where are you off to?" She closed her laptop.

"I'm going to meet with Wright for another interview and then I'm off to Hampton's building."

Isabelle pushed the computer aside. "Cool. I'll get my stuff."

"No." Andy shook her head. "You have to stay here. You have to rest."

"I'm not tired enough to sleep."

"Go sit with Jam then. Or go to the gym. Get tired." Andy got up, looking at her watch. It was three in the afternoon already. The day was running away from her.

"Why are you going back to Arlene's apartment?"

"I have to go check on something that bothered me last night, but it means I have to sneak back into the crime scene. You're not trained for that yet. You shouldn't even have been at Hampton's apartment last night. I should have dropped you off first."

Andy could see Isabelle stiffen at the words. "You had no time to take me home last night, so don't go there. And exactly how long is this 'not trained' going to be your excuse for everything?"

"Until you pass René's three-month course. Make no mistake about that."

"And your excuses for not sleeping with me?"

Andy didn't know how to respond. Did Isabelle really want her, or was it just their weird set of circumstances talking?

Isabelle blew out an angry breath, stood up, and walked to Andy. She tugged at the hem of her black T-shirt. "Will you at least promise to be careful?"

"Absolutely. And René, Iona, and David will be there. Marc as well, in between interrogating Sharapov. A whole team looking after little ol' me. So don't worry."

Isabelle chewed on her bottom lip. "I don't like sitting here doing nothing."

"Continue the work on your algorithm. Maybe it can help us."

"Okay."

"You've had a hell of a time the last few weeks. Why don't you just take it easy for a bit?"

Isabelle let go of the T-shirt. "I'll see. But you be careful, please."

Andy kissed her on the cheek without thinking. "Promise. I'll try and be back before midnight."

"No diners?"

"No diners. I'll send in René. She'd love the opportunity to kick some butt again."

❖

As soon as Andy closed the door behind her, Isabelle picked up the phone and called Jam. Andy was right. Her algorithm could be of more assistance than she'd initially considered. And if it was the only thing she could contribute, apart from dreaming, then she would give it a try.

"I have a proposal for you," she said when Jam answered. "It's about my algorithm. The one with Detective Wright's detail."

"Uh-huh." Jam forced out a laugh. "Am I going to regret giving you that data?"

"Nope. All I need from you is a few more bits of information. That's all."

"Okay." Jam perked up. "I can help you in ten. After that I have to sleep. Seems like this is going to be another very long night."

Chapter Thirty-five

Getting into Arlene Hampton's building was going to be a challenge. The tags René had, the ones they'd stolen from the estate agent, were voided when Jam crashed the security system to erase the CCTV footage.

Andy wanted to see the crime scene again, without the police breathing down her neck. Something had felt out of place last night. Too perfect, almost. She hadn't told anyone exactly what was bugging her, only that she needed a second look.

The problem was how to do it without being spotted. The building's security guards would be more alert after what had happened, and they couldn't just force their way in, deleting the surveillance footage again. That would prove way too suspicious.

Luckily, Jam had found a way in. She scoured Tinder and other hookup apps until she found the perfect target—a hotshot corporate lawyer living on the fourth floor of Hampton's building. Jason Hall was single, a big fan of random sex with strangers, and he owned a car, which was a nice bonus as it would give them a way into the building.

Iona had said she was prepared to play the part of the seductress. David had agreed, as long as things ended before it got too physical.

Tracking Jason Hall's cell phone, Jam had found an upmarket bar in Manhattan he frequented. From his credit card bills, it was clear he often paid for two people. Scotch was a staple order, while the other drinks varied between cocktails and wine. It probably meant Hall drank whiskey while he plied his dates with alcohol. His social media accounts didn't mention a partner. He seemed every inch the young, alpha male—handsome, rich, and not willing to settle down.

As it was Thursday, Andy hoped Hall would be on the prowl again. Seemed like he loved getting primed for the weekend with a quickie on a Thursday.

She looked at her watch as she popped into the elevator. She wanted to check on Sharapov before she and Caroline met up with Detective Wright again. She found René downstairs, staring through the two-way mirror at Marc Bunt leaning back in his chair, observing the Russian like he was a dead slab of meat. Loud techno music was playing, enough for the mirror in front of her to vibrate.

Sharapov was still dressed in nothing more than a T-shirt. He was blue in in the face from the cold. Bunt was wrapped up as if it was the Arctic.

Sharapov's head was dipping forward, as if he was about to fall asleep, when Bunt slapped his hand down on the table. Sharapov's head bobbed up in slow-motion, curse words flying from his mouth.

"We've been taking turns to keep him awake," René said. "He's about to break."

"I don't know about that. I'm starting to wonder if he has anything to confess."

René cocked an eyebrow. "Why do you say that? You know something we don't?"

"Look at him. He's a low-level enforcer. He's not trained to withstand Bunt, and you guys have been going at it for more than a day. If Sharapov hasn't said anything by now it's because he doesn't have anything to say."

René contemplated Andy's words. "Could be," she admitted reluctantly. "He says he doesn't know why he and his buddies followed Hampton or why anyone would want her dead. He's never heard of her before." She rolled her shoulders as if loosening the muscles. "The bad news is that it seems that he works for Natalya Kuznetsova. He says she's the one who sent them to follow her, with the emphasis on *follow*. He swears they had strict orders not to touch Hampton. Says he has no idea why his little friends would go into her apartment."

"You're not serious."

"Dead serious."

"Fuck it. The Russian mafia."

"Exactly. And you don't even know the full story. Kate seriously pissed them off last year. Ma Soeur got one of their pimps arrested for murder. We were supposed to stay out of their business and they out of ours."

"We can't do that if they are involved in Hampton's murder."

"Yeah, I know, but it will make everything that much more complicated. Apparently, Natalya does not play nice."

Andy leaned against the mirror and looked from Bunt to René. "Why don't we apologize and let him go? See where he leads us? Unless you seriously think he's going to cough up anything of value."

René rubbed a contemplative thumb over her mouth. "It could work. But I'll have to speak to Kate and Marc first."

"Good." Andy pushed her body away from the mirror. "Ready? Apparently, you are my primary babysitter for the day."

René ran a hand over her hair and sighed in exaggeration. "I would have preferred keeping a leery eye over your girlfriend, but your ugly mug will have to do, I guess."

❖

René waited in the SUV as Andy walked into a coffee spot just around the corner from 1 Police Plaza where Detective Jane Wright and the Major Case Squad were based.

Caroline was already there, the sole of her four-inch Jimmy Choos tapping the ground impatiently. Around her, young men and women were typing away on their computers, headphones insulating them from the world.

Caroline looked up as Andy approached, waving a quick hello. She arched her eyebrows. "I won't bite, you know."

Andy leaned down and kissed her hello, inhaling expensive perfume. She sat opposite her at the table for four.

Caroline was dressed in a tailored black skirt, the red blouse showing off her cleavage and a bit of the Italian lingerie she preferred.

"And this?" Andy pointed to Caroline's attire.

"Jam and Kate said to show a bit of skin. Seems like your cop likes blondes."

"Ah. And of course we have to cash in on that."

"Well, old habits are hard to break if one of the only weapons you've had for millennia has been your body." Caroline tilted her head and regarded Andy with a smile. "But yes, seems like people are increasingly challenging your mother's methods."

"Are you one of them?"

"I'm not interested in power, Andrea. You know that." She traced a red fingernail down Andy's arm. "I'd much rather submit."

"And we both know who holds the true power when you do that," Andy said, playing along.

The door of the coffee shop banged open, an ice-cold gust following Detective Wright as she stalked inside. She smoothed over her hair and straightened her collar, lifting her suit jacket to expose the butt of a matte black pistol.

"My, my," sighed Caroline. "I've always liked a woman who knows how to handle a gun."

CHAPTER THIRTY-SIX

Jane sat down across from the two women. "Ms. Bouchard. Ms. Diaz."

She blew out a tired breath, envious at the espresso Andrea Bouchard had in front of her. She lifted two fingers in an attempt to summon a server.

"Don't worry. We already ordered for you. Americano? Three sugars?" Diaz said with a smile.

Jane's envy turned into suspicion. "How do you know that?"

"I paid attention to what you drank last night."

Similar to the last time they'd met, Diaz was dressed as if she owned a Fortune 100 company. Bouchard changed her black jeans for blue ones, her shirt covered up by a tightfitting black leather jacket that hugged every angle and curve.

Jane wanted to argue with Diaz, but a cup of coffee appeared before her, along with three brown sugar packets.

"Bless your soul," she murmured to the retreating back of the server. She dunked the sugar into the coffee, stirred vigorously, and took the first sip like a caffeine junkie.

"You do like your coffee, Detective," Diaz remarked as she leaned back in her chair.

Jane put down the cup and pointed at her. "You're nice. Last night—this morning—you treated me like crap. What's up?"

Diaz sipped from the glass of water in front of her, one eye squinting slightly as the slice of lemon got in the way. She switched to the black tea, steaming in a light blue cup. Finally, she answered. "I was tired last night. And perhaps unnecessarily rude. I'm sure we can all work through this in a civilized way. It's only a misunderstanding, after all."

Jane pointed at her. "I spoke to my colleagues at One PP about you. You never play nice. So stop it. You're making me nervous."

Diaz frowned, clearly taken aback. Bouchard laughed, of all things. She tried not to, but she did, until Diaz silenced her with a glare that could whither daisies.

Diaz fiddled with the teaspoon in the saucer. "Your choice, Detective. How about you tell us then why you dragged all of us down here this afternoon."

Much better, Jane considered. She trusted this searing hot version of Caroline Diaz much more than the polite, cool one. In fact, she rather liked her.

"I wanted to see if Ms. Bouchard's memory had improved in the light of day." She pointed to the November gloom outside. Last night's snow was lying on the roadside, treacherous ice patches dotting the sparsely populated sidewalks.

She looked to Andy's black eyes, the face that should be young but looked older somehow. "Sometimes we remember better when we're somewhat removed from the heat of the moment."

Bouchard had the good manners to fake thinking about it. Then simply said, "No."

Jane drank from the blue mug again and prevented a sigh of contentment from slipping from her tongue. "Let me then raise a few issues that have been bugging me since last night."

"Fire away," Bouchard said.

"Ms. Hampton's partner at Fortress, Philippe Lautrec, said he wasn't aware that she'd employed any private protection. He said there was no need for it as far as he knew."

Bouchard looked to Diaz. Diaz shrugged, then nodded.

"As far as I know, my being there had to do with the visit from the Norwegian prime minister, who is also Ms. Hampton's old friend," Bouchard explained. "They go way back. Ten years. More. Maybe Ms. Hampton never bothered to tell her partner about it."

Jane was surprised she'd answered at all. No doubt it was carefully considered though. A strategy even.

"The prime minister—Ms. Siv Sandberg—is giving a speech at the United Nations on Monday," Bouchard continued. "Ms. Hampton was aware of the contents of the speech. It seems as if it is bound to upset quite a number of people, possibly placing her and Ms. Sandberg in danger."

Bouchard moved uneasily in her seat. "I'm only giving you this information as it may help you to catch her killer. You have to understand that this is a highly confidential matter."

Jane rested her chin in her hand. She felt the caffeine waking her up slowly, kicking her mind into gear. What was up with these two? Were they offering her real information or were they attempting to guide her off course, away from what had really happened?

"What's in this supposed speech?"

Jane watched as Bouchard again glanced at Diaz.

She didn't buy it. A woman like Bouchard wouldn't constantly seek permission from Diaz to speak. It hadn't been the case last night, and it was unlikely to happen now that the sun was up.

"Ms. Sandberg can tell you that," Bouchard finally said. "Let's just say it would upset the American government. And it appears as if she would have the reluctant backing of the Russians on this issue, and possibly also the Chinese, as it offers them the opportunity to push the US into a corner. So, the purely hypothetical question is, what if Ms. Sandberg had something to make the Russians play ball? What if Ms. Hampton was killed as a warning to Ms. Sandberg to ensure that she doesn't force the Russian president's hand in supporting her? That she doesn't make that speech on Monday? Or, at the very least, tone it down? The second, perhaps more urgent question is, what would happen if Ms. Sandberg refuses to do so?"

For the first time, Jane got the feeling that Bouchard was telling the truth. From murder to international politics. This case was getting stranger by the minute. And quickly escalating into something that could soon have the State Department up her ass as well. "What could the prime minister of Norway possibly have on the Russian president?"

Bouchard searched for the server, lifting her empty cup. She raised a questioning eyebrow at Jane. Jane nodded and drained her mug, then played tag and looked at Diaz, who stared at her with something bordering on irritation.

No.

Neglect. Caroline Diaz hated being ignored while she and Bouchard had their little tête-à-tête.

"What about you, Ms. Diaz?" she asked. "Would you like a fresh cup of tea?"

Diaz snapped her head away, clearing her throat. She looked past Jane at the coffee shop entrance. "Why not? Earl Grey tea. Black. Honey."

"Of course. Honey," Jane teased her.

There was the slightest of smiles on Diaz's lips, but it disappeared as the server took the order from Bouchard.

Back to business. Bouchard leaned forward in her chair. "I don't know what Sandberg has on the Russian president. All I know is that Sandberg, Hampton, Popov, the Russian president, and Phillipe Lautrec all crossed paths at Davos at some point for a few weeks about six years ago. That's the only place we can put the four of them all together in one spot."

"Davos? The big annual politics and investment schmooze fest in Switzerland where the world's CEOs and presidents go to live it up every year?"

"Yes."

Jane waited for the punchline, but it didn't come. "So?"

"I don't know any more. At this point it's the only connection I've managed to make between these people."

"And based on these random facts you believe Ms. Sandberg may be in danger?"

"Yes."

Jane contemplated Bouchard's earnest expression and decided to give her a bone. "Ms. Sandberg called the police commissioner this morning. She and her wife are extremely upset by the murder of Arlene Hampton, as you can imagine." She watched Bouchard's face closely. "It seems Ms. Sandberg is indeed concerned that she would no longer be safe traveling to New York. Mr. Philippe Lautrec has also advised her to reconsider her itinerary."

"Then perhaps you should do the same and ensure that they don't make the trip," Bouchard said.

"I can try, but put yourself in my shoes. Why would I do that? Based on the word of a suspect in a murder inquiry? As I said, Mr. Lautrec doesn't know anything about you providing personal protection to Ms. Hampton. And I also have a number of questions about who you are exactly."

"What do you mean?"

"You came here recently from London?"

"Yes. I work there mainly."

Jane fished a notebook from her coat pocket and looked at the information the uniforms had given her last night. "And your home address here in New York is that of a nonprofit organization?"

"Correct. I stay there sometimes. They have rooms available as long-term rentals. It provides an extra source of income for them."

"But it seems you also work there, as I understood from the receptionist. I called there this morning."

Bouchard shrugged as if it didn't matter. "She's mistaken. I did some work for Ma Soeur, as I said, but the last time was around three years ago. Personal protection is an unfortunate side business when you look after the rights of women. When you have to protect them and remove them from dangerous situations. You know most women are murdered by someone they know."

"Of course, yes," Jane agreed. Very smooth answer, she thought. Well rehearsed. "So, you're no longer with Ma Soeur?"

A moment's hesitation. "I'm considering a job offer from them. We'll see."

Bouchard crossed her arms, the biceps in her arms straining against the leather. She shook her head. "Detective, I'm not involved in Arlene Hampton's murder. If I were you, I'd be more interested in the fact that Phillipe Lautrec advised Sandberg to reconsider her travel plans. It seems rather convenient. It could stop Sandberg from giving that speech on Monday."

Jane hadn't told Bouchard anything that wouldn't be in the newspapers or on the news websites this afternoon. Sandberg was about to publicly grieve the loss of her friend, using her murder as a platform to slam her climate opponents.

She decided to let the matter of Ma Soeur go. For now.

"Why do you think Lautrec is involved?" she asked, also dropping the honorifics. All these niceties were exhausting. "Did Hampton mention that she was worried about him on any level?"

"No. But she was very private. They could have been a couple for all I know. All I'm saying is that he says he doesn't know about me, but apparently he knows enough to tell Sandberg not to come to New York."

Jane nodded her thanks as the server brought them their coffee. She opened the sugar packets and dunked the contents into the piping hot liquid.

"Hampton's neighbors said they heard only women's voices around her apartment," she said. "Not in the apartment, as that is pretty soundproof, but on the way from the elevator and in the stairwell. Security says the same. Her visitors were almost always female. Arriving at night and leaving in the morning. So, we don't believe she and Lautrec were sharing a bed. Not at all."

Diaz looked at Bouchard with the slightest of frowns. Bouchard blinked.

Jackpot, Jane thought. She'd touched a nerve. She stretched in her seat, moving the gun in her side an inch toward her back. "Now, I'm wondering, Andy—may I call you Andy?—whether you are one of those women? Perhaps even, THE woman?" She contemplated the coffee in front of her, the crema on top. "Maybe you and Arlene had a lovers' tiff. Maybe you imagined her and Siv Sandberg all cozy somewhere in bed. Maybe you killed her. Maybe those men in black work for you. Maybe you rushed down the hall, leaving through the parking garage and coming back up through the front door to give yourself an alibi. Maybe you erased all the CCTV footage to cover your tracks."

Bouchard had the audacity to smile. "No. Not me, Detective, I can promise you that."

But thanks for the information on Hampton, said the expression on her face.

Fuck.

"Okay. Do you know who Arlene Hampton's current lover is?" Jane scrambled to recover. "Maybe you saw her around when you supposedly guarded her."

"No. But I'll ask around."

"And where will you do that?"

"People who might have known her." Bouchard shrugged.

"Know many of those?"

"One or two."

Diaz put her hand on Bouchard's leg, probably telling her to shut up. The gesture seemed intimate and familiar.

Jane felt an unexpected surge of jealousy. It had been 631 days since she and Amy had called it quits. More than 500 since the divorce. Probably close to one thousand nights without someone in her bed.

She didn't like quick and dirty. Never had. She blamed her parents. Decent people who loved her no matter what. It's always difficult to disappoint nice people.

Jane sat back, crossing her legs and watching Diaz and Bouchard closely. "Talking about your illustrious career as a bodyguard. We found a document on Hampton's work computer. Seems like a contract with you. It is unsigned, however."

Nobody showed any emotion. Neither Diaz nor Bouchard seemed glad Andy Bouchard might be in the clear. It was almost as if they expected it, as if someone planted the document there.

"Seems very convenient," Jane said.

"As I said earlier, I didn't want to sign any document," Bouchard said. "I had an oral agreement with Hampton and that was sufficient for me."

"You never fear getting screwed?"

Bouchard gave a gentle shake of the head. "By the time payday arrives, I know too much for my clients not to pay."

Diaz leaned forward to see if her tea had steeped sufficiently. Her red blouse opened, showing a strip of tanned skin and lace, the swell of a breast.

Jane felt her lower abdomen clench involuntarily.

Diaz looked up, her eyes hot and smoldering.

Jane glanced away. It was a trap, her mind warned, but her body was not so eager to listen.

Amy was also a blonde. Gorgeous. Soft and gentle, until she got angry.

The silence lingered, became awkward.

"Is there anything else, Detective Wright?" Diaz asked as she poured her tea. She drank it black, no sugar. "Any news on the DNA?"

"If we're lucky I'll get it tomorrow. We've fast-tracked the forensics."

Diaz smiled. It warmed only when it finally reached her eyes. "Sandberg putting pressure on the department?"

Jane finished her coffee, not willing to admit anything to Diaz.

"What about ballistics? The guns used by the men in black? Did you find anything yet?" Bouchard asked.

"Why would I tell you anything about the casings?" Jane said. Why the hell was she answering questions all of a sudden?

"Just wondering. The sooner I'm in the clear the better."

"You're not. And you better stay away from this case. If I catch you anywhere near any other person of interest, I'll haul your ass in front of a judge as quick as you can say obstruction of justice. Got it?"

Bouchard didn't react.

"Same goes for that redhead of yours," Jane said. "Tell me. By the way. Does she still dream?"

Bouchard's mouth became a thin, contemplative line.

"Andy," Diaz warned her in a low voice.

Bouchard waved a hand at her. "I have no idea what you're talking about."

When her hand came down, she placed it on Jane's arm.

The unexpected touch almost made Jane reach for her gun.

So much for pushing Bouchard out of her comfort zone. Here she was, thrashing around in the deep end.

"Detective," Bouchard said in a sudden gentle tone.

"What?" Jane snapped, shifting her arm out from under Bouchard's touch.

"That said, should you run into a diner in the next few days with your gun drawn, perhaps just turn around and walk away."

Jane stared at her, waiting for the punchline.

Diaz puffed out a breath, as if Bouchard had disappointed her.

"A diner? Are you serious?" she asked.

Bouchard just stared at her, her face unreadable.

"How…Of course. Isabelle Templeton." Jane closed her eyes for a second. She couldn't believe she was about to ask the question on her lips, but she'd always trusted her gut, and that very same gut had saved her life on two previous occasions. "Tell me. Did she…did Isabelle Templeton dream about Arlene Hampton's death?"

Diaz, clearly miffed, signaled for the bill and stood up hurriedly. Bouchard followed, tugging at the back of her leather jacket as if to cover a weapon.

Diaz dumped a wad of bills on the table. The server was going to party for a week with that tip.

"Let's go." Diaz waved Andy to her side.

"I don't know anything about Hampton and a dream," Bouchard said as a parting shot, "all I'm saying is that you need to be careful." She hesitated. "Please."

Jane looked on as they left the café, Diaz clearly about to kill Bouchard. If she'd wanted to upset them, she'd certainly managed that, but not in the way she'd expected. Not at all.

❖

Andy walked out of the coffee shop, Caroline in a huff.

"What the hell, Andy? Are you insane? Dreaming 101. Shut the fuck up about Ma Soeur. It's bad enough that Wright picked up on our scent through Ma Soeur. It was a damn smart move calling there this morning."

"Isabelle would kill me if I didn't warn Wright."

"Doesn't mean you can break the rules as you please." Diaz dodged a pimply kid, eyes locked on his cellphone. She walked to the curb in search of a cab. "I thought this was a quick in and out for you. Why does it sound as if this girl has already clawed her way in under your skin?"

"It's not like that. And don't talk about Isabelle like that. She feels guilty about Hampton's murder. I can't let her add Wright's death to her conscience as well."

Diaz swiveled around, taking a deep breath in a clear sign to steady herself. "How is she doing?"

Andy dug her hands into her coat pockets. "Not too well. She's questioning us. Herself. Everything."

"What about your…death? How does she feel about that? How do *you* feel about it?"

"You heard?"

"I know everything that goes on at Ma Soeur."

Andy shivered as a gust of wind cut around the corner of the building. She kicked at a pile of ice that had collected around the bottom of a signpost. The white snow from last night had become dirty, nasty stuff, so far removed from its initial fairy tale beauty.

"Andy?"

She shrugged. "I've got people on me. Don't worry."

"That's not what I asked."

"I'm too stubborn too die."

A cab pulled up to the curb. "What does Kate say?"

"Nothing."

"Now that I believe," Caroline whispered. She headed for the cab, then turned around, walked up to Andy, and kissed her on the cheek. "Please, promise you'll be careful."

CHAPTER THIRTY-SEVEN

The vehicle that pulled up to the side of the road three minutes later was all Jam—a black BMW M3 that skidded to a halt in front of Andy.

"What are you doing here?" Andy asked as she got in. "Where's David? He's supposed to pick me up for the gig with the lawyer tonight."

"Something came up. I've got a job for you first. Won't be long—an hour? I dug up something on Phillipe Lautrec that could be useful."

"What did you find?" Andy locked her boots into the corners of the footwell as Jam rapidly pounded the shift up and down, reaching speeds that seemed impossible in the early evening traffic.

"Lautrec made a payment to a dodgy restaurant in Little Odessa. One that belongs to Natalya Kuznetsova."

Andy groaned. That name again. Marat Sharapov's boss. Did the Russians really kill Arlene Hampton as a warning to the Norwegian prime minister?

Jam nodded. "Yep. The one and only. Anyway, Lautrec tried to cover his tracks, but I found the payment. Problem is, I think the cops will also discover it pretty soon." Jam tilted her head in Andy's direction. "Better you get at it before Wright starts to ask the questions."

"What was the payment for?"

"I can't quite figure it out." Jam looked tortured by the thought. "It's like we have a lot of pieces of the puzzle but we're unable to put it all together. All I know is that this is too much of a coincidence, and Kate agrees. The Russians following Hampton. Her murder. Sandberg's UN speech. Her trying to strong-arm the Russian president. And now Lautrec is also somehow involved, even though I don't know what he would gain by working with the Russians. Maybe he gets the Fortress business to himself? Maybe there's a money trail I'm not seeing? A huge payment from the Russians for him to help get rid of Arlene Hampton? Who knows? Anyway. That's why we're sending in the troops. Cue you, Captain Fantastic."

Andy tightened the seat belt around her torso as Jam skidded around a corner, hitting the brakes at the sea of red lights in front of her. Jam consulted her phone, reversed a few yards, and turned left.

"Okay. Where exactly are we going?" Andy couldn't plot a course from Jam's haphazard driving.

"The Crimson Parlor is an upmarket strip club in Midtown." Jam pushed a flash of purple hair from her face. "Lautrec normally goes there early on a Thursday. Seems like he has a standing arrangement for a private dance by Kandy, with a K. She's an edgy Mistress type. All leather and kinky boots up to her armpits. And one dirty little secret."

Jam's grin told Andy everything she needed to know. "Kandy with a K is one of us?"

"Yeah. She promised to be late tonight so we can talk to Lautrec. Only one thing, though. We—you—have to be careful. Kandy says you're going to ruin five years of work if you blow her cover. She gets us stock tips from heaven. Kate says she's one of our highest earners. Probably pays your salary. And she's already locked up two fraudsters, one rapist, and one bank robber. Funny what people will confess to when a strange woman ties you up and whispers 'bad boy' in your ear."

Andy reached for the grab handle as Jam took the impossibly narrow gap between a garbage truck and a UPS van.

"We've got René on you," Jam said. "And Marc will be her sidekick for this one."

"Great." Andy nodded.

"Kate said to make sure nothing happens to you."

"She said nothing to me."

"You know she won't. But it will be my head on the block if you don't come back in one piece."

"Isabelle's dreams only come true in two, three days. Maybe more. So, there's time. Don't worry."

Jam shook her head. "You hope. We haven't yet determined any pattern for her dreams. So, for heaven's sake, don't do anything stupid, like run into a diner."

Andy gave a mock salute. "Will do."

"And keep in contact. Don't switch anything off." She pointed to the communication device in Andy's ear.

"I hear you."

Andy waited for more instructions, but there were none forthcoming. She decided to use the few minutes of alone time with Jam. "When is the election?"

"For your mom's spot?"

"Yes."

"In a week."

"I heard René is running against her. She doesn't seem the type."

Jam turned in the driver's seat, staring at her is if wondering why she'd ask such a question.

Andy wished she would look at the road again.

"Are you asking me if I'm behind it?" Jam's voice had an edge to it.

Andy pointed at the road. "Cab. Stopping."

Jam swerved left.

"From what I heard you and René had something going on a year ago," Andy said.

"Not really. Those were mostly rumors. I'd check my sources if I were you. We're friends. Nothing more."

Andy looked for another entry point. "Aren't you interested in the job? You're very diplomatic about Kate, but people talk. You think she's rash, irresponsible. And you didn't agree with her taking Isabelle. And my sources are good on this one, thank you very much."

Jam smiled wanly. "As I say, don't believe everything you hear. Also not the fact that Kate wants to continue in her job. From what I've been told she wants to retire. She and Claire have been talking about buying a place in Napa Valley."

She slammed on the brakes, turned right, and shot down an alleyway. She parked in front of what looked like a hotel.

"Enough sweet talk. Go in, press two in the elevator, and go to the room at the end of the hall. You have an appointment with Mistress Helen, if anyone asks. Go in at exactly six twenty. René and Marc are already inside, disguised as customers. Good luck. I'll be listening and waiting."

Andy looked at her for the info she really needed.

"Kate said to go in hard," Jam confirmed. "Time's of the essence. Especially in light of Isabelle's dream."

"Okay." Maybe Andy was wrong. Maybe the old woman cared more than she'd let on.

"Keep safe."

"I'll do so. Lautrec was ex-military."

Jam blew out a questioning breath. "Seems he was more a paper pusher than anything else. From what I gathered, he exaggerated his military career on the battlefield to sell himself to Hampton. Still doesn't make him a pushover though."

❖

Andy walked into the upmarket space, decorated in hues of black and white, punctuated with the odd dash of purple every now and then—a painting, the bartender's top hat. A silver cage swung from the roof, the woman inside wearing a skimpy leopard print thong, her breasts large and heavy.

The music was soft, electronic, the beat steady and seductive.

It was a decidedly straight male environment, the few suits that made up the early Thursday evening crowd sitting around on sofas, being kept company by sparsely clothed women lounging at their feet.

It seemed the shedding of clothing and other associated services happened in the privacy of rooms not visible from here.

Marc was sitting at the bar, having an animated conversation with the bartender, a statuesque blonde in a blue dress. He was dressed like he belonged in an office, wearing a light blue suit and crisp white shirt.

Andy couldn't see René anywhere.

A voice crackled in her ear. "Well, well. Good evening, Ms. Bouchard. So nice of you to join us."

Andy smiled. She'd missed René. And she knew she'd messed up by slipping away in the night like a convict three years ago. She should have done better, especially with the people who cared about her.

"Beware the shark," René signaled a warning. "Almost had me kicked out until they could find young Ashley here to entertain me."

"Shark?"

"Yeah. Great white. She hunts to kill."

Andy looked over her shoulder. A woman in heels and a killer white dress was trying to catch up with her.

"Hi there. Can I help you?" she called as if Andy was lost.

Damn it. She'd almost made it to the elevator without pinging anyone's radar.

"I haven't seen you here before," the woman said, curiosity on her face. In her forties, she was substantially older than the other women in the Crimson Parlor.

Andy pointed to the elevator. "I'm going to the second floor."

"Ah. You have an appointment?"

"Yes," she said.

"With?"

"Mistress Helen."

The curiosity made way for a fake smile, a red fingernail that lazily drifted up her arm. "Well, then. Enjoy."

Andy faked a smile back. "Thanks. I'm sure I will."

On the second floor, she stepped into the hallway, the sounds of her footsteps muffled by a thick gray carpet. The black-and-white prints on the wall were of various sex positions, the women in them all younger than what felt appropriate. Only one showed two women in action.

She kept her head down and walked to the end of the hall. She stood in front of the white door and looked at her watch.

Six twenty.

She opened the door.

The man sitting chained on the chair wore a blindfold, a pair of black pants, and not much more. He was in his fifties, with a graying goatee and shaved head. Square face. His arms were ropey, ending in hands that were balled into fists, as if being tied scared him.

His crotch said she was wrong. Maybe excited was a better word.

He perked up as Andy closed the door, his breath quickening.

She said nothing.

Two minutes passed.

Lautrec stirred in his chair. "Mistress Kandy? I did as you commanded. Do you not find it pleasing?"

Lautrec's voice was surprisingly light and modulated.

Andy had ten minutes before Kandy would walk in, screaming, startled by the intruder who slipped in while she went to collect fresh, hot wax.

She walked over and tightened Lautrec's restraints. She needed them to be real, not for show. He reared up as she came closer, fighting against the leather straps that kept him tied to the chair. He sat in the middle of a mirrored room adorned with a massive bed and an array of whips and chains against the walls.

"You're not Kandy," Lautrec said.

"Bravo."

Andy picked a riding crop from the bed and tested it in her hand.

Ow.

"Tell me about Arlene Hampton," she said.

Lautrec stood up, the chair like a tortoise shell on his back. Using his shoulder, he tried to scrape the blindfold from his face, his excitement rapidly turning into panic.

Andy yanked him back down. "I only want information. That's all, Lautrec. Play along and I won't hurt you."

He frowned at her tone. "Who are you? Untie me and we can talk."

"I won't be long. I want to know who Arlene Hampton was dating."

"You're mad. Why would I tell you anything?" he snarled.

Andy hit him with the riding crop on the top of his legs, alarmingly close to his now wilting hard-on.

"Fuck. You bitch!"

"Now, now. Who was Arlene seeing?"

"I'll fucking kill you. And sue this place. Everyone here."

"What makes you think anyone knows I'm here? Mistress Kandy has run into unexpected problems and won't be here for a while."

He snarled, yelled for help.

Andy chuckled. "Soundproof rooms. Made for disciplining. Or torture. You're not very perceptive for a former military man, Lautrec."

"Fuck you."

"Tsk-tsk." Andy looked around her. She inhaled the fresh scent of roses sitting in a vase on a desk in the corner of the room. Kandy must love flowers. "So, let's recap. You're all alone. In a soundproof room. With a mad woman as your only company." She stood behind Lautrec. She knew it wouldn't be long before Kandy barged in here. She leaned down and whispered into Lautrec's neck. "Tell me who Arlene was dating. And who knows, maybe nobody has to know you spoke to me."

His arms fought against the restraints.

"Give me a name."

He groaned.

"Come now, Phillipe. Don't let me punish you. *Really* punish you."

"Okay. It was a woman. That's all I know."

"Name."

"Don't know it."

"Age, race. Anything."

Lautrec was turning red underneath the blindfold. "I don't know. White? Arlene didn't talk about her private life. She had some obsession about anyone knowing anything about her. I only knew that she was gay because a photo popped up on her phone during a meeting. A photo of her and another woman and it was clear they were more than friends, but I couldn't see her face."

Andy sat on the bed behind him. Damn thing was rock hard.

"Okay. Now tell me about the money you paid to a restaurant in Little Odessa. The one owned by the Russian mafia."

He didn't answer.

"Now, now, Phillipe."

Andy stood up. She unlocked her phone and took some photos of him, the room. "If nothing else, consider how difficult it would be for your two daughters to digest their dear old dad in this particular setting." She took another photo, close enough for him to hear the audible snap of the shutter.

"Tell me about the money you paid to have Arlene Hampton killed."

Lautrec almost choked. "No. No way!" He stood up again, chair tied to his body.

Andy slapped him down, her hand leaving a red mark on his cheek. "The money."

"It wasn't to kill Arlene." He spoke rapidly, his voice becoming increasingly high-pitched. "It was…is…gambling debts. I have gambling debts."

"So why was the Russian mafia following Arlene?"

"To threaten me. They did the same to my daughters. They thought Arlene and I were sleeping together."

"I don't buy it."

"It's the truth!"

"Put yourself in my shoes, Lautrec," Andy said, returning to a casual tone. "It all seems very convenient. Norwegian Prime Minister

Siv Sandberg is coming to town along with the Russian president. Sandberg's got some nasty stuff on him and hires Arlene and Fortress to look after her. Then the Russian mafia starts following Arlene, killing her in her apartment. What's that? A warning to Sandberg to shut up? You can see why I don't believe you."

"Why would I lie to you?"

"You could have a million reasons to fucking lie to me."

Andy considered her options, then pulled out her gun. She cocked it and pushed it against Lautrec's head. Time was running out. For her and Detective Wright. "Why was the Russian mafia following Arlene?"

He inhaled sharply, almost choked. "I told you. My debt. My gambling debt!"

She increased the pressure against his temple. "One last chance."

"My debt! For fuck's sake. Please." He started to cry.

She swore. "Tell me this then, what does Sandberg have on the Russian president?"

"Something about an affair." He sobbed. "That's all I know."

Andy stepped away from Lautrec, evening out her breath. She'd pushed Lautrec to the edge and she didn't think he had anything else to offer. She put away her gun and unlocked the door, then closed it softly behind her.

"Is our shark still swimming?" she asked René and Marc.

"The water is clear," Marc said in her ear. "Exit the elevator and keep to your left all the way to the door."

"Thanks," she said. "And would you be so kind as to order some Ingrid Bergman roses for Mistress Kandy? Two dozen. We owe her a big thank you."

CHAPTER THIRTY-EIGHT

Isabelle closed her laptop and put on her running shoes. It was early evening and the perfect time for a jog, before the cold settled in for the night. Only problem was, she doubted Ma Soeur would allow her to simply walk out the front door unaccompanied.

René and Jam were busy looking after Andy, so the only hope she had was to ask Claire if she could leave. Not Kate. She didn't like Kate. Not after what Andy had told her about Victoria and what had happened. And sending her out like this tonight, despite the dream she'd had? No. Didn't like her at all.

Isabelle put on a tracksuit and running shoes, and tucked her gloves into a beanie, along with her phone. She left her earpiece and took her earphones. She wasn't part of the operation Andy was involved in tonight, so she couldn't follow the feed, no matter how hard she'd tried to bypass Jam's security protocols.

She found Claire in Kate's office, sorting out paperwork. Their offices were decorated in muted browns and beiges, the carpet underfoot thick and luxurious.

"Hi," she said.

"Hi. This is a surprise." Claire looked up from behind her mahogany desk, slightly startled. Behind her the door to Kate's office was open, but it was dark inside, Kate probably gone for the evening.

For the first time since Isabelle had known them, she wondered what their relationship was like. There must have been a twenty-year-plus age difference between them. Was Claire in love with the power Kate swayed, the elegant, sophisticated confidence she had? She didn't even know if Kate was rich. Sure seemed like it from the way she dressed.

Isabelle liked confidence too, but something more akin to Andy's swagger. Something a little bit more careful and sensitive, more respectful of other people. The acknowledgement that no one existed in a vacuum.

And what Andy lacked in sophistication she made up for in sheer grit and power.

She ignored the flush of heat traveling down her body when she remembered Andy's body on top of hers.

"I want to go for a jog," she told Claire. "I think it would help me sleep."

Claire swiveled her chair to the right, gathering the swoop of her yellow dress as she stood in a single fluid movement. Her lipstick was freshly applied, the scent of just sprayed perfume, something with spices and oranges, hanging in the air. Her chestnut hair hung loose to just below her shoulders. The diamond around her neck was expensive, at least a few carats of perfectly cut pear-shaped beauty.

A gift from Kate?

Claire pointed to the window where the darkness had settled in. The snow had stopped, but the cold remained. "In this weather?"

"I don't mind." She looked at Claire with what she hoped was sufficient desperation. She'd never been a good actress. She stepped closer, reached out, and touched her arm briefly, hoping it would convince Claire of her intentions. "Please?"

Claire inched back, pulling her arm to her body. Isabelle blanched at the action. Perhaps Claire was scared she would dream of her death too.

Claire looked at her with a piercing gaze. "No funny stuff?"

Isabelle shook her head. "No. Promise. I don't want to leave. Not with Andy in danger," she said candidly.

She was being honest. She didn't want to escape. What she had in mind was something completely different, and perhaps a little bit more dangerous.

❖

The guardian Claire had assigned her was young and handsome in a rugged, squarish kind of way—shoulders, jaw, hands. He was twenty-two and a keeper in training, waiting to be paired with a dreamer he already had his eye on. She was about his own age and the love of his young life, Claire had said.

Claire had made sure that Isabelle felt responsible for Warrick—both his life and his future. That she knew what was at stake if she disappeared on him. He would probably be kicked out of Ma Soeur—his family's home for the past four generations.

Warrick was fit and had no trouble keeping up with Isabelle. He'd asked if she had a route in mind. She lied and said no.

Earlier, on her laptop, she had used the algorithm she'd been developing to predict where Andy and Detective Wright might be attacked. Rethinking the dream carefully, she could put down a few more parameters, such as the red and white color scheme, to determine the diner's possible location.

Adding Detective Wright's and Andy's patterns and previous known locations, gleaned from social media and cellphone records Jam had given her, she'd managed to strengthen the algorithm. She'd also fed it everything she could gather from the comm room on the Russian mafia, Siv Sandberg, as well as any information she could get on Arlene Hampton's historic movement patterns, largely based on which cellphone towers her phone had pinged.

Lucky for her the old-fashioned New York-style diners, such as the one she'd seen in her dreams, were slowly dying out, but there were still too many to provide her with a sure-fire hit. The algorithm had given her three options, all, sadly, with a less than sixty percent probability. Tonight she wanted to take a look at the first two, both located in Brooklyn. The other one was in Hell's Kitchen. How she was going to get there was a different story altogether, but she'd figure something out.

Warrick kept a steady pace next to her as they ran a route she hoped seemed random, but was, in fact, going right past the two diners she wanted to check out. The first one, Roman's Diner, was nearer than she'd imagined. In fact, it was a block away, and offered a distant view of Ma Soeur's front door.

Isabelle stopped in front of a nearby pizza place, as if lost.

Next to her, Warrick ran on the spot, frowning. "How far do you want to run? I've got a five-mile route I normally do," he said in a New York accent she'd only heard in the movies before, dropping his r's all over the place.

"Just looking. I live in Jersey City. I've never been here before."

She surveyed her surroundings. Detective Wright could probably sit here and watch Ma Soeur from one of the window booths. It offered a clear view of the official comings and goings. Ma Soeur's back door, however, remained out of sight.

They jogged farther, the evening becoming colder by the minute, their breathing white clouds in the night air as they picked up the pace. Little Pete's was four blocks away in a newly gentrified part of Brooklyn. Apparently, the owner, Peter Foggerty, had been holding out on a developer offering him seven figures for his restaurant.

Isabelle mapped the route in her head, turning with precision until they finally passed the red and white colors of the eatery on the bottom floor of a three-story building. Little Pete's Diner, it said in flashing lights.

She stopped across the road, hands on her knees, breathing deeply. She'd been pushing Warrick, and he was red in the face, puffing air from thin lips.

She scanned the window surreptitiously. Nothing and no one seemed familiar. Nothing stirred in her memory.

Maybe she was stupid in thinking this would produce results. Didn't matter. She was going to keep at it. She was going to give Hell's Kitchen a go as soon as she could. If she couldn't play with Andy and René, she sure as hell wasn't going to stay home like a good little girl either.

"Let's go back," she said, Warrick nodding his head gratefully. "It would be three miles in my app going back the way we came."

"No problem," he said.

She touched his shoulder even if she didn't want to, thanking him. "You've been great. I just had to clear my head. Thanks."

He nodded, managing to crack a smile. "Don't worry about it. Always glad to help."

CHAPTER THIRTY-NINE

Jason Hall, the lawyer who lived in Arlene Hampton's building, spent a lot of time in the gym, but clearly not with a personal trainer who could have provided him with some much needed advice. Puffed, popcorn shoulders and arms towered over scrawny legs that were in dire need of equal bulk. The imbalance made him look like a smooth-talking hero from some cartoon network.

He had a good smile, however, and he knew it. He reserved it for petite blondes with long hair, throwing it at them across the room, clutching his heart when they smiled back, as if surprised that someone so incredibly beautiful would frequent the same wannabe suave Manhattan dump as him.

A lot more women fell for his stunt than Andy considered smart. Lucky for them the first woman who drifted toward him was sidetracked by David, who looked like a Greek god in his perfectly cut suit Iona had selected for him. She even got him to shave his beard.

Andy didn't know where Kate had found Iona and David, but they were the most beautiful specimens of human beings she'd ever seen. They belonged in science books and on alien ships as prime examples of what people who populated Earth looked like.

The Bull and Bear brimmed with the adrenaline from a day spent making and losing money. High-powered types, mostly of the gorgeous, well-groomed variety, drifted around the crowded room, drinking and laughing, some on the edge of intoxication, others already there, as they blunted the sharp edge of the day into something more tolerable.

No doubt some had already moved beyond alcohol as Andy watched the telltale pinprick eyes, the slightly dulled body language.

But not Jason Hall. He was an experienced hunter, which meant he would never be more drunk than his target. When Iona had walked in, stilettos in hand as if they had been hurting her feet, flax blond hair slightly mussed, and a hint of little-girl-lost in her eyes, he'd swooped in with no regret over the woman now crooning in David's ears.

Within five minutes, Iona was sitting at his side, laughing at his jokes.

Andy sat watching them in silence, nodding only that the table next to her was indeed available when a woman asked her if she could sit down.

"You're not from around here," the woman of Indian descent said, her voice light, lilting upward at the end of the sentence. She had flawless skin, with an inquisitive smile creasing her eyes. She was older than Andy. Beautiful hands. Narrow, long fingers ending in fingernails the color of young peaches.

Andy's eye strayed from Iona. She wondered what to say. She'd been born in New York, Brooklyn, before it became all la-di-da.

"No," she lied. "London."

"Ah. Could have guessed."

Andy would be blind to miss the spark of interest. For a moment she wanted to say yes. Anything to burn off the edge Isabelle had placed in her body this morning, the ache still pooled between her legs looking for release.

The woman had money and she'd dressed to flaunt her wealth, exuding a quiet, strong confidence that would have seen Andy crawling into her bed in a heartbeat a week ago.

The woman pointed her chin toward the bar. "I can do with another G&T. And some company." She lifted her almost empty glass.

Andy sighed, laughed ruefully. "I'm taken. Sorry."

"I don't see a ring."

Andy didn't want to explain her rather unique situation. Didn't even really want to think about what she'd said about being taken, why she hadn't asked for a telephone number.

She got up as Jason Hall asked for the bill. She had to be ready and waiting near his car. She nodded to David, who placed a hundred-dollar bill on the table, apologizing to the woman next to him.

Andy faced the woman next to her. "I'm really sorry. Another time, yes. Absolutely, yes."

The woman believed her. "I hope she's special."

Andy didn't know what to say, so she settled for the most mundane of answers. "Sorry. Really sorry."

❖

Hall and Iona walked to his vehicle. In a city where not a lot of people owned a car, Hall did—a black Mercedes-Benz AMG with twin chrome exhausts and red-rimmed wheels that screamed money but fell short on taste.

Jason opened the door for Iona, unashamedly looking down the front of her ice-blue dress as she climbed in. He walked around and got into the car. She leaned over, took hold of the lapels on his jacket, and pulled him closer to kiss him.

Next to Andy, David groaned something incomprehensible. They were standing on the sidewalk, as if they were looking for a taxi. Every now and then the odd passerby would stomp by, despite the freezing cold.

"You know she's just doing her job." Andy tried to soothe his anger.

"Yeah, I know. But, man, that's my favorite dress on her and that guy…He's like grease that's never going to come off." Again, the angry grunt.

"Hey, you're helping me out. I'll never forget that."

He grimaced but nodded.

The Mercedes pulled away, turning left into the first available alley as per Iona's plan.

A black truck pulled away, turning across the road to park close to the alley's entrance. René and Marc were there to keep an eye on Iona should Hall not fall for her suggestion for a quickie nearby.

Seems their fear was unfounded. Iona had her man, hook, line, and sinker.

Andy hooked her arm through David's. They walked away as if they'd decided to give up on the taxi.

They turned into the alley.

In front of them, the Mercedes was steaming up, Iona straddling Hall. Under her fingers, Andy could feel David's arm turn to stone.

Behind them, the black truck inched forward. The door to the Mercedes opened and Iona got out, signaling them over.

René and Marc moved the truck to fully block the view into the alley.

Iona must have managed to inject Hall with a cocktail containing ketamine—a dose small enough not to cause harm, but sufficient to knock him out. The evening's events would be nothing but a blur tomorrow, Hall left only with a note that suggested he'd met a gorgeous woman, drank too much, and that she and some friends had driven him home.

Nothing would be stolen and there would no evidence of any physical encounter. It wasn't ideal, but it was the only plan they had been able to cobble together on such short notice.

Andy had to get into Hampton's apartment. She hadn't explained why to anyone, just said that she wanted to go over things one more time. Kate had believed her, sanctioning the op.

David strode to Hall's car. Andy hung back, giving him and Iona a moment of privacy. Iona looked at David, her face worried. She leaned in to kiss him. He stood still, anger settling like concrete in his shoulders, then he relented and kissed her back.

She pulled back and looked at him, said something Andy could only imagine. If it was Isabelle, she would…

She would do nothing. Isabelle wasn't hers.

She walked over. David leaned into the Mercedes and dragged a barely conscious Hall to the passenger side.

❖

It was a quick drive to Arlene Hampton's building. David used Hall's security tags to enter the building and park in the basement in a space marked with a number corresponding to his apartment address. René and Marc parked in the street, at the entrance of the building, just in case.

"He's an ass, but he's got a nice car," David said appreciatively as he exited the vehicle.

Andy tied back her hair and put on a cap, covering her face from the CCTV cameras before she got out. David slung his arm around Hall, with Andy doing the same on the other side as they started the process of lugging their "drunk friend" home.

Iona followed in their wake, holding the elevator door as they walked a semi-conscious Hall inside. After arriving on the fourth floor, she walked ahead to unlock the heavy front door of number forty-one. They walked in. David dumped Hall on his bed. He looked at his watch as he spoke to Andy.

"Is fifteen minutes enough? It will be difficult to explain staying here for longer than that."

"It will do."

Iona looked at her inquisitively. "Are you sure you don't need any help?"

"Yes. I just want to see the scene again. Get a better picture of what happened. Maybe I can spot something that can help Isabelle."

Iona nodded. She was also a dreamer. She understood what it meant to lose a mark to the dragon. "Then I hope you find it."

Andy smiled at them. "Thanks. You two kiss and make up."

Iona scrunched up her face as she looked at David. "Did he complain? I said nothing two months ago when he had a Bulgarian pole dancer all over his lap."

David squirmed.

Andy laughed, putting her hands in the air. "I say nothing. See you in fifteen."

❖

The front door to Arlene Hampton's apartment was crisscrossed with crime scene tape. There was no police guard. The Major Case Squad probably believed they had everything they needed. Andy slipped on nitrile gloves and picked the lock to the door, thanking her lucky stars there was no CCTV in the hallways, and stepped through the tape.

She closed the door behind her softly. She still couldn't pinpoint what had forced her to return to the scene of the crime, despite the risk to her, Iona, and David. She only knew that something bugged her. Something that got lost in last night's chaos of blood and uniforms.

She stepped into the apartment, rubbing her neck tiredly. Her muscles were tense, her senses not as sharp as they should have been, just like last night. She was in desperate need of a full night's sleep. Eight hours of bliss.

She closed her eyes for a second and inhaled deeply through her nose, steadying herself mentally. All she needed was two minutes of being alert and awake. Of seeing everything as if for the first time.

Victoria had this thing she did that could steady Andy. Where she could make Andy see properly and without the cloud of emotion. Where she could make her place everything around her in context, making her join the dots from random information she'd gleaned over the course of the investigation into a coherent mesh—an answer.

Victoria was a Buddhist. Andy, on the other hand, had faith of another kind. A complicated relationship she didn't always understand. She fished under her shirt for the tiny silver cross and held it until it became warm between her fingers.

She took another breath, just as she would have done had Vic been around. She managed ten easy, steady breaths and then opened her eyes, waiting as everything in Hampton's apartment came into sharp focus. The round table in the kitchen with…nothing on it. Yesterday there was a bottle there, and two glasses, one with lipstick. The bottle of red was expensive. She waited as she tried to remember.

Domaine de la Romanée-Conti Grand Cru 2010.

That was about $10,000 a bottle. More. You only shared that with someone very special. Very, very special. And you drank it when you celebrated. Or had someone in your bed for the first time.

She smelled the air. A hint of chemicals, probably the police forensics crew.

She walked to the kitchen. Two empty plates in the sink. Looked like it could have been spaghetti. Not something you necessarily ate on a first date, unless you could trust that your date was pretty handy with her cutlery.

The fridge was full. Stocked to the brim with fruit, vegetables, and freshly squeezed juices of some variety. Healthy. Andy closed the door. She looked at the calendar, held by two fridge magnets of dachshunds.

Hampton hadn't seemed like a dog person. Andy looked around. Nope. No sign of a dog. No water bowl, bed, or indication of hair. Ditto for evidence of a cat.

The calendar itself was also interesting. All the days up to the twenty-first of November were crossed out even though today was only the twentieth.

That bugged her. Why do that? She lifted it, looked underneath. Put it back.

The clock was also a concern. It was stuck on 2:59. Was it broken?

She moved deeper into the apartment, to the spot where Hampton had died. The blood had turned into a rusty, brown spot on the floor. No handbag. The cops would have taken that as well.

It troubled her that Hampton hadn't fought back. If it was the Russians who'd stormed in here, wouldn't a woman like Hampton make an effort to fight back? She felt like the type who would fight to her last breath. Instead she died here, almost as if in surprise. As if she might have known her attacker.

But then again, she'd buzzed the Russians up.

The scent of flowers lured Andy to the main bedroom. A vase filled with red roses stood on a small table at the window. Both sides of the bed were a mess, the sheets tangled. Dinner and sex? Sex, dinner, sex?

The bathroom sink featured one toothbrush. The small medicine cabinet held expensive makeup, one brand of tampons, and a prescription for sleeping pills, largely unused. There were, however, two distinct empty spaces in the cabinet as some items had been removed.

Whoever Hampton dated had cleared out without leaving any clue to their existence, except maybe for DNA.

Who had been Arlene Hampton's mystery guest? Andy had a feeling that Hampton's lover might be the only one able to provide the answer to what had happened last night. She wondered if Detective Wright had already closed in on whoever it was.

CHAPTER FORTY

It was almost midnight when Andy got home. Isabelle was up, working on her laptop, sitting cross-legged on the bed, her hair twirled into a bun and held there with a pencil.

She looked up when the door opened, Andy ready to sneak into the room.

"Any luck?" she asked, her voice filled with hope.

Andy looked at her turned head, her neck, so frail in the soft light from the bed lamp. "No. But it seems the cops were right. Arlene had a girlfriend. We also learned that Philippe Lautrec had some gambling debts with the Russians and that they were following Hampton to scare him—says he. Sharapov swears his people were only supposed to follow Hampton, not kill her," Andy said as she flopped down on the bed. "Why aren't you sleeping?"

Isabelle put the laptop on the bedside table. "I'm studying. I can't just drop everything I've worked for the last few years."

"How close are you to wrapping up?" Andy asked.

"I'm basically done."

"Right then. Let's get some sleep." Andy jumped up and headed for the shower.

When she came out of the bedroom, only the lamp on her side of the bed was left burning.

"Don't even think about the couch, buster," Isabelle said from under the duvet.

She was too tired to argue. Too tired to think. She switched off the light and slipped in between the crisp white sheets. Isabelle immediately rolled on her side and rested her head on Andy's shoulder.

Andy felt a calmness wash over her she didn't even realize she could muster. She closed her eyes, only for them to fly open as the bedding shifted and Isabelle slid onto her, nestling between her legs.

"Isabelle. No, wait."

"It's still my birthday and you owe me." There was a smile in Isabelle's voice.

"Sex?"

"Oh, what arrogance," Isabelle teased her as she looked down at her, her face framed by her fiery hair, her eyes unreadable in the faint moonlight that fell through the window.

She was light and heavy in all the right places. She shifted slightly, and her breasts almost spilled from the top of her camisole, the tiniest glimpse of hardened nipple brushing up against Andy's black T-shirt.

Andy swallowed, then moved to release the pressure on her center, but Isabelle just moved along with her, intensifying the pressure on her clit with her hip.

"My birthday present, Andy Bouchard, is that you'll live. Not die in a diner, shot in the back." Isabelle tugged her hips firmly, deeper into the vee of Andy's legs. "That means I have to dream. A better dream. A stronger one. Can you give that to me?"

Andy's throat was too dry to answer, unlike the rest of her. She could feel herself flood with a wetness that begged for more of what Isabelle was offering. She groaned as Isabelle slowly started to rock against her, her hair enveloping Andy as she lifted her upper body, increasing the pressure on Andy's clit in a slow, certain rhythm.

Isabelle's left breast escaped the confines of her spaghetti-strapped top and fell, ripe and full against Andy's chest. She had to stop her hand from reaching for it, sensing she wouldn't be able to turn back once she'd done so.

She groaned in frustration as she flipped Isabelle over and pinned her down, her hands around Isabelle's wrists, her knees on either side of her legs.

Isabelle moved under her, frustration in her undulating hips, seeking the pressure of Andy's body. "Sweetheart, please. Just…why are you fighting this?" she pleaded. "I need to know what will happen, and for that I need more than that one dream. Don't you understand that?"

"I can't," Andy said, her voice raw with emotion—with need, she suspected.

Isabelle's body stilled. "Why? Am I that ugly? Is it that difficult to touch me?"

"No! Please don't think that. You are the most beautiful woman in the room, every time. In every possible way."

Isabelle fought against Andy's grip. "What then?"

"It's me. I don't want to stay. I don't want to be stuck here again doing this job, watching people die," Andy said, her voice almost a whisper. "Please understand."

"But I must keep on dreaming about random, violent deaths? Without you? Every time?"

"Walk away then. Don't stay here."

"If I do, will you come with me? Because the dreams won't stop."

Andy looked at her hands clenched around Isabelle's wrists. She released her grip somewhat but didn't answer.

"Coward. I have no way out and you know it."

"Yes." Andy sighed in submission. "I hate…Fuck it. Yes, this is the best place for you."

"Even if it kills me."

Again, Andy had no answer.

"I'd be safe if you were here," Isabelle said. "I trust you. Completely. More than that. When I dreamed about you months ago, I knew you were the one. Why do you think I came here? It wasn't anything Kate had said or done. Or Claire. I agreed to do this because you were here. The woman I had dreamed about. The woman who could hold me. All of me."

Andy let go of Isabelle's arms. Vic was gone. Her first dreamer was killed in a shooting. She was seventeen. And Isabelle…She was smart enough to know that Isabelle was a very different woman altogether. That this was—could be—more than anything she'd ever felt. A potential A-bomb waiting to detonate.

"I can't do this again," she said. "I really can't. Please understand."

Isabelle looked out the window, at the moon disappearing behind a passing cloud. "Then you better make sure we wrap this case up as soon as possible." When her gaze returned to Andy her eyes were on fire. "It's my birthday." Her voice was dark and rough. "I need this. I need you. Now." She wrapped her arms around Andy and lifted her upper body, crashing into Andy, seeking her mouth, but finding her shoulder instead, biting down into the muscle.

Andy's body unexpectedly verged on an orgasm, as if desperate to end the torture from the last few days.

"Forget everything I said. I'm not asking for forever," Isabelle snapped. Her legs fought with Andy's knees, then she screamed into Andy's neck, primal and loud. She threw her head back to look Andy in the eye. "I'm just asking you to do your fucking job."

Andy looked at the face below her, stark and angry and stripped from all warmth.

She sat back on her knees, staring at Isabelle. She cleared her throat and calmed her body. Her job. That's all.

"Okay then. If that is what you wish."

She willed her hands to move to Isabelle's white lace panties. She inched the material down her legs, breathing in the heady scent of Isabelle's sex. The insides of her thighs were slick with her arousal.

Andy didn't wait. There was no need. She tentatively slipped her middle finger into Isabelle, steadily inching deeper. Isabelle was tight, her body tensing as Andy entered her. Andy stopped. She wanted to ask but didn't know how. She pulled out. Isabelle hissed, locking eyes with her as if she wanted to kill her.

Andy placed a pillow underneath Isabelle's hips, urging her to open her legs wider. She gently pushed inside again, slowly, gaining a centimeter at a time. Once fully inside, she moved from the left to right, stretching Isabelle's entrance slowly. Then she inched out again.

She waited.

Isabelle's eyes were murky with want, desire, and pent up anger.

She again pushed inside, a little bit faster this time, her thumb touching Isabelle's swollen clit briefly.

Isabelle moaned in something like a mix of rage and unwanted pleasure. Andy picked up the pace, confident Isabelle was comfortable with her length and width. She thrust into Isabelle again, harder this time, curling her finger to finally find the spot inside she'd been seeking, the muscle contracting under her finger.

She circled around it, faster and faster, her thumb connecting with Isabelle's clit with every thrust.

Isabelle's breathing was raspy, desperate. She grabbed the sheets. She tossed her head back, seemingly lost in time and space, her hips bucking under Andy's hands.

The scream when she let go, when she came, wild and unthinking, was at once the most beautiful and most terrifying thing Andy had ever heard.

❖

Isabelle had never allowed a woman inside her. One of the two dates she'd had with women had ended in a quick, unsatisfactory fumbling without even undressing properly. The other date hadn't even gotten that far. But Andy was different. She'd wanted Andy to enter her. She wanted to feel her move inside her, taking her without hesitation.

Without hesitation.

Why did Andy continue to fight her? Did she not see what Isabelle knew? Had known months ago already?

Damn stubborn woman.

As she slowly came down from her orgasm, Andy held her until her breathing steadied.

She moved her arm that covered her eyes. "I knew you were going to be an excellent lover."

Andy lifted an eyebrow, her eyes dark and unreadable. "You okay?"

"Absolutely."

She wasn't going to thank Andy. That would imply a service, a task, and despite what she'd said earlier, that hadn't been what she'd wanted from Andy. She'd had time to think since Arlene's death. Running away from who she was wouldn't make the dreaming disappear.

Problem was, she would never allow anyone else in her head and in her bed but Andy.

She also knew that she needed more than Andy was prepared to give at the moment. She wanted everything, even if that notion was clearly going to present a problem or two.

But she'd never been one to shy away from a challenge. She wanted to be with Andy, here at Ma Soeur, or anywhere else Andy wanted to be. What she couldn't have, was Andy running away again. Didn't she realize how much she deprived herself because of something that had happened years ago? By denying what Isabelle knew she felt for her?

Andy dipped her head to lock eyes with her. "Are you sure you're okay? It felt as if…" She cleared her throat. "As if it might have been your first time. Or close to it."

"Close to it." Isabelle blushed, hating every moment of it. She was sure Andy was used to far more experienced women. "Inside. First time."

There was concern on Andy's face. "Did I hurt you in any way?"

She put her arms around Andy's neck. "Not at all. You were you. Strong. Certain. Gentle. And I wanted it to be with you."

Andy said nothing.

"Promise."

"If maybe you're sore…"

"It would be okay. But I'm not."

"Sure?"

"Yes. I would know. No pain…Just happiness." Release, finally. And hopefully a dream. A really, really scary dream where Andy again died in front of her eyes.

Andy managed a smile. She turned and swung her feet over the edge of the bed. "Okay then. I'm going to shower."

Isabelle caught her shirt, tugging her back to bed. "No way, sweetheart."

Andy sat back down on the edge of the bed, looking at her, one eyebrow cocked.

Isabelle slipped in behind Andy's back, putting her arms around her waist. "I don't care how much you fight me. We're in this together, much more than you think, and if you'll just admit to what I know you're feeling, you'll make it easier on both of us."

Andy's eyes narrowed into a scowl, but she didn't say anything.

Isabelle slipped her hand under Andy's T-shirt. "And I know you're right on the edge, so there's no way you're going to shower right now." Isabelle's hand moved lower, her nails slowly running up Andy's thigh. "If you want to come, I'll be the one to make it happen, not you. And I'm right here if that is what you want. Anytime."

Andy shifted uncomfortably, an involuntary groan escaping her mouth.

"I am happy to help you out," said Isabelle as she moved to sit next to Andy, watching where Andy's gaze lingered.

She felt her nipples harden, her clit contracting again. The left strap of her camisole fell from her shoulder, exposing most of her breast. "I can take this off anytime. All of it. You can come any way you want. Hard. Fast. Slow. On my mouth. In my hand. I'm an excellent student."

Andy looked away and swallowed audibly.

"No," she said finally. "No. I'm okay. Good. Thanks." She backed up past Isabelle and slipped into the sheets, then cleared her throat. "Time to sleep."

Isabelle watched as she turned off the light, then slipped in behind her, her arm tightly wrapped around Andy's tense body.

CHAPTER FORTY-ONE

It was her, but not her. She was Andy, standing in her shoes, moving in her body. She was strong and running fast, fear pushing her along. Like the spring tide, the terror was relentless, eating away at the shore. Her sanity. Pounding at it again and again.

She ran, gun in hand, dodging people on the sidewalk. Left, right, rushing past shop fronts—a deli, dry cleaners, shoe shop. Left, right, the bright colors merging into a blur, passing in a steady stream of blues, oranges, and reds, people laughing, then hurriedly stepping out of the way as if she was a madwoman.

"She's got a gun!" someone called. A man. Young and pimply, he scurried away from her.

A left turn. Faster. Lungs on fire, breath exploding, legs churning the air. Through a glass door, fighting the people on their way out. Straight to the corner booth.

A woman in a pantsuit and hair the color of wheat—Jane Wright—was lying on her stomach in a pool of blood. The air smelled coppery, heavy, nauseating. Andy—Isabelle—turned around, ducking, scouting her surroundings. The shooter must be here, close by.

To her left were two more women. One was dead, the other alive.

From the corner of her eye, she could see René rushing across the room, gun drawn. She crouched down to feel for a pulse. Detective Wright was still breathing. She was whispering something.

She looked up at a gut-wrenching sound. Isabelle was outside, running toward her, screaming a warning.

Andy turned.

Too late.

The sound of the gunshots came only a microsecond before the burn. The fire in her chest, then above her left ear. She fell to the ground, the Sig falling from her grip, her forward momentum seeing it spin away from her, leaving her helpless.

❖

The scream that exploded from Isabelle's lips made Andy reach for her gun where it rested on the bedside table. She jumped from bed, cocking the Sig in a single, fluid movement.

She stared in stunned silence at the picture in front of her. Isabelle's eyes were rolling back in her head, her head tossing from left to right and back again, her hands reaching out to something, someone. Her eyes were open, staring at an image that was scaring her to death.

Andy dropped the gun and jumped back in the bed. She crawled to Isabelle, sneaking in under her flailing arms to embrace her.

"I've got you, baby. I've got you. Come back. Please, come back." Andy was scared. She'd never seen anything like this before.

Someone was pounding on their door. "Andy! Isabelle?"

Not now. Can't now.

Isabelle fought with her. Pounded her with her fists, her nails, scratching them down her neck and chest. Andy fumbled, trying to catch her hands, pinning her arms to her body. Kissing her.

"Andy! Open this door!"

Wood splintered as someone attacked the door.

Andy kissed Isabelle. Her mouth, her eyes. Breathed into her as if resuscitating her. "It's okay. I'm here. I'm here. Isa. I'm here."

A body burst through the door. Another.

René, gun in hand, followed by David.

They stopped, frozen as they watched Isabelle screaming from a primal place inside her.

Andy felt something like tears on her cheeks. "Please, Isa. Come on. Please, come back."

Isabelle choked, coughed, spluttered. Breathed in deeply, and then started to cry.

Andy held her, rocking her gently. She looked at René and David standing helplessly at the foot of the bed, weapons in hand.

"We're okay. I think we're okay."

She could feel Isabelle's body relaxing, melting. Hear her crying. She should have never, ever made love to her.

René's fighting stance melted as she let go of a breath she must have held for a long time. "You sure?" she whispered.

Andy nodded. *Thank you*, she said silently, wondering what the hell she was supposed to do now.

❖

They sat under a steady stream of hot water. Isabelle had emptied the contents of her stomach into the toilet, after which Andy had carried her to the shower so that she could stop shivering. Isabelle could feel Andy's arms around her as she sat nestled sideways between her legs, hear the beating of her heart where she rested her head against Andy's chest.

She wished she could get warm.

"Maybe we should undress you?" Andy whispered in her ear. "Would that be okay?"

Andy leaned back and tugged at the hem of Isabelle's top, then slipped it over her head. The panties were more difficult, but she managed to get rid of them when Isabelle lifted her hips to aid the process.

Andy took off her own shirt, then dragged Isabelle back to the heat of her body. Blindly, Isabelle traced the goose bumps on her skin, felt the involuntary shudder when Andy captured her hand, kissing her wrist, lightly, gently.

"Are you okay?" Andy asked.

"Yes," she said, her voice hoarse. "But can we sit here a bit longer?" Isabelle loved it here. It felt safe, whole.

"We can sit as long as you like."

Five minutes later, the steam rising, her skin red and hot, Isabelle opened her eyes. The world was still reeling, the edges painted black, but the dizziness and disorientation had lessened.

Andy was watching her, concern etched on her face. Isabelle averted her eyes and sighed with something like contentment. Then she remembered the dream, and a fresh wave of nausea flooded her body.

"You need to eat something," Andy said. She helped Isabelle to her feet, turned off the water, and carried her out of the shower. She sat her on the closed toilet and toweled her down.

Isabelle didn't have the strength to fight her. She watched as Andy tenderly dried her hair, her shoulders, her arms and legs.

"Come on," said Andy. "I'll put you in bed while I make you something to eat."

She lifted her again and carried her to bed.

"The usual?" Andy asked.

"Yes," Isabelle heard herself croak the single word. "But more strawberries this time, please."

❖

Andy ate her cereal as she watched Isabelle eat—drink—the strange concoction her body craved following her dreams. As she ate her oatmeal and sipped her coffee, she could still smell Isabelle on her hands, sweet and salty all at once.

She wondered what Isabelle would taste like, then admonished her wayward mind and focused on drinking her black, bitter coffee, feeling herself settling into the day. Her stomach had protested against blending almost raw meat with strawberries at five in the morning, but that was her job and she was damn well going to do it.

If Isabelle could face dreaming, she could give her whatever she desired.

She watched as Isabelle ate hungrily, then slipped into a dreamless sleep until eight o'clock, Andy too nervous to take her eyes off her.

What a strange mix of fragile and fierce. Of brilliant and innocent. How would she ever forget her when it was time to leave?

CHAPTER FORTY-TWO

"It was you in the dream, but I was you." Isabelle looked at Andy as if she wanted to make sure she understood what she was saying. "I felt everything you felt. The adrenaline, the fear, the love, the pain."

"Love?" As soon as Andy had said the word she regretted it.

Isabelle didn't hesitate. "What you felt—feel—for me."

Andy didn't know how to respond, so she got out of bed and walked to the apartment window and stared at the bustling streets below. Today—Friday—was warmer than yesterday, the mellow sun peeking through the buildings, blinding her for a moment as she scanned the horizon from east to west, as if looking for a threat.

A way out.

She felt restless. She needed to move, to breathe cold air over the fire in her stomach, the worry eating away at her. The other, unnamed emotion building inside her like a perfect storm.

Love. What a word. Love was never simple or unconditional. That was people's first and biggest mistake. It had a lifetime of expectations and dreams attached to it people never even knew existed.

"Andy?"

She turned on her heels, struggling to look Isabelle in the eye.

"You can forget about everything else. It's okay. The only thing you have to remember is that the attack on you and Detective Wright happens in the diner one block down. Roman's Diner. And it's going to be soon, maybe in the next few hours. The dream was vivid, more real."

Andy frowned. "How do you know where it will happen?"

"I went jogging with Warrick last night, scouting possible locations."

Who the hell let Isabelle roam free at night? Andy swallowed the sudden surge of anger. "How did you even know where to start looking?"

"My algorithm. And Jam helped with some data points." Isabelle sat back, sheets tangled between her legs. "Will you please come with me to the diner? I want to show it to you so that you know what to expect."

"I don't know if that's wise. We can talk through it here, as always."

"Being there would be better. Besides, I need to get out." Isabelle crawled from bed.

Andy inspected her for any signs of trauma but detected none. Isabelle stood her ground, head slightly turned, a soft smile on her face, but her eyes ready for battle. She knew what she was doing. What she wanted.

Andy was amazed at how she had grown into her skin over the last few days.

"Okay," she said. "But first we go and let off some steam in the ring with René. It will help you recover. And we have a meeting with Kate. Then we can go to the diner."

Isabelle nodded in agreement. "And maybe then you can tell me what's been bugging you. You didn't tell me everything that happened last night. Something has upset you."

"What's new?" Andy deflected the question.

Isabelle was right. Something was eating away at her—something new. She just didn't know if she wanted to put it into words.

❖

"Ouch, Bouchard. Lady's got a beautiful left hook. Do you want my glasses? How did you not see that one coming?"

René was leaning over the boxing ring, watching as Andy and Isabelle sparred, both of them slick with sweat. Andy's hair was plastered to her neck, Isabelle's tied back in a ponytail that swung from right to left as she moved in to punch Andy's midriff.

Andy danced back just in time. Isabelle was fit, and she was trying to tire her out with pure staying power, darting away every time Andy wanted to tackle her to the ground, forcing them to box rather than wrestle. Andy had always tried to end any fight as soon as she could, rather than waste her energy on big shows of endurance.

She stopped all of a sudden, dropping her hands and speeding up her breathing to a notch under exhausted.

"I give up."

Isabelle frowned and turned to René. René shrugged, suspicion on her face.

Andy dashed forward, grabbing Isabelle around the waist and slamming her to the floor. She lay on top of her, knees on either side of Isabelle's torso, holding Isabelle's right wrist in her left hand and pushing down on her throat and her left bicep with her right forearm.

"Yield," she demanded.

Isabelle's surprise transformed into anger. She tried to lift her lower body with her legs in an attempt to throw Andy off, but Andy's bulk kept her there, solid and unmoving.

"Hmm-hmm," said Andy. "Got you. Yield." She applied more pressure to Isabelle's throat. "No more Ms. Nice Guy."

Isabelle's body relaxed. She smiled up at Andy. "But you were such a nice guy last night. Making me come like that, inside me. Anyone ever told you you're an excellent lover?"

Andy leaned in and whispered in her ear. "Every time. I've never left a woman unsatisfied. Not one of the hundreds of women I've taken to bed."

Isabelle swore with white-hot anger. She wriggled and kicked under Andy, but with little success.

Andy laughed at her. "Two can play this game."

"Are you ladies going to move it along, or should I give you the room?" René called from the side of the ring. "Isabelle, do you know how to get out from under Andy?"

Isabelle squirmed again, then threw her head back on the floor. "No. And she's getting frigging heavy."

René jumped into the ring. "I'll show you what to do."

She touched Andy's shoulder, indicating to her to move to the side. The smile she gave Andy was pleased.

Andy shook her head. "It's not what you think."

Rene laughed. "Oh, it's exactly what I think."

❖

Isabelle packed up her training gear, watching as Andy threw her gloves into her sports bag and zipped it closed. Apart from being gorgeous, stripped down to her exercise gear, her body looked pleased and satisfied. Confident.

No. Damn cocky, almost like the Andy Bouchard Isabelle had dreamed about weeks ago.

She liked it. The idea that she'd sparked that swagger in Andy, that Andy was returning to herself, to the woman of her dreams.

She took off her training gloves, reached out, and gently touched the scar on Andy's side. "Where did you get that?"

Andy's muscles contracted, but she didn't retreat from her touch. "A stubborn Fijian who almost stabbed his girlfriend to death."

"But you were in time?"

"Yes. We got lucky. It happened at the restaurant where she worked as a sous-chef and I pretended to storm into the kitchen to complain about the soup." Andy lifted her bag over her shoulder. "Make no mistake, a lot of this is luck."

Isabelle nodded but said nothing.

"You don't believe me."

"No."

"Let me ask you something else then. Do you think we cause any harm?"

Isabelle considered her answer. "No," she said eventually. "Where you—we—get it right, it helps. I think." She frowned. "You said we. You've never said that before. Does that mean you'll stay when this is done?"

"Probably not. Don't know. And you? Made any decisions on your future yet?"

"I know that I won't stay without you. I don't think I can trust anyone else with my body," she answered as honestly as she could.

"You'll learn," said Andy, not looking her in the eye.

"I've not dreamt of anyone but you, ever, so no, I'm not going to learn."

"The pay is good. You'll see. You can continue your studies and live a good life. It's not always this hectic."

Isabelle didn't answer. She didn't want to blackmail Andy into staying. If she was going to remain at Ma Soeur, she would have to do so of her own accord. She wiped down her face and shoulders with a fresh towel she fished from her bag, then waved René down as she walked past.

"I wondered if I could also learn to throw knives, like Andy. Just for fun."

René looked at Andy.

Andy shrugged. "I have a spare set. I'll give it to her. We can see if we can fit in some training tomorrow." She weighed Isabelle's hands and body. "You should be fairly good at it."

René nodded. "Okay then." She looked at Andy. "I know you have a meeting with Kate, but do you have five minutes for a bit of sparring?"

Andy sighed. "Nobody else left to kill in the entire building?"

"Nobody willing to fight as hard and dirty as you are."

Andy looked at Isabelle. "You go ahead and shower if you want. I'll be there in ten minutes. The knives are on the first shelf, under my T-shirts, if you want to take a look at them."

"Okay." Isabelle hiked her bag over her shoulder.

"Leave some hot water for me."

Isabelle laughed. "Only if you win, sweetheart."

❖

René knew all her tricks. Apart from her army training she'd mastered Krav Maga, judo, and a variety of other fighting forms. She was ruthless in the ring and her first contact showed it. She forced Andy into a corner, pumping her fists into Andy's upper body, leaving her blocking as best she could, struggling to absorb the blows that slipped past her arms.

"Don't want to spoil that pretty face for the missus," René joked, her breathing steady.

Andy didn't respond, just ducked and stormed into René's body, taking a blow to the head, instantly feeling blood trickling down her face.

She slammed René onto the floor, trying to sneak in behind her to execute a choke hold. René swiveled, then lifted her feet—her body—in one swift movement and summersaulted backward, over Andy's body, breaking the grip.

Andy scrambled forward to avoid René taking her down from behind.

"Not bad for an old woman," Andy teased her.

René waved her closer. "Let me show you who's the old woman in the ring."

Andy was taller than René, so her reach was better. She danced in, faking a blow to René's side. As René drew her body away she exposed her head, and Andy jetted forward, grabbing her behind the neck with her left hand, pushing her backward, holding her close as she hit her body with a number of short, sharp punches with her right fist.

René returned the embrace and tried to push her back, repeatedly slamming her right knee into Andy's ribs.

Neither of them let go.

René was putting everything into her kicks. Andy could feel her ribs taking a hell of a bruising.

She let go of René's neck, then caught her leg as she brought it up for another kick. She dove forward and landed on top of her, both of them squirming and grappling for the upper hand.

"Yield," Andy said as she finally had a grip on René's head and torso, the blood dripping down her right eye, blurring her vision.

"Only if you stay," René heaved.

"Is that what this is all about?"

"Maybe. But I also want to make sure you're sharp. That you don't get killed out there." René's voice was rasping, her throat struggling against Andy's arm.

"I'm okay."

"You won't be if you leave and you know it. Don't be so stubborn. Go see Victoria. Get some peace. Move on with your life."

Andy shot to her feet. "Fuck it, René. What do you know?"

René coughed, sat up. "I know you better than you know yourself. We've been friends since you were sixteen. If you let this go, if you let Isabelle go, you're going to regret it. And you'd be monumentally stupid." René smiled wanly. "And I'd kind of miss you, you know. Again."

"I'm okay with being stupid." Andy climbed through the ropes of the ring and snatched her bag from the ground.

"And regrets? You okay with those too?" René called after her.

Andy wiped the blood from her face and walked out of the gym without answering.

CHAPTER FORTY-THREE

Isabelle couldn't quite fathom what had happened between Andy and René after she'd left the gym, but she knew it had upset Andy. In fact, both of them seemed on edge. And that cut over Andy's eye wasn't deep, but it meant that René had managed—wanted?—to draw blood. And René had groaned as she sat down, so Andy hadn't played nice either.

But nobody was talking about the elephant in the room. No, they were all sitting around the table in Kate's office, talking about Arlene Hampton.

Perhaps the dead should be left to fend for themselves, she considered. She was much more worried about Andy.

"Do you think Lautrec was honest with you?" Kate looked at Andy as if she didn't believe her. "Do you really think the Russians followed Arlene purely because of his gambling debt, and not because of a connection to the Russian president?"

"He could be telling the truth, yes," Andy said. "And you know Natalya Kuznetsova. She's strong on collateral damage. Hurting the ones you love." She turned to Jam. "Did you find anything in Lautrec's records to indicate he has a gambling problem?"

"You mean big amounts disappearing and appearing in his account for no good reason? Yeah, sure. But his phone doesn't place him anywhere near any casinos. If he gambles it mirrors his sexual appetite. All hush-hush. Don't let the good folk with the pitchforks know who I really am, that type of thing." Jam flicked her purple bangs from her eyes.

Isabelle thought she looked better today, as if she'd had some rest. The only people still looking haggard from lack of sleep were Kate and Claire.

She realized that her dream was probably only one of many Ma Soeur was currently working to resolve. She didn't know how Kate kept it all together. She wouldn't want the responsibility for that many people's lives in her hands.

Andy sat back in her chair, hands on her legs. She looked calm, calculating, the playfulness from earlier in the gym gone. Whatever René had said or done must have angered her tremendously.

"I can go check with the Russians if you want," she said. "I can go to Little Odessa to talk to them. I've told René that I think we should release our guest downstairs. Maybe we can track him to see where he goes, what he does. If he really is one of Kuznetsova's men."

"They're going to be upset we took him," René said.

"I got your request to let Sharapov go," Kate told Andy. "And yes, I agree, it's probably the best option, given the time we have available. I'll make a phone call and arrange a meeting for you. Perhaps we can make some monetary amends. That should help."

Claire shook her head. "Natalya would want cash and our funds are low. We are, after all, also a real charity, doing work in thirty-three countries."

"Then we have to find a way. I can't let Andy walk in there with nothing." Kate bristled. "Letting Sharapov go won't be enough. You know Natalya."

"Okay. Whatever you say. I'll see what I can do." Claire looked down at her notepad, hiding her irritation. She wrote something Isabelle couldn't decipher.

Clearly, René and Andy weren't the only ones who'd had a falling out this morning.

Isabelle looked to the sunny morning outside the window, almost blinding in its brilliance. The sky was a deep, cold blue, split in two by the contrail of a plane passing by to the east. Kate had a corner office on the top floor of Ma Soeur with a beautiful view of Brooklyn and what lay beyond.

"When you're done in Little Odessa I need you to go see Dr. Sandberg," Kate said.

"The Norwegian prime minister?" Andy looked at her in surprise.

"Yes. She and her wife have arrived in New York, despite what they'd said in public about not coming. They want to know what happened to Arlene, and it seems Sandberg is intent on delivering that speech at the UN. You would be the best person to answer their questions. Ma Soeur was instrumental in getting her elected, and she has been a generous sponsor of ours for a number of years. She is aware of the fact that Detective Jane Wright and the NYPD do not necessarily have the full picture."

Kate's eyes locked onto Isabelle's. "And take Isabelle with you when you go. We need a soft touch. Sandberg and Arlene went to Harvard together. They were good friends." She turned her gaze to her hands clasped together on the table. "It seems Sandberg's wife was Arlene's first girlfriend. Arlene introduced them to each other. So be nice. These people are in mourning." Her mouth took on a tired, twisted line.

Isabelle reached out to touch her, but Kate pulled her hands back and rested them on her legs, just as Andy had done, the only difference being that her fingernails were longer, a deep red, just like her lipstick.

"We'll be as comforting as we can be," Isabelle assured her.

Kate nodded sharply. "How is the case progressing? Do the police have any new leads?"

"It doesn't seem like it," Jam said.

"Nothing from forensics yet? What does our contact in the lab say?"

"The DNA hasn't been tested yet. The results are expected this afternoon. But don't worry. There's nothing that will implicate Andy."

"Implicate Andy?" Kate faltered for a moment.

"Yes. She gave her DNA to the police."

Kate turned to Andy. "Are you insane? We most certainly don't want you on any DNA database!" Her furious eyes burned into Andy's.

"There was no other way," Andy replied. "Not giving it to Detective Wright would have made me look guilty. I already cleaned up my brass, thinking I would get away, but then I got stuck there, doing CPR, the empty shells in my pocket."

Kate looked away, at her shoes, her anger palpable. Then she visibly pulled herself together.

"Anything else I should know?" she clipped.

"Yes."

Everyone looked at René.

"Isabelle dreamed again last night."

Claire shifted her gaze to Isabelle. "Why didn't you speak up sooner?"

Isabelle looked at Andy and shrugged. "It was the same dream, just more vivid. All we have extra is a possible location. Nothing more. No look at the killer, or the date."

"Where?" Kate asked.

"The diner down the road," René said. "Roman's Diner. We're all going to check it out later today."

Kate looked at Andy, the concern on her face fleeting but intense. "Are you okay?"

"Yes. Don't worry."

"No Victorias?"

Andy's face remained straight. Isabelle slipped her hand into Andy's, feeling the strong hand relaxing under hers.

"No Victorias," Andy said.

❖

"This predictive project of yours is a kickass algorithm. Man, I'm impressed," Jam said as they all left Kate's office and walked to the elevators. "The AI on this is amazing. Can I steal bits of it for our predictive analysis?"

"Sure," said Isabelle. "Just don't share it with anyone else. I still want to get my doctorate with it."

Jam stabbed the elevator button with two fingers. "You're going to ace it. They should just give it to you right now."

"It helped that I could use Ma Soeur's supercomputer to crunch the numbers," Isabelle said. "The university doesn't have nearly the firepower you've got."

Jam nodded, pleased with Isabelle's assessment.

"Plus, you gave me some information that normal people don't have access to."

"The cops have the same information. And the intelligence agencies."

Isabelle nodded. "I know, but I don't want my research to go anywhere near any of those places. How long before they input race parameters to determine crime patterns? Or sexual orientation? Before they start making all kinds of wild assumptions about people?"

"I've got news for you," Jam said, frowning at the elevator still not arriving. "They're already doing that. Predictive crime combatting is starting to happen all over the world. I may be out of a job soon."

Andy leaned past Jam and jabbed the already lit button for the ground floor again. They needed to go to Little Odessa and it was ten in the morning already. "What we're doing is different, and you know it. We don't profile. We act, no matter who we dream about."

"Defending Ma Soeur. Can't believe what I'm hearing," Jam teased her. She leaned against the wall, lifting her hands when Andy scowled at her. "I know. Not funny. I was just yanking your chain."

"Are you ready for today?" Andy asked.

"Yep." Jam rubbed her eyes. "Last night was the first time I got some decent sleep since this thing started, so don't worry. I'll be in your ears the whole time. And René and Marc will be on your asses like glue. Gonna be another fun day in New York City."

CHAPTER FORTY-FOUR

Andy looked at the few brave souls walking on the Brighton Beach promenade. They were all wrapped up warmly, except for a shaggy haired teenager on a skateboard doing sloppy 360s. He'd fallen twice already, which was probably why he was out in this weather alone. Wouldn't want epic fails on a bright, sunny day when the girls were out.

She turned to Isabelle, sitting next to her in the white van with its tinted windows, and big, blue print on the sides proclaiming that Jay's Plumbers were in the neighborhood.

"Will you please wait here?" she asked.

"Why?"

"You know why." Andy pointed to René sitting in the front before Isabelle could protest any further. "René? Up for some fun and games?"

René nodded. She jutted her chin in Marc's direction, who was their driver for the day. "Will you keep an eye on Isabelle?"

Marc nodded.

"Why can't we all come along?" Isabelle asked.

Andy glanced over the knee-high brown boots, the tight jeans tucked into them, the dark green top, revealing a triangle of smooth skin adorned with a simple, thin gold chain. "If we show up in numbers, nobody will believe it when we say we come in peace. It's never good for negotiators to arrive in a posse."

Isabelle scowled at her.

René nodded in agreement. "What Andy really means is that the Russians most definitely cannot realize that you are her soft spot. It would make her appear weak. Perhaps even make us vulnerable. We don't need to give them that kind of leverage right now."

Andy swore under her breath, looking at René as if she wanted to kill her.

Isabelle's eyes narrowed. "But you guys be will safe, no? This is just a negotiation, not a gunfight?"

"Don't worry," René said in a calming voice. "We were born to do this. And nobody more so than Miss Personality over here."

Marc chimed in. "And I'll be on standby. Don't worry. And Iona and David are also nearby."

David had released Marat Sharapov just after this morning's meeting, following him as he'd limped to home base. Andy had the payment to apologize to the Russians hidden in her coat. Two hundred thousand dollars in untraceable, used bills.

"Okay then," Isabelle agreed reluctantly. She gave Andy a kiss on the cheek. "Be careful, please. And patient. Don't lose your temper."

Andy nodded. She exited the van, René on her heels.

They walked down the boardwalk, hands dug deep into their coat pockets. The day was clear, the air crisp, carrying the scent of the ocean in the slightest of breezes pushing against their bodies.

Andy turned to René. "Why do you keep on…" She sighed and let it go. "I'm going to save my energy for the Russians, but it's time for you to stop interfering. I've just about had enough of your nonsense."

"I kept quiet last time and look what happened."

"Everyone kept quiet."

"Exactly. You don't think some of us feel guilty for not standing up to Kate? She's the one who let you walk into that subway tunnel knowing full well what would happen. Who kicked Victoria out knowing what it would do to you."

"Is that why you're running for CEO?"

"That and other reasons. Kate's been slipping lately. Pushing us further and harder than should be the case. The teams need to rest and recuperate, but it's as if she's got to prove to everyone and herself that we're still relevant." René sidestepped an old woman at a grocer haggling in some Eastern European language over the price of tomatoes.

Past a pharmacy—an anteka. The shops turned into a swimming academy. Restaurants.

"You know she's turning sixty this year," René said. "She's been working since she was sixteen. I… A lot of us think it's time she retired."

Andy had forgotten about the big landmark birthday. Kate had had her late in life. She'd used some sperm donor and raised her with Elaine—gregarious, kind Elaine—for ten years before departing that relationship in a swirl of never-ending fights and incriminations.

The blue and white sign of Tatjana's appeared.

Andy wasn't looking forward to this, but there was no way out. She put her game face on, looked at René, nodded, and opened the door.

❖

Natalya Kuznetsova was an attractive woman. Closing in on fifty, she had a runner's body, lithe and trim, even if a bit too thin for Andy's liking. She'd always liked her smile, though. When she smiled it was the smile of a younger woman, warm, open, and inviting, smoothing out her sharp edges, turning her into someone you could almost trust.

Almost.

She glanced up from her borscht as Andy opened the door, easing her frame into the door and adjusting her eyes to the dim light inside. She waited for René to follow, then closed the door.

Tatyana's was still closed, the tables empty, but a pleasant, homey smell wafted from the kitchen, indicating it would not remain so for long. Andy counted two men at the kitchen door and one standing to the right of them, his hand tucked inside his jacket pocket, as if resting on the butt of his gun.

She only recognized one of the men, the taller one of the duo at the kitchen door. It was Tea Guy, the lanky fellow she and Isabelle had seen in Greenwich when they'd followed Arlene and they'd captured Marat Sharapov.

He smirked at her, hoisting a middle finger in salute, the gesture shielded from Kuznetsova's view by his body.

Kuznetsova had always insisted on good manners. As if *please* and *thank you* mattered when you killed and tortured someone.

Andy took pleasure in Tea Guy's blackened eyes, the big white bandage covering his nose. She definitely broke his nose that day in the alley.

Andy counted three seconds before Kuznetsova gave her her trademark smile, pushed back her chair, and walked over. The smile was slow in coming, as if fighting another, stronger emotion. She wore it with equal grace as she did the wine-red dress and the black pumps with their silver stiletto heels. Andy waited to see if the smile reached her wide, pale blue eyes, punctuated by thin, elegant eyebrows held aloft by a touch of Botox.

It did not.

"Andrea Bouchard, welcome." Her accent was decidedly British, betraying her Oxford education. "I could not believe my ears when your mother said she would be sending you over." Her hands feigned surprise at seeing René. "And you brought a friend." She held out her hand. "Natalya Kuznetsova." She waved a finger in the air. "Not Talya. Ever."

"I'll remember that, ma'am," René nodded as she shook her hand, then gave a small bow.

Andy had warned her to show respect to Kuznetsova, to make eye contact at first, and to then look down.

Today was not a day for fighting the Russians.

Kuznetsova remained standing in the middle of the room. "Normally, I would immediately invite you for tea, but in light of what has happened, I would require you to surrender your weapons first." She pointed to the empty table next to her.

Andy hesitated for a moment, then lifted the Sig from her side. René looked at her as if she were mad. They were breaking her second rule: Never surrender your weapon.

Andy gestured to the table.

René shook her head, rubbing a hand through her cropped hair in a stubborn gesture. "If you don't mind…"

Kuznetsova swung around on her heels and strode into Rene's space, almost bumping into her. She looked her in the eye. "But I do mind, René. I mind very, very much."

She smiled. This time it barely got past her mouth.

René looked at Andy, grimaced, and then took out her own Sig. She leaned past Kuznetsova to place it on the table.

Kuznetsova leaned in, touching René's hip in an intimate gesture, as if she were pulling René toward her. "And your backup piece," she whispered into her ear.

René didn't move.

The men at the kitchen door shuffled closer. Tea Guy had something like joy etched on his face.

René stepped back, kneeled down, and took the Browning from her ankle.

Andy stripped the seven knives, held in a special pouch, from her back.

Kuznetsova turned to the table, fingering the barrel of the Sig. The array of knives. She looked at Andy. "And the other one, darling?"

How did she know about it?

"Sorry. I forgot," Andy said. She bent and retrieved the knife from her boot, then handed it to Kuznetsova, still on her knee, as if handing over a gift.

If the object was to humiliate them, to get them on their knees in front of her, perhaps it was best to play along. Subjugation only truly existed in the body, never the mind.

She rose to her feet again.

Kuznetsova's smile was a hint, a playful lift of her wide mouth, but her eyes revealed a deep satisfaction.

Andy wondered who kept her bed warm at night. She had a huge appetite for younger men, if the rumors were correct.

"Anything else hidden away?" Kuznetsova asked. "I would hate for our meeting to break whatever little trust still exists between us and Ma Soeur."

René shook her head. Andy did the same.

"Let's continue then."

"How is your mother?" Natalya asked as they walked to her table in the back of Tatyana's. She gestured for one of the men at the kitchen door to clear her plate and sat down, crossing her legs, smoothing down the short red dress showing them off to perfection. She pushed a lost strand of dark hair from her face, then checked a small golden watch on her wrist.

"She is well, thank you," Andy said. "She sends her regards."

She sat down opposite Kuznetsova, René remaining standing behind her, keeping an eye on the three men in the room.

Andy had worn her usual black jeans for today, but with a button-down shirt under her black leather coat and checkered scarf.

René looked as if she'd stepped from a combat zone, with light brown fatigues and layer after layer of white T-shirts, long and short, underneath a dark brown coat.

Andy did not waste time. She slowly reached inside her jacket pocket, taking out $100,000 in a brown paper bag. She placed it on the table and pushed it over to Kuznetsova. It was only half the money she had on her, but she'd never been tempted to reveal her hand in the first round.

"Kate expresses her sincerest apologies for detaining one of your men beyond his desire to stay. She would have never kept him if she knew that he was…family of yours."

Kuznetsova rested her hands on her lap, leaving the money untouched. She turned to the man who'd cleared the table. "Please ask Olga for some tea and honey cake." She pointed to Andy and René. "Our guests must be thirsty for some Russian hospitality."

Tea Guy's stocky companion disappeared into the kitchen.

The silence grew.

Andy knew it would be impolite not to drink with Kuznetsova. "Again, our apologies," she said, locking eyes with Kuznetsova in an attempt to determine what she was thinking.

"Marat said you were rather unkind during his stay," Kuznetsova said. "That your hospitality lacked…warmth." She emphasized the last word.

Andy nodded. "It did perhaps, yes. We did not realize he was with you, otherwise we would have treated him much better," she lied. "He, however, as you can imagine, refused to speak with us."

"He did?"

Andy straightened her coat. Was Kuznetsova worried about what secrets Marat Sharapov could have possibly spilled while in their basement?

"Indeed, he didn't say a word. It was quite admirable, actually. One would almost hope he worked for us."

The tea arrived. Kuznetsova pointed to the fine china. "Shall I pour?"

Andy nodded. "Please. Milk, no sugar for me."

Kuznetsova looked at René who stood scouting her surroundings.

"Hmm?" René lifted a questioning eyebrow. "Black, with honey. Please, ma'am."

"A woman with taste." Kuznetsova smiled appreciatively, glancing over René's body with something like admiration, inching to hunger the longer it lingered.

René cleared her throat and shuffled a step back.

Andy smiled. René talked a hundred miles an hour with her fists, but she knew little about the bartering it sometimes took to survive as a keeper. The subtle diplomacy, role-playing, and strong-arming demanded to navigate a number of often fraught relationships.

The rules were less clear here than on any battlefield. Less black-and-white. Less honorable.

Kuznetsova offered Andy the teacup. She held on to René's before relinquishing it, making sure her fingers touched hers.

She was trying to throw René off balance, and Andy feared it might be working. Even worse, the delicate teacups also kept her and René's hands where everyone could see them. You only needed one hand for a mug of coffee.

Andy looked at René, her eyes asking if she remained present, aware. René's eyes widened a bit, but then she nodded.

Kuznetsova sipped from her teacup. The early afternoon light was seeping through the windows, yellow and gentle, illuminating the dust in the air.

"Marat told me something interesting," she said.

"Yes?" Andy asked.

The $100,000 rested on the table, untouched.

"He told me about a redhaired woman. A dreamer, I think your colleagues called her." She studied Andy over the rim of her cup.

Andy wanted to keep quiet but realized Kuznetsova would only persist until she gave her something. Anything.

"He must be mistaken. We don't have a redheaded woman in our employ in New York. As for the dreamer—what a strange word. Are you sure your colleague heard right?"

"Andrea. You were with the redhead. She was gorgeous, smart. And she insisted on touching Marat as if she held some power. It was almost as if she was an important asset to Ma Soeur. And it seemed she meant something to you as well." She gave a coy smile. "It's about time. After Victoria."

Andy said nothing.

"You know." Kuznetsova put down her tea. She stuck a cake fork into the slice of rich, layered honey cake in front of her, breaking off a piece and placing it in her mouth.

"Hmm. Delicious. You should have some."

She pointed to the other two slices on the tray.

Andy didn't move. René stepped forward, placed her cup on the table, then stepped back again.

Kuznetsova smiled. "You know I've always wondered what Ma Soeur really does. I've never really believed that it's merely a charity focusing on women's issues. I've persistently encountered you in places where you don't belong."

The last three words came out flat and angry, the British accent falling away to reveal an almost guttural Russian undertone.

"Again," Andy said calmly. "We apologize. Sincerely. If what we offer is not sufficient an apology, I can negotiate with Kate to increase the number to your desire."

Kuznetsova stood up. She came to sit on the edge of the table, as close to Andy as she could manage. The men in the room inched closer.

"What I desire, Andrea Feraud Bouchard, is to meet this redhaired woman. I want to understand who Ma Soeur is. Perhaps we can be of assistance to one another, you never know."

"We are exactly who we say we are," Andy said, her hands in the air. "We were merely responsible for Arlene Hampton's safety, as per her request, and saw that your men were following her. We thought they were thugs intent on hurting her and intervened. We meant no harm. We didn't know that you were keeping an eye on her to ensure Phillipe Lautrec paid his gambling debts."

She looked up at Kuznetsova, glad for the opening to test Lautrec's story.

Kuznetsova blinked, slightly surprised at Andy's words.

"We were, yes," she snapped. "But we wouldn't have hurt her. Never."

"I believe you." Andy didn't flinch, only gently signaled with her hands for Kuznetsova to calm down. "I just need to be certain. The night of Arlene Hampton's death I saw two men leave her apartment in a hurry. I wondered if they were your men. I would like to be able to tell the police the truth when they interrogate me again."

Andy could see her body tense, the gentle pulse in her neck accelerating. She crossed her arms and looked to Tea Guy, who shook his head in a clear warning: *No.*

Kuznetsova stared at him, then shrugged as if offering an equally silent apology. "Hypothetically speaking, they could have been my men."

Andy betrayed no emotion.

Tea Guy looked to his left, fists clenched in front of his body, disgust on his face. He made a strange noise in the back of his throat.

Kuznetsova ignored him. "Perhaps these men were too late," she said. "Perhaps they were on their way up to deliver a message to Ms. Hampton for Mr. Lautrec. It would seem that Mr. Lautrec was very, very fond of Ms. Hampton, even though she did not return the sentiment. Perhaps someone imagined that he would respond best to a…request from her to pay his debts, rather than from us. Perhaps these men arrived just after the shooter had left, long enough for you to come across them." She lifted one shoulder. "Perhaps."

"The men I saw had security tags for the building."

"Could be that a security guard sold it to them. It's plausible. This guard seemed as if he'd done it before."

Andy mulled over her words.

"You know there are no absolutes in our world, Andy," Kuznetsova said.

"I see. But you are willing to vouch for this to be the truth? Hypothetically speaking."

"Yes."

That was big, Andy knew. "Did these men perhaps see anything of interest? Anyone of interest?

"No. Whoever it had been, was gone when they arrived."

"How disappointing."

"Indeed." A slight pause. "Do the police think we are involved in Ms. Hampton's death?"

Andy did her best not to smile. Kuznetsova's information came with a price then, after all. "Not as far as we can see, no."

"And you are certain of that?"

"At this point, yes."

Kuznetsova returned to her seat. "As you can see, we had no hand in what happened to Ms. Hampton. None whatsoever. Mr. Lautrec owes us almost half a million dollars in gambling debt. We only wanted to ensure he understood the gravity of his situation."

"We understand. Fully. I assure you." Andy hesitated for a moment. "And I will convey this to my mother."

Kuznetsova nodded. She looked at the bag containing the money, then pushed it back in Andy's direction. "As I said, Phillipe Lautrec had a thing for Arlene Hampton. Tell Kate that too. He was fascinated with her sex life. And mightily upset that she wasn't interested in him. In men."

She inhaled deeply, as if regaining her composure and flashed Andy a cold, hard smile. "Tell your mother that I'll arrange a meeting with her. One hundred thousand is simply not sufficient to cover the mental damage Marat suffered at your hands. The man-hours lost to my business. And bring the redhead with you. I'd like to meet her."

"I can arrange the meeting. I don't, however, know about the woman." There was no way in hell the Russians would ever know about Isabelle. Andy would die before they got their hands on her.

Kuznetsova stood up, dismissing them with a wave of her hand. "I don't think it's up to you. This is between me and your mother."

CHAPTER FORTY-FIVE

Siv Sandberg was a striking woman in her fifties who moved with statuesque grace. Her blond hair, peppered with gray, tied back on her neck, revealed a determined chin, matched by steel gray eyes that pinned you down, demanding the truth—and even more so when talking about Arlene Hampton's murder.

Her wife was almost inconsolable. Isabelle hadn't had her heart broken by a lover yet, she had to admit, but she wondered if you should really be that upset about the death of your first girlfriend in the company of your wife of twelve years? Should this not happen in private, the doors and windows closed?

But she was here to provide the soft touch, the gentle tone and soothing voice Kate seemed to think Andy was incapable of delivering, not judgement.

"I'm really sorry," she said again, rubbing Nilla Sandberg's left hand between her own, coaxing some warmth into the cold fingers. Both Sandbergs were still in the clothes they had traveled in, their suitcases remaining unpacked next to the enormous bed in the hotel's presidential suite.

The diminutive Nilla sat upright, opening her brown eyes, murky with a mixture of sorrow and lack of sleep, under straight blond hair. "I'd hoped it would have been a gentle death. Quick and painless. Not this…not fleeing in terror from whoev—" She broke down again.

Siv moved in, stroking her back. "I know, darling, I know." She looked at Andy, who had remained on the periphery since their introductions, allowing Isabelle to answer all their questions.

Andy had asked Isabelle in the elevator if she would mind taking the lead in talking to the Sandbergs. She'd agreed to do so. Whatever had happened at Brighton Beach had upset Andy. Nobody else had noticed, she was sure, but she could spot the anger in that tiny twitch in the corner of Andy's mouth, almost like a trapped animal snarling at whoever dared to come close.

She hadn't pried. Perhaps she'd felt like giving Andy a break. Perhaps she'd felt it was time she proved to her that she could also do some of the heavy lifting in this relationship.

René was downstairs, in the lobby of the Hilton Hotel, with Marc patrolling the hotel's exits.

Siv looked at Isabelle, then to Andy, as if determining who carried the power between them. She seemed at a loss to decide.

It made Isabelle smile. The world was a funny place and it kept on evolving. She kept on evolving. She almost liked who she had become over the last few days. Except for Arlene. She'd carry Arlene with her for the rest of her life. Her death was her failure. Her constant reminder to do better.

"Do the police know anything yet?" Siv asked.

"Nothing significant, it seems," Isabelle said. "We are tracking their lead investigator and will let you know as soon we know more."

Siv took a deep breath. She abandoned soothing her wife and moved to the window in three long strides. She wore a red pantsuit, the color a crimson contrast against the earthy tones of the Hilton Hotel's penthouse suite.

Outside the hotel room door there waited a contingent of staff and security personnel, gently goaded out when Andy and Isabelle had arrived.

Andy shifted where she was standing like a military statue posing at rest, hands clasped behind her back. "Kate asked me to request you not deliver your speech on Monday. She is scared that the Russians may make an attempt on your life. That Arlene Hampton's death was perhaps a warning for you to step back from whatever announcement you wish to make."

"I thought you said Arlene's death may be linked to her partner's gambling debts?"

"It may. But the opposite may also be true. We're not quite sure what's going on at the moment."

Siv contemplated her answer for a nanosecond. “I can’t do that.” She shook her head vigorously. “It’s time to clean up our act, otherwise there will be nothing left of this planet. We’re all on a slow train to hell, with no one eager to make it stop.”

“Are you sure there is no other way to deliver your message?”

“Absolutely. I will not keep quiet until I have a deal on the table.”

Isabelle could see that Andy had anticipated her response. “Okay. But perhaps you can help us then. Are you sure you haven’t received any death threat? Perhaps a phone call asking you not to make the speech, hinting at what had happened to Arlene?”

Nilla looked up from where she was sitting, her face imploring Siv to say something.

Andy looked from her to Siv. To Isabelle.

Isabelle walked to Siv. She wanted to touch her, to connect with her, but Siv remained detached, rage simmering just beneath the surface. In a way she was a little like the Andy she’d first met, pissed off at everything and everyone.

“You must tell us, please.” She searched Siv’s eyes. “It is important. To lose you at the helm of the coalition in Norway could see the right-wing conservatives take over. That would be a tremendous loss. Not only for your country, but for the climate and Ma Soeur as well. We were, after all, instrumental in mobilizing the women’s vote for you, especially online.”

Siv’s mouth hinted at a smile. “You did your homework.”

Isabelle simply nodded. You couldn’t play the game if you couldn’t calculate the odds. And to calculate the odds you had to know what was going on.

“I owe a lot to Kate Bouchard,” Siv admitted.

“And what about Arly.” Nilla spat out the words, standing up. “What do you owe her? Our kids? She was their godmother. What if your job gets us killed? Them killed? All because of you and your fucking principles?” She stomped over to Siv. “You tell them. Tell them about the woman who called you to warn you to back off that asshole of a Russian president. About him fucking men at Harvard when he was visiting there. The same hypocritical old man now hunting down gay people in Moscow.”

Siv’s face contorted into something like rage. Then she turned to Isabelle and Andy. “My wife seems determined to show you our entire playbook today. Please forgive me.”

Nilla stepped forward, looking as if she wanted to kill Siv. Siv looked at her with a sudden tenderness that made Isabelle envious.

Siv opened her arms. Nilla lowered her eyes, her body tense, that of an athlete readying to run a long, long distance.

"Nilla."

Nilla broke down as she stepped into Siv's arms.

Siv held her as she cried. She kissed the top of Nilla's head, looking at Isabelle. "Before you ask. I don't know who this woman was. She said to back off the Russian president or face the consequences."

"She?"

"Yes."

Isabelle thought about what Andy had told her about this morning. Natalya Kuznetsova. Surely, she had no reason to protect the Russian president?

"Did you recognize her voice?" Isabelle asked.

"No. It could have been his wife for all I know." Siv smiled, exhaustion tugging at her face. "Will you please leave us alone? It has been a long day and it's Arly's funeral tomorrow morning."

"We just need to know—" Andy jumped in.

Isabelle stopped her. "Certainly. And we're really sorry to ask, but would you perhaps, please, reconsider the speech? Use the funeral as an excuse. It would be difficult to go to the funeral of such a close friend and still deliver a speech of such magnitude at the UN on Monday."

Nilla stirred against Siv's chest, turning her head to look at them with the saddest of smiles. "It's no use asking. Siv Sandberg never backs down. That's what I love and hate most about her."

CHAPTER FORTY-SIX

Whatever it was that had bothered Andy about Hampton's apartment still gnawed at her. It rested at the murky bottom of her mind, unwilling to be named. She pushed the empty plate aside and sat back in her chair. She watched as Isabelle ate her chicken pie in a café they'd stopped at as they were making their way to Roman's Diner. René and Marc had opted to stay in the van.

She pushed her empty soup bowl away, tuning in to the conversations around her. To her right, a young woman sat next to an older man, a lovers' tiff in full swing. Her eyes followed them as they paid and left, the man reaching out to the angry woman in a silent peace offering once they got outside.

When her gaze returned to Isabelle, she found herself being observed with a bemused smile.

"When are you going to tell me?" Isabelle asked.

"Tell you what?"

"What's been bugging you ever since you and Iona went out to the bar with that corporate lawyer. You've been stewing over it all day." A last bite of the pie. "And you believed that Russian woman when she said her men didn't kill Arlene, despite what you told Siv."

Andy finished her Americano. She didn't stop to think when exactly Isabelle Templeton had started to excel so much at reading her body and her mind.

She mulled over the multitude of loose threads in her mind. Maybe she should test her theory. See if it sounded as outlandish to someone else's ears as it did inside her head. She could trust Isabelle. Isabelle was new to Ma Soeur. There was no history tainting her perceptions.

She blew out a slow breath. "The calendar in Arlene's apartment."

"What about it?" Isabelle folded her napkin in half, looking down at the frail white paper.

"Don't you think it's odd that the days on it were marked off past the day of Arlene's murder?" Andy asked. "Past the date that you dreamed it? Why would she do that? Why mark off something ahead of time? Surely you mark one day at a time if you are counting down to an event?"

Isabelle tilted her head as she digested the thought, biting down on her bottom lip.

Andy was getting used to the gesture. It was the sign of a mathematician weighing the odds, considering her words carefully, not willing to spend them unwisely.

"The calendar was marked off until today, the twenty-first," Isabelle said. "Until the Sandbergs' arrival in the city. Arlene was supposed to look after them while they were here. Maybe that is why the days were crossed out."

"Maybe. But what if we are being manipulated? What if someone tried to control the way we would react to your dream? There is nothing to suggest that Arlene valued paper calendars. Or paper for that matter. There were no physical books in her apartment, and there are no online photos of her. The Fortress office indicates it to be the same there. All her appointments were made on an online diary."

Andy tapped the table with two fingers. "There was nothing in that calendar on the fridge, except the crossing out of a list of fourteen days in succession up to today, and some other random days during which nothing of significance happened in Arlene's life, both personal and professional. Jam checked as best she could. And there was no writing on it, no birthdays and holidays, almost as if somebody knew they wouldn't be able to mimic her handwriting. That it would betray their presence. Their game. It's almost as if the calendar was placed there."

Andy considered her next words. "And the clock is interesting. It was stuck on two fifty-nine p.m., even though the attack happened at night. Did someone do that deliberately? Did they hope it would throw us off the scent?"

Another fold in Isabelle's napkin, a quizzical tilt of the head in the other direction. "Why would someone do that?" she asked.

Andy stroked her chin, her jaw. "They expected us there and they wanted to manipulate our perceived timing of Arlene Hampton's death." She couldn't believe she was saying it out loud. "They wanted to make sure they got away with it. That we didn't interfere."

Isabelle sat back, the folded napkin clutched in her hand. Concern had pushed the curiosity aside. She worried her hair, tugging it behind her ear. "You know what your theory would imply, don't you?"

"Yes."

"Whoever killed Arlene knows about Ma Soeur. Who we are. What we do. How we operate."

"Yes. Or…" Andy waited to see if her worst fear would dawn on Isabelle.

She didn't have to wait long.

Isabelle ran a hand over her mouth. "Or someone within Ma Soeur murdered Arlene Hampton."

❖

"Who would do such a thing? And why?" Isabelle asked again, not satisfied with Andy's vague guesses.

Andy shrugged, stepping to the curb to wave down Marc and René in the van. Isabelle stood next to her, swaddled in a brown coat that ended to reveal her knee-high brown boots. "Who? Come on, I know you have a name swimming around inside that head of yours."

"I don't," Andy said.

"When will you learn to stop lying to me?"

Marc tried to make a U-turn across the road. "All I know is that there is a leadership struggle at Ma Soeur. Some people want Kate gone. If they could set her up, make her seem incompetent and weak, they could open the door for a takeover. Right now that is exactly the case. She seems vulnerable."

"Because of me? Because her little imported protégé got it wrong? She gambled and lost?"

"Anybody would have gotten it wrong if the scene was manipulated."

Isabelle walked up to her and slid her hand down Andy's arm into her coat pocket. Her fingers were cold. Andy wrapped them up in hers, rubbing them warm.

"Who are the people who want Kate's job?" Isabelle asked.

"Surely you heard the rumors."

"Andy."

"Okay. René is interested." A frustrated groan. "And she's acting with Jam's help, I gather."

Isabelle pulled her hand from Andy's grip. "I don't believe that René or Jam would murder anyone. Not for a second."

"Neither do I, but right now I don't know where else to look."

"What about the Sandbergs? Arlene had a girlfriend and Nilla Sandberg seems particularly heartbroken. And the Sandbergs know a lot about Ma Soeur. They could have had an argument. Nilla could have killed her in the heat of the moment—then made the effort to set up the scene to fool us?"

Andy considered the option. "Do they know about the dreaming as well?"

"I don't know. Your mother will know."

"But they've only just arrived in New York."

"As far I can see that's the case for Siv. I heard from Jam that Nilla's been here since last week for a Harvard class reunion."

❖

The diner near Ma Soeur was homey and warm, with white and red the most prominent colors. Sixties memorabilia hung from the ceiling and a jukebox in the corner played an Eagles song at low volume. The scent of fresh bread and stale coffee mingled into something largely pleasant. At almost four on a Friday afternoon, most of the tables were empty, so Isabelle dragged Andy over to a booth in the corner that overlooked the street to the left and the diner's entrance to the right.

René and Marc were outside, keeping guard.

Isabelle took a deep breath as she sat down. "You are walking toward this table when it happens. Detective Wright is on the ground, shot in the back, and you put your gun down to check on her." She inhaled sharply. "And then someone shoots you too. In the chest and in the head, as you are turning toward them. It changed from the first dream. You're no longer shot in the back."

Andy looked around her. At the servers gathering at the bar, enjoying the slowdown at the end of their shift. At the cook in the back, visible only when he slapped down a plate of eggs and bacon, calling out the order. Clearly, someone woke up late today.

She counted the exits. She could only spot the door they'd used earlier but knew there would be one in the kitchen too, probably leading to an alleyway. If she were to bend down to check on Wright where Isabelle had said she would, she would find herself with her back to the room. She wouldn't be able to see anything—not the entrance or the kitchen.

She trained her ears and listened carefully.

The main door made a double squeak as it opened. A silent whoosh as it closed. If she was crouched on the floor as Isabelle had explained, the window would be in front of her, with an aisle, meandering through a row of booths, to her right. To her left would be this corner booth and behind her another aisle leading to the front door.

She didn't like the setup. Not at all. Too open. She wiped at her neck, her skin crawling with unease.

She looked at Isabelle.

Isabelle failed to wipe the terror from her face in time.

Andy reached out, enclosing her hands in a tight grip. "It will be okay. This helps. It does. I didn't think it would, but it does."

"Really? Because it feels so futile to me. Like a runaway train I can't stop." Isabelle attempted a half smile. "Let's just hope I continue to be crap at this. That I'm zero for two in a few days' time. I got Arlene's date wrong. Maybe I mixed you up with someone else. Someone bad who deserves to die."

Isabelle tried to blink away the tears. She wiped at her eyes.

Andy shook her head. "Someone set you up to fail with Arlene, but they can't control everything, and they'll find that out soon enough. And once we have her killer, who knows how we change things going forward?"

❖

Andy stepped out of the diner to take a phone call as Isabelle finished her tea and paid the bill.

It was Kate. As usual, there were no pleasantries.

"What did Natalya say?" she asked.

"The money was not enough. She'll contact you later to discuss proper compensation." Andy held her breath. "She hinted at knowing something about Ma Soeur. About what we do. I suspect she's going to hold you to ransom for information. And she wants to meet Isabelle."

"That will be the day." There was the muffled sound of a voice in the background, probably Claire's. Then Kate returned. "Did she say when she wanted to meet?"

"No. But knowing her it would be soon."

"Probably, yes. She's never been the patient type."

A moment's silence.

"Kate," Andy said.

"Yes?"

"She was angry. Be careful. Don't meet her alone."

"We've never trusted each other enough for that. We've always chosen public places." Again, the muffled voices. Were she and Claire fighting? "How is Sandberg doing? And her wife?"

"They're upset. Sad. As can be expected."

Andy dodged a running toddler on the sidewalk, a dad in sweats chasing her down. "Are you going to the funeral?"

"Yes."

"And Sandberg's speech on Monday?"

"That too, yes."

"Could be trouble."

Kate laughed, but it wasn't a warm sound. "Darling, I can't remember a time without trouble."

Chapter Forty-seven

Jane closed the door to her apartment in Tribeca. Lieutenant Monaghan had ordered her home for something to eat and a good night's sleep. She'd been working forty-eight hours straight.

She'd objected perfunctorily and then left, even though it was only afternoon.

She listened for the din of tinny voices from below. Situated over a twenty-four-hour corner bodega on Broome Street, her apartment was never really quiet. The owner watched Korean TV most of the day, and the bell over the entrance would chime at regular intervals as customers entered and left the store.

The bodega had been robbed twice in the more than twenty months she'd lived here. The owner almost died the second time. Lucky for him, she'd reacted swiftly to the single gunshot just after one in the morning and saved his life. Third time she had to use CPR in her career. Got the perp too. Two in the chest when he turned his gun on her. Earned her a lifetime of how-are-you-really-feeling assessments and paperwork, and free dinner from the store's fridges whenever she wanted it.

Johnny Bahk liked her. Said he'd marry her. Too bad he was seventy-two and she as gay as they come. And not of the happy variety either, she'd been forced to explain as he'd held her hand a moment too long as he thanked her.

She could have moved months ago already, to somewhere quieter, but she didn't have the energy to do so.

Amy-the-bitch got the house after she cheated on her. In fact, she got the girl—their neighbor, what poor taste—*and* the house. And most of their friends. Especially those who knew Amy had been cheating on her but said nothing as they sat across from her at Saturday barbeques sipping their dainty glasses of chardonnay while checking their investment portfolios.

Jane had just wanted to get out of there. She'd packed two suitcases and her gun and came to Tribeca because she didn't know anyone here. It seemed as good a place as any if life was forcing you to make a U-turn. Because this sure wasn't starting over. Nobody ever started over. Not even in fairy tales. You picked up your shit, went somewhere else, and tried again—everything that had happened either part of you, or running alongside you like a rabid dog waiting to strike as soon as you dropped your guard.

Funny how forever could turn into a messy pile of paperwork, recriminations, and contribution calculations. Not that her contribution amounted to much, according to Amy—financially and otherwise.

Jane placed her gun on the coffee table, walked to the fridge, and opened a beer. She took the last one from the empty shelf. Shit. She would have to stop at Bahk's place to stock up. And she needed milk. As it was, she would have to crunch down on dry cereal for breakfast tomorrow morning.

She lifted her shirt and peered at the flat stomach underneath the white button-down. She was getting too thin again. Maybe she should go out for dinner, a nice greasy steak or something.

Maybe not.

She sat on the couch and lifted her feet onto the steel chest that doubled as a coffee table and switched on the TV. She flipped through the channels as she drank the beer slowly, savoring the taste, hoping the hunger would go away.

Nothing on TV caught her interest. The beer finished, she rose from her seat, her stomach growling. Time to face Bahk. If she was lucky his son would be working tonight.

She picked up her gun and walked out of the apartment, locking the door behind her. She didn't have much, but she'd become quite fond of what she'd accumulated over the past few months. It was her stuff. *Her* frigging stuff. Her own hand-picked furniture from secondhand markets, restored to their original state. Her pride and joy was the mahogany bookshelf in the bedroom. She loved that. She was still working on the teak dresser, sanding it down by hand to smooth perfection.

She put on her coat and rushed down the stairs into Bahk's place. She sifted through the ready-made meals in the freezer, selecting five different ones. Then she loaded apples, cereal, beer, coffee, and milk into her arms and struggled to the counter. Bahk came to her aid as soon as the customer he'd been serving left.

He took the pile of goods from her arms and walked back to his spot behind the counter. He added a handful of the sour cherry lollipops she liked so much, putting them in the bag without ringing them up.

"Mr. Bahk, those things give me a sugar high."

He scowled at her, making an indiscernible noise in the back of his throat and put two more lollipops in the bag.

She took out one while he rang up the rest of her shopping, popped it in her mouth, and turned to look out the window. "Things been quiet here?"

"Yes. No problems." He frowned at the lasagna she'd chosen, walked back to the freezer, and came back with another, more expensive version of the same meal. "Everyone tells me this one is nicer." It went into the bag without a charge.

"You really shouldn't do that, Mr. Bahk. I'm eating all of your profits."

"Johnny. And no. It's a gift. For a beautiful lady." He flashed her a smile, his sturdy square face happy behind the rimless glasses.

He'd always looked like a doctor to her.

She'd wondered what he was before he came to New York. What he could have been. Wanted to be. His children were studying something in IT. Both of them. His wife had died ten years ago.

She picked up her bag, then froze as she felt a tingling at the back of her neck. She turned her head just in time to see a woman standing beside an old Chevy looking directly at her. Realizing she'd been busted, the woman opened the car door and slid into the vehicle.

Jane frowned, leaving the bag on the floor as she stepped out into the cold, hand on her gun. Around her, passersby swore as they were forced to step around her.

The Chevy sped away.

"Jane…what is it? Everything okay?" Johnny called, tension in his voice.

She punched the plates into her phone, and frowned as she tried to think. She hadn't been able to tell the age or much about the appearance of the woman before she got into the car. She was swaddled in a coat—an expensive coat, if she remembered correctly. And she wore gloves and a fur hat, as if she had been out in the cold for quite some time.

She put her phone away and stepped back into the bodega. She tutted at Bahk as she picked up her shopping. "Just someone I thought I knew. Don't worry."

He sighed with relief.

She popped the lollipop back into her mouth. "Thanks for these. I owe you."

Bahk smiled broadly, a twinkle in his eye. "Enough to go out with my son?"

She returned his smile. "You'd need about a million more of these. And I'd need to suffer from some serious amnesia."

❖

Back home, she phoned the Major Case Squad to run the plates. Russo was still at the office, chasing down some leads on a Russian they'd identified prowling near Hampton's building the day before her murder.

The Chevy was a company car, he said. Belonged to an NPO named Ma Soeur.

That name again. The place with Andrea Bouchard, the furious blond lawyer, and the mysterious redhead and her funny dreams.

Why would the woman be watching her? She hadn't been there by accident. No way. Jane had never believed in coincidence. No good cop ever did. No cop who lived to retirement, anyway.

"I'll have some news on that Bouchard woman's DNA later," said Russo. "The lab said it should be ready anytime now."

"Great. Thanks."

"Yeah, yeah. You coming in later?"

"Yep. I only left you to the wolves because Monaghan ordered me home. Said I was shouting at everyone. I'm going to sleep for a couple of hours and then head back in. I'll be there as soon as Monaghan has left. Let me know, will you?"

"Will do," he said before hanging up.

She put the phone down and inched open the blinds in the living room. A quick scan of the street below revealed nothing but normal people doing normal things for a Friday afternoon. Rushing home as the sun was closing in on the horizon. Shopping. Taking their dogs for a walk.

There was no sign of the woman.

She stripped as she walked to the shower, exhausted to the bone. She put the shower on full blast, scrubbing down her body under the steaming hot water. She stepped out of the bathroom and put on sweatpants and a T-shirt she fished from the laundry bag.

She studied her reflection in the mirror, the thinnish line of her mouth, the angular Roman nose. Her skin was not too bad for someone on the wrong side of forty. There were a few crow's feet around her eyes, but she liked it. It looked good on her, as if she was forever squinting the truth out of someone. As if she'd seen stuff, and you couldn't lie to her. No, sir. Not Detective Jane Wright. Built-in bullshit detector, that one.

No single gray hair, either. She could thank her father for that. English genes that had refused a single gray hair on his head till his fifties.

Stubborn man. Retired English professor. She should call him. Maybe even go visit as soon her caseload allowed her to do so.

She flipped through the channels until she found a repeat of the Olympic ice skating finals. She settled down to watch until she fell asleep, her alarm set for eight.

Halfway through her lasagna and second beer, her phone rang.

It was Russo.

"Monaghan gone?"

"Yeah."

Something in his voice made her sit upright. "What's up?"

"It's the DNA. Got something funny here, Janey."

She stuck the fork in the pasta. Russo would know not to yank her chain. "Funny how?"

CHAPTER FORTY-EIGHT

Isabelle and Andy were a block from the diner when Andy's phone rang. It was early evening, dusk settling in around them. Isabelle had threaded her arm through Andy's, and they were wandering back to Ma Soeur, stopping at a brightly lit store window every now and then, in no rush to go back home.

Andy felt like a normal New Yorker wandering down the street with her lover, despite René and Marc following them at a respectful distance.

The idea made her frown. Had the one orgasm she'd given Isabelle made her her lover? She knew what Isabelle believed, what she wanted. She'd made that pretty clear.

But what did she want for herself? The thought of going back to London and the Black Sheep suddenly felt empty. Void of meaning. Besides, Jimmy was taking great care of the place, it seemed.

Staying here, at Ma Soeur, would mean she'd be with Isabelle. She'd be able to look after her. Make sure she'd be okay. Would that be so bad? Would it be so bad to give in to what she was feeling?

But what *was* she feeling?

She'd known by the jealousy she'd felt in the She Bar the other night that Isabelle had gotten underneath her skin. Same for the pure desire that had surged through her last night, the satisfaction of feeling Isabelle contracting, spilling over. Perhaps she also realized it from the deep-seated need she felt to surrender to someone.

No, not to someone. To Isabelle.

Just don't call it love. Never call it love. Then she wanted to run.

She unloved Isabelle.

Was that even a concept?

Next to her, Isabelle sighed as Andy's phone rang. She flashed an apologetic smile and fished the phone from her right pocket. Isabelle was on her left, as René had taught her, leaving Andy's gun hand free.

"Bouchard."

"Miss Bouchard…Andy. It's Detective Jane Wright. Mind if I call you Andy?"

"No. Please go ahead."

Isabelle looked at her.

"Wright," she mouthed silently.

Isabelle nodded.

They turned the corner to Ma Soeur's building.

"I have something to ask you. It's rather urgent. I'm at Ma Soeur, but they say you're out? In fact. It seems as if everyone has left for the weekend."

Andy looked up from her phone, straight at Wright, her lean frame wrapped in a black polar fleece jacket. She was standing at the entrance of Ma Soeur, milling around impatiently in tight blue jeans and black boots. She was dressed as if she'd rushed out without considering the weather properly.

She could almost feel Isabelle's irritation at the phone call turn into apprehension when she saw Wright.

Andy put away her phone. "It is Friday, you know," she called to Detective Wright.

Wright looked from her phone to Andy, relief on her face. "I know, but I thought I'd come over and see if you'd be willing to talk to me."

"Should I have my lawyer present?"

Andy and Isabelle came to a halt before Wright.

"You could phone Ms. Diaz, yes, but I don't think it's necessary. We have officially cleared you as a suspect. Scout's honor." Wright sketched a silent greeting to Isabelle, shuddering against the wind. "Would you mind if we talk inside? I'm freezing."

Andy was a bit surprised at her acknowledgement. "Certainly."

A frown appeared on Wright's face as she leaned back on her heels, looking past Andy.

"Who's your entourage?" She squinted at René and Marc.

Andy didn't even turn to look. She decided not to explain. "Don't worry about them." She pointed to the glass door that led into Ma Soeur. "We can sit and talk in the reception area."

"Okay. I suppose," Wright said reluctantly.

Andy allowed Wright to walk in first, Isabelle following in her wake.

There was a woman she didn't know working the reception desk. A youngish keeper, if she remembered correctly, no doubt armed. CCTV would also be keeping an eye on them. René probably already had Jam tuning in to the lobby. Jam would have no ears on the conversation, but she would be able to keep an eye on them.

Andy nodded a greeting to the keeper and pointed toward a small reception area in the corner. Caroline would kill her for speaking to a cop alone, but something brought Detective Jane Wright here on a Friday evening, and she wanted to know what it was.

Besides, from what she remembered, Caroline went to bed at five on a Friday, sleeping off the week's crazy work hours. Dragging her out was not a pretty sight. All that Armani took a while to assemble.

René walked into the lobby and headed toward them.

Andy pointed outside.

René's jaw dropped. It was a cold day, with the temperature decreasing rapidly.

Andy shrugged.

René mouthed something like "I'll kill you" and then walked out the door, Marc following her reluctantly.

Wright looked around her. "This is nice." They all sat on faded blue sofas underneath a set of posters advocating the use of clean water in rural Bangladesh. "Practical."

She almost sounded disappointed, as if she'd expected more. She settled back on her chair, looking from Andy to Isabelle, raising a questioning eyebrow. "You guys seemed a bit peeved with each other the last time we met. Did you kiss and make up?"

Andy gave a practiced, non-committal smile. "What can I help you with, Detective? It is a Friday, and we would like to go out for the evening."

"Ah. Do you live nearby then, or also at Ma Soeur?" Wright asked Isabelle. "Somehow I imagined you two shared a bed."

"Detective," Andy said in a warning tone.

"Yes, okay." Wright leaned forward, placing her elbows on her knees, pinning Andy down with her hazel eyes. "As I said, it seems that you are free and clear. We found no significant traces of your

DNA at the scene. Not on the wine glasses, in the kitchen, or in Arlene Hampton's bed. Same for the bathroom. We only found some DNA on the body, as can be expected when you administer CPR."

"And you came all the way to Brooklyn to tell me that?" An unease stirred in Andy. She could feel the same tension radiate off Isabelle, growing in magnitude as the seconds ticked by.

"Not exactly." Wright's mouth twitched in satisfaction. "We found DNA related to you—genetically speaking, family of yours—in Arlene Hampton's apartment and on her body. Lots of it." She shifted closer, a gleam in her eyes. "As I understand it, your mother is the head of Ma Soeur, correct?"

❖

It had been quick, a glimmer of emotion on the otherwise stony face, but Jane knew she hadn't imagined it. There had been a faint hint of surprise, then shock, followed by disappointment.

Disappointment that Andy Bouchard was…right?

Then it was gone, as quickly as it had appeared.

Jane sat back in her chair, keeping the heel of her right boot from tapping up and down in anticipation. She was closing in. She was on to something. Something big. There was something to this place. Ma Soeur. It didn't feel like a nonprofit, even though it appeared so on paper. Active in thirty-three countries. Clean water, education, self-defense, and voter education programs for women. Bullshit.

The problem was the people in Ma Soeur's orbit. None of them quite fit an organization aimed at charity work. A redhead who spoke about her dreaming the future and a tall, angry bodyguard. That woman with the short hair hovering outside in the cold, keeping a close eye on them, looked like she was ex-military. And the man with her. Well, he looked like a whole different kettle of fish. He looked like he'd slinked in from a place where government agencies became murky abbreviations with shadowy paymasters.

"I tried to get hold of your mother—Kate, is it?—but her phone is off," Jane said.

Bouchard shrugged as if it didn't matter. "It's a Friday evening. I'm sure she's resting or spending time with her fiancée. I'll give Caroline Diaz a call. We'll track Kate down and bring her to your office tomorrow."

Jane was convinced Bouchard was scrambling to buy time. "You can understand that we have to speak to your mother as quickly as possible." She hesitated deliberately. "And although we don't necessarily believe that you had any direct involvement with Arlene Hampton's murder, the fact that your mother spent time in her bed raises some interesting questions about any role you might have played in assisting her to cover up the crime. Like picking up your bullet casings. Perhaps even hers."

"There were other bullet casings on the scene. I left those."

"Yes. Those belonging to three Walther PPKs."

Bouchard didn't blink, didn't flinch, but Jane could see the pulse in her neck quicken. Templeton turned to Bouchard as if she could feel it happening. She placed her hand on Bouchard's.

"Your mother has a PPK registered in her name," Jane said, watching her closely. "And it was a PPK that killed Arlene Hampton."

Bouchard's pulse slowed down, becoming a faint contraction in her neck in what seemed an act of sheer willpower. "Why then did I not pick them up, if I were covering up for her, as you put it? Besides, one of the men I told you about, the men fleeing the scene, had a PPK. It could be a coincidence. A mistake."

"I suppose so." Jane leaned forward. "But somehow I don't think so."

"Oh, stop playing games," snapped Templeton. "If Andy left the PPK's casings you most certainly can't suspect her of covering up for her mother."

Bouchard looked at her with a hint of surprise in her eyes.

Jane was equally impressed. And she had to give Templeton that one. "Yes, perhaps you're right, which is why I'm not going to arrest her. Yet. But I may change my mind about that tomorrow. In the meantime, it will help your cause if you can tell me where your mother is."

"I really don't know," Bouchard said.

"This building is stated as her home address, same as yours. Maybe we should check and see if she's here. As you said, she may be resting and not paying attention to her phone." Jane stood up, tilting her head in the direction of the receptionist who hadn't taken her eyes off them for the entire duration of their conversation.

Bouchard also got to her feet, followed by Templeton. The man and woman at the front door walked in.

Jane resisted the itch to reach for the cool steel of her gun. Maybe she should have brought backup. She'd told Russo she'd come alone. He'd wanted to wait until tomorrow. She'd been impatient, as usual. Or maybe she was the only one in the Major Case Squad who didn't have anyone to go home to at the end of the week.

But Bouchard surprised her. She looked at the receptionist, nodded at her. "Could you please check if Kate is here?"

Bouchard didn't call her "mother." Interesting.

The receptionist hesitated, then picked up her phone and dialed a number.

She waited for almost a minute. "No answer."

Bouchard turned to them. "My apologies. Seems that is all we can help you with for the moment."

"Perhaps not. I would like to go knock on her door."

"If Ms. Diaz was here she would advise me against such action." Bouchard stretched to her full length, stepping closer to Jane in the process, forcing her to look up.

Jane didn't flinch. She wasn't in the habit of being intimated. "I can come back with a warrant for her arrest."

"Then you should do that. As I understand it, Ma Soeur is always happy to assist the NYPD."

"I'll do so. In the meantime, tell your mother to contact me immediately." Jane flashed Bouchard a smile. Oh, she loved a challenge.

"I'll do that as soon as I locate her."

Jane didn't believe her. Bouchard had known her mother wasn't home, otherwise she wouldn't have risked the call.

She looked from Bouchard to Templeton. The serious faces of the man and woman behind her. What the fuck was this place?

She pushed her hands into her pockets and walked to the door, dreading the cold outside. She turned on her heels just before she exited. "Don't go anywhere now. I won't be long."

Chapter Forty-nine

"What the fuck was that?" René erupted.

Andy didn't answer. "I need to go and find Jam, and then we must locate Kate, as fast as we can."

"What did that cop want fr—"

"I'll explain later." Andy signaled to René and Marc. "Please wait here while I find Jam."

"No way," René said.

Andy took a moment, then turned to face her. Detective Wright's information changed everything. With what she knew now, she could probably clue Jam and René in on her theory. They were leading the revolt against Kate in the CEO election. They had no reason to protect her.

"I can't tell you everything right now, because I'm still trying to get my own head around it, so will you please trust me?" She looked over René's shoulder to Marc. He stood stone-faced, hands jammed in his pockets, head still covered by a black beanie.

He took a while, then nodded.

Andy had known him for many years. He'd developed the ability to think for himself, despite his background. Turned out he wasn't one for blindly following orders after all.

René had recruited him, if she remembered correctly.

Andy took a deep breath and signaled her thanks to Marc with a tiny nod. He managed a vague smile, then turned around, facing away from them, and stood there as if he was completely deaf.

René looked at Marc, then back to Andy. "Fuck it, I hate you sometimes."

Andy reached out and held René's hands between her own. "I won't ask anything of you today, except to keep Isabelle and me safe. That's all. Nothing you weren't supposed to do anyway, I promise."

"Nothing is ever that black-and-white with you, Bouchard," René grumbled, then groaned in frustration. "What do you want us to do?"

"Get the car ready. Two cars. We may need to split up. And wait for us here."

There was a plan forming in Andy's head, but she first needed to locate Kate. And for that she needed to speak to Jam.

"Okay," René said. "Go."

"You're a lifesaver. Thanks."

Andy grabbed Isabelle by the arm and rushed to the elevator. They got in and pushed the button for the comm center. Hopefully, Jam was there. She didn't want to use their in-ear comm systems to find her. Kate had access to all of Ma Soeur's comm systems.

"I can't believe your mother would do something like this," Isabelle whispered. "Is she capable of murder? Murdering someone she may…might have been involved with?"

Andy didn't know what to say. Kate sleeping with Arlene Hampton would certainly explain her anger and frustration over her death. She'd imagined it had to do with the risk of bringing Isabelle here and the upcoming election. She could kick herself for being so blind.

Isabelle's eyes opened a bit wider. "Kate did send you into that subway station, knowing what would happen. I guess murder may not be far off."

"She does what needs to be done. That's what makes her so scary," Andy said, a weariness settling deep into her bones. "Who knows what happened between my mother and Hampton. And it wouldn't be the first time my mother cheated on her partner. Not by a long shot."

The elevator doors opened and they rushed into the comm center.

Jam looked up from her laptop. She shot up from behind her desk when she saw them, her yellow sneakers hitting the floor with a loud thud. The comm center was empty except for her and three other people. Andy looked at her watch. It was after six and quiet for a Friday.

Andy turned to the two men and one woman behind their computers. "Could you please give us the room?"

They glanced at Jam. Jam ran her hands through her purple hair, over the row of studs in her right ear. "We're not tracking any serious operations at the moment, so yeah, why not? Take the rest of the evening off. The next shift will come in at eight, so that should be okay."

When the last operator disappeared, Jam turned to Andy. "What's up? I saw Detective Wright downstairs."

"Yes, and she's coming back with an arrest warrant for Kate."

"What?"

Andy hesitated, then rubbed her mouth in a sharp, uneven movement. "I'm trusting you here."

Jam frowned. "Of course, yeah."

"Kate's DNA was found on the Hampton murder scene. Everywhere in the apartment."

It took a while for the words to sink in. "She did it again. Cheated again."

"Seems like it."

"But do you think...Does it mean..." Jam cleared her throat and looked from Andy to Isabelle. "I'm not too fond of Kate, but I don't think she's capable of murder. Messing around, yes. Murder? No."

Andy tilted her head and exhaled sharply. "Not even if Hampton threatened to expose Ma Soeur? Or if she cheated on Kate, in turn?" Andy held her breath for a moment. "I've had my suspicions for a while now that this murder scene was staged by someone who knows how we operate. That paper calendar, the stopped clock, it was too convenient. Too unlike Arlene Hampton. It gave us a time and date. A deliberately misleading time and date."

Jam frowned at Andy's words. "It's a possibility, I suppose. But it's your mother, Andy. And Ma Soeur's CEO. How can we be standing here talking about her killing someone? That goes against centuries of ethics."

"All I know is that she must have been very upset about Isabelle's dream," Andy said. "It was a completely unexpected turn of events. Kate handled Isabelle during her abduction, true?"

Jam thought for a second. "Yes."

"And Isabelle hit Kate when we were released from the green room."

"Yes."

"That could have been enough to prompt Isabelle's dream. Yet Kate went ahead and murdered Arlene, despite the dream. Her plan must have looked pretty bulletproof to her. Besides, we wouldn't even be investigating Hampton's death if it wasn't for Isabelle's second dream. My death. We would have left it to the police. Kate would have been free and clear."

"What about the Russians at Hampton's place then?"

"A coincidence. Fate intervening. Wouldn't be the first time." Andy shrugged. "All I know is that we have to find Kate and talk to her. That's all that matters right now."

Andy felt Isabelle slip her hand in hers, giving her a reassuring tug as if she knew what Andy was planning.

"We need to find Kate before the cops do, Jam," she said. "We have to know what's going on. But we need to hurry. Detective Wright is probably getting that warrant as we speak."

❖

"It's no use. Kate's phone is dead." Jam stabbed at the enter key.

"What about Claire's? Maybe they're together?"

Jam's hands again flew over the keyboard, then paused. "Nope. Nothing. Also dead. Maybe they're busy. They are engaged, after all."

"What about their bracelet trackers?"

"That may be a bit of a problem." Jam scrunched up one side of her face. "They're not active in the field anymore so they've both asked not to wear them every now and then to get a break from work. I couldn't argue. They're normally at it 24/7. Your mother hasn't taken leave in five years."

Andy didn't know that but left it there. "Where did their phones last ping? Both of them?"

"That I can do," Jam said.

Andy turned to sit next to Isabelle, who was watching Jam's every move.

"You okay?" she asked Isabelle.

"Yes. But I still don't know about this thing with your mom and Arlene."

Andy gave a half smile. "Your mom dropped you off at an orphanage."

"Yes, I suppose. I just...why do I always expect them to do better? Parents, you know. Why have kids if you are not going to bother with them?"

Andy immediately felt sorry for reminding Isabelle about her own unhappy childhood. She put an arm around her and kissed her on top of her head. “Sorry. I didn’t mean to…you know.”

“I know.”

“Got it,” Jam said. “Your mom’s phone says she was here half an hour ago. Then it went dark, though. And I don’t know if it helps, but her diary shows she has a meeting with Natalya Kuznetsova at eight.”

“Where?”

“Doesn’t say.”

“Doesn’t matter. It’s more than we had before. I’ll go break that up if we can’t find any trace of her sooner.” Andy nodded, somewhat relieved. “In the meantime, we can track Kuznetsova’s phone to see where she is. What about Claire?”

“She’s somewhere in the city, shopping it seems, according to her phone and credit cards. I’ll give you the address of her last ping.”

“Great.” Andy turned to Isabelle. “Are you game to help? It wouldn’t be anything dangerous, promise.”

Isabelle looked at her with something like disbelief. “Now all of a sudden I’m allowed to help?”

Andy shrugged. She knew she could only trust a handful of people if it involved the Ma Soeur CEO. “Please?”

“In that case, of course,” Isabelle said with a smile.

“Thanks. I want you and Marc to go look for Claire. Maybe she’ll lead us to Kate. Don’t engage if you find her, just give me a call.”

“Will do. Are you going after Natalya?”

“Yes.” She grimaced. “And I’m going to search Kate’s office to see what I can find before the cops arrive.” She pointed to Jam. “Maybe you can work out where Kate was the night of the murder? Maybe her phone records can exonerate her.”

“And if they don’t?” Isabelle laid a hand on Andy’s arm. “What if she did kill Arlene? You can’t remove any evidence of your mother’s guilt. You know that, don’t you?”

Andy felt a jolt in her stomach, her chest. “Yes. I know.”

“Despite the scrutiny a case such as this will bring to Ma Soeur?” Isabelle said.

“Kate…this…it may jeopardize everything we have worked for,” Jam said from behind them. There was a fragile sound in her voice, a sense of loss for a life built around Ma Soeur.

Jam arrived here at age twenty, if Andy remembered correctly. She had an arrest record as long as her arm, because she was continuously looking for something—anything—to challenge her mind and the restless energy she had inside her. The burning desire for more.

Kate had saved so many souls. Screwed up some others too.

Vic got here at eighteen. A strong dreamer, her first dream leaving her in tears at sixteen. It would be enough to drive anyone over the edge, no matter how old they were.

"If Kate murdered Arlene Hampton she'll have to pay for it. She has to," Andy said grimly. "There is no other way. We'll undo everything we stand for if we let her walk."

Jam groaned. "I'm hoping the Russians did it. Really. They were there and they had guns. Good enough for me."

"I'm with you," Andy said.

Isabelle moved closer. Andy could smell the heady scent of jasmine and tilled soil after the rain. Fresh, crisp. Intoxicating.

She pulled Isabelle close to her. Held on to her. "Be careful," she whispered.

"You too," said Isabelle. Andy could hear the strain as she forced a smile into her voice. "Don't go near any diners."

"I won't," she said.

"I love you," Isabelle whispered in her neck. "Please come home safely."

"I'll do my very best," Andy promised.

CHAPTER FIFTY

Marc gave Isabelle a quick, staccato wave. "Nice to see you again."

There was respect in his voice. Isabelle liked him, but also feared him a bit. There was something dark in him, something he managed to hold at bay, if only barely. His face sometimes betrayed his struggle. His smile was genuine, but tired. His strides long, but somehow faltering, as if he was running a marathon with no end in sight.

She held his hand for a moment longer and looked at his eyes, the small patch of hair his razor missed this morning just above his upper lip.

"Are you okay to work with me tonight?" she asked.

Surprise flickered in his eyes. "It will be my honor, Ms. Templeton. I have great respect for your work."

"Isabelle, please."

He simply nodded. "I'll do my best to look after you as well as Andy would. Please let me know if I can do anything to make our time together more comfortable."

She wanted to hug him, to wrap him in her arms, but she refrained from doing so, sensing he wouldn't like it. Instead she ran her hand down the length of his arm.

He flinched but didn't pull away.

She imagined that he wasn't touched often, that he didn't like it, but still longed for human warmth on some level.

"Shall we go find Claire?" she said.

Claire's phone last pinged in Tribeca. Once there, however, Isabelle didn't know where she and Marc would have to go to look for her.

They drove in silence to the spot where Claire's phone last produced GPS coordinates. The site was in the heart of the normally lively neighborhood, the mood seemingly sedated by the cold. The weather forecast predicted snow later tonight. Already the clouds had started to move in, the clear skies from earlier gone. Isabelle wasn't particularly fond of the cold. She loved the rain, though.

Marc parked the SUV across from a café, the sounds of slow jazz seeping through the closed doors when they stepped out of the vehicle. A man stood smoking on the sidewalk, head hidden under a hoodie. He dragged on the cigarette like he was in a hurry to get out of the cold and back to wherever he came from.

Isabelle zipped up her coat. What did they do now? Look around? Ask if anyone had seen Claire? The shops on this particular street were closed by now, except for a single set of inviting lights a block away.

She walked down the street, Marc a vigilant presence on her right hand. It would probably be a dead end, but it was the only bread crumb to follow. They stepped inside the bodega. The man behind the counter looked up. He was older, Asian, his practiced smile reflecting a lifetime of customer service.

It died when he saw Marc.

Isabelle turned around, signaling for Marc to wait at the door as she approached the man.

"Evening," she said and smiled. "My name is Isabelle Templeton."

"Hi." The gentleman thawed somewhat but didn't offer his name. He rubbed his hands together, his eyes still fixed on Marc.

"I wonder if you can help me? I'm looking for a woman. Maybe you saw her around here earlier today? Maybe she came in for a water or something to eat." Isabelle realized she had to do better. She loathed to tell the lie but did so anyway. "It's my older sister. We fear she may be in danger."

"Ah," the man said. This time the smile was warmer, more genuine. "My name is Johnny Bahk."

She shook his hand, then showed him a picture of Claire that Jam had sent to her phone earlier. He studied it carefully. "I don't know. I don't think so. No. I haven't seen her."

"Are you sure? Maybe she didn't come in here. Maybe she just walked by on the street?"

"No," he said, shaking his head with conviction. "I haven't seen her. I'm sorry."

Isabelle nodded and put her phone away. She bowed slightly. "Thank you for your time."

At the door, the man called her back. "Are you married?"

She turned. "Uhm…no."

He beamed. "My son is studying programming."

She held up her hands, laughing. "I'm taken, Mr. Bahk. Sorry. As good as married. Just don't have the ring yet."

It didn't feel like a lie—not if she trusted the dreams, like she'd started to do.

His face fell, but he managed an anemic smile. "Ah, well. All the good ones are always taken."

She waved good-bye and she and Marc walked back to his car. Back in the warmth of the SUV, she wondered what to do next.

Next to her, Marc looked at her expectantly. "We could knock on some doors. Fake an emergency and talk to some shop owners where Claire had used her credit card?"

Isabelle looked at her watch. She had a bad feeling about tonight. "I don't think it would help Andy in time."

"Then I have one more suggestion," he said.

She looked at him expectantly.

He called Jam on the comm system and synced it with the car's audio system. "Jam, does Claire often shop in Tribeca or around here?"

"Her credit cards don't suggest that, no."

"Okay. Does she have any friends or family in Tribeca?"

"No luck in finding her?"

"No, there's no sign of her, and I'm unwilling to leave before we've tried every angle. Maybe Claire is visiting someone here. Or maybe Kate sent her on an errand. You know she's completely devoted to Kate. Anything is possible."

"I suppose," Jam said.

"Perhaps you should also check if any of the people involved in this case—Kuznetsova, Hampton, Lautrec—doesn't matter who—live or work in Tribeca?"

"Why go that far?"

"I don't know. Devotion is a strange emotion. One I encountered many times in interrogation. It's powerful leverage."

Isabelle cocked her head at the sudden glint of emotion in Marc's voice.

"So, you're saying…" Jam's voice trailed off.

"Nothing. Just covering all the bases."

Marc had pulled away as he spoke. He drove slowly through the neighborhood. Isabelle looked out the tinted window, on the lookout for Claire's chestnut hair, her steady gait.

"I'm running the search," Jam said. "Might take a while."

"No problem. We'll stay in the area."

CHAPTER FIFTY-ONE

Jane got in her '68 Mustang. She loved the machine, all black and newly overhauled. It smelled like worn leather and hot steel. Better yet, it felt like home—more like home than any other place.

She pulled away from Ma Soeur's HQ and drove around the block. She parked farther away from the building this time, out of sight of the surveillance cameras at the front door.

Funny place that. Tried its best to look like a nonprofit but couldn't quite pull it off—almost like a little rich girl trying to pose as a twenty-dollar hooker. That receptionist looked like she could dig out your eyes with a teaspoon and devour you with a side of spinach. And all those cameras. In the foyer, outside. Plus the elevators had a biometric ID system.

There was much more to Ma Soeur than met the eye, and she was damn well going to find out what it was. She also suspected that Andy Bouchard knew more about her mother's whereabouts than she'd let on.

Jane fished her phone from her pocket and called Russo. She had just about enough juice left to make the call. The battery was about to die. "How's that warrant going?"

He grunted something unintelligible. No doubt some Italian swear words he'd picked up from his ninety-seven-year-old grandma.

"Getting there," he finally managed something she could understand.

When the Ma Soeur receptionist couldn't locate Kate Bouchard, she had Russo start the process to secure a warrant for her arrest, only calling Andy Bouchard afterward. She hadn't been able to resist stirring the pot while she was forced to wait. She wanted to see what happened if she pushed the Bouchards into a corner.

She had to give it to Andy Bouchard. Must be a bitch playing poker with her. Not that she could imagine Bouchard as a gambling woman. She looked like she planned, weighed, and measured everything. But she was sure there lurked some recklessness in there. Something that would strip down to brutal and ruthless when cornered. Or when someone touched that redhead next to her in any way but with a great amount of respect.

"Just get the paperwork, will you," she said to Russo. "As soon as you can. And track Kate Bouchard's phone as soon as you can. I need to find this damn woman."

"And bring the paperwork where exactly, Your Highness?" he grunted. He must be walking up the stairs or something, because he sounded out of breath.

"What are you doing?" she asked.

"Taking the stairs." The Major Case Squad was on the third floor. "Doc says I got to lose fifteen pounds. Jenny wants another kid and well, yeah...whatever."

"Okay. Cool." She cleared her throat. Russo was the only one on the force who knew she was gay, which often made him share odd, intimate details of his life with her. "I'm at Ma Soeur when you get it. Not in the building, but close by. Just look out for the 'Stang."

"You're going to freeze your ass off in that car."

"Don't worry about me. Just bring the warrant as soon as you've got it."

❖

"I still can't believe Kate would kill someone. She is a dreamer. They don't kill people. To them life is sacred. Something to protect at all costs." René rummaged through a drawer in Kate's desk without really looking at its contents.

"I'm not saying she necessarily killed anyone. All I'm saying is that it's pretty clear she had an affair with Arlene Hampton." Andy flipped through the books in her mother's bookcase, looking for anything that would give them a clue as to what had been going on between Kate and Hampton. Her mother always stored keepsakes in books. She shrugged. "And you never know. Kate could have revealed too much about Ma Soeur. They could have argued. Hampton could have threatened to expose us. Maybe she blackmailed Kate. Or maybe Hampton cheated on Kate. Anything is possible."

"Maybe it was a one-night thing."

"That's also a possibility, although I doubt it. It felt like Hampton made an effort with her guest. Roses. Expensive wine."

"You don't wine and dine someone you're blackmailing."

"Also true," Andy agreed.

She put back the stack of books she'd just searched and took down five new ones. Typical Kate Bouchard books. Warfare, battlefield histories, boardroom strategies. All the stuff she grew up with.

"How often did Kate...you know." René suddenly ran out of words.

Andy completed the sentence for her. "Cheat?"

"Yeah."

"I know of two affairs as I grew up."

"All forgiven?"

"No. One was, but the other broke up the relationship. It was before you arrived. It was a woman I really liked too. More of a mother than Kate ever was."

"Sorry."

"Why? It happened. I survived."

René opened another drawer. She peered over the rosewood desk at Andy. "Do you think Claire knew?"

"About Kate and Hampton? It's possible. On some level we always know, don't we?"

"Claire is much younger than Kate. Younger than Hampton."

"I know. And much younger than Kate's typical pattern, which makes me think Hampton was maybe something more. A surprise. Something real. And if you're not used to that emotion, the depth of it, you're probably not used to the level of jealousy and uncertainty that can go with it. The degree to which you are suddenly not in control. And at almost sixty, do you still have the capability to develop all of that emotional control?"

René considered her words. "Okay. Maybe you're right. Maybe Kate lost her temper and did something stupid." She blinked at Andy.

"Is Isabelle's age the reason you're scared of her? Do you think that you might be repeating your mother's patterns?"

Andy retrieved a new set of books and sighed heavily. "Maybe. If you live long enough it's always your mother staring back at you in the mirror, isn't it?"

René sighed. "Fuck, yeah."

Andy recalled René's mother being a retired army general, and a mother to four equally rock-hard daughters.

"What would you do if Isabelle cheated on you?" René asked.

"Technically, we are not together."

"Fuck technically."

"I would probably pack up and leave."

"Do you think that's what Claire will do when she finds out about Kate and Hampton? Because this is going to come out, make no mistake." René pointed to the other desk in the room next door, the smaller one, belonging to Claire.

Andy frowned. "I don't know Claire. When did she and my mother get together?"

"Just after you left. Kate was depressed and lonely, although she'd never admit to it. Claire was a young keeper who'd just lost her dreamer." René cleared her throat. "Suicide. Anyway. Kate had a rare dream and Claire was there to help her."

Andy frowned. "How deeply connected are they?"

"Kate is Claire's life. Her purpose. I wouldn't know if the reverse is true. I guess not."

Andy put down the books in her hands. "Jam says Claire's phone was dark the night of Hampton's death, just like Kate's. We assumed they were together, but maybe that was not the case. And Claire would have access to Kate's gun, true?"

"The PPK? Yes. I suppose so." René considered her words. "But what about the Russians then? The men we saw at Hampton's apartment. They also had PPKs. Did Kuznetsova tell the truth? Was it all just coincidence that night Hampton was killed—her men showing up at a murder scene?"

"It's possible. Unlikely, but feasible nonetheless." Andy pointed to Claire's desk. "See if you can find anything that suggests that Claire knew about Kate's affair. I'll phone Isabelle and warn her to not engage Claire."

"Marc can handle Claire. And Isabelle is no wilting little flower."

"I know, but…"

"Technically, you don't need to say any more." René grinned at her as she steamed past Andy to Claire's desk.

Ten minutes later, she called to Andy from next door.

"You better take a look at this."

Andy walked next door to Claire's office. René held a book on Italian grammar in her hand. Inside was a photo taken through a window from a few feet away. Snapped in what appeared to be a hotel, it was a photo of a half-naked Arlene kneeling in front of Kate, her mouth clasped on Kate's left breast, Kate's head thrown back in pleasure.

CHAPTER FIFTY-TWO

Isabelle nudged Marc as Jam beeped in her ear. She held an imaginary phone against her ear. He shot up, nodding at her to take the call. For some reason he hated carrying his earpiece. Maybe it reminded him of his past, who knew.

"Jam?" she asked over the car's speaker phone.

"Bad news. There's someone related to the case who lives in Tribeca. In fact, quite close to where you are now. That bodega you should be able to see from the car?"

Isabelle peered out the window to the shop they'd visited earlier. "Yes?"

"Detective Jane Wright lives in the apartment right above it."

Isabelle glanced at the darkened windows directly above the twenty-four-hour shop.

"Do you know where she is?" she asked Jam. She prayed the detective had gone home and to bed after her visit to Ma Soeur.

"I'll start a trace."

"And Claire?" Marc chimed in. "Has she surfaced yet?"

"Nope. Her phone and bracelet are both still dark."

Isabelle watched as Marc mulled over the information Jam had provided. "So, are we saying that Claire might have been following Detective Wright?" he asked.

"Maybe," Jam said. "Or maybe it was a coincidence?"

Marc's eyes narrowed. "I don't think so. Claire's a planner. I've always known her to be meticulous and precise."

Isabelle didn't know Claire but felt that she agreed with Marc. She sat back in her seat, eyes closed. Claire? Here? Why would she be follo—

The dots suddenly connected in her mind, surging forward in a maddening, disconcerting realization.

"Claire was worried," she said. "She knew about the affair. She knew Andy gave her DNA to the police. She knew that would make Kate a suspect in Arlene's murder. And if Kate was implicated, it meant Ma Soeur could potentially be unmasked. The police would go through Kate's documents, her office. Turn her life upside down. Maybe Claire followed Detective Wright to keep tabs on the investigation. To see how things were progressing."

Marc nodded silently, as if he agreed.

Jam digested the idea. "Could be," she said. "Does it mean she suspected Kate of killing Hampton?"

"Maybe," said Isabelle slowly. "Or…"

"Yes?" Jam snapped impatiently.

"What if Claire was the one who killed Arlene," Isabelle said. "What if she knew about the affair and she wanted to get rid of Arlene? There was no way she would have approved of Kate sharing Arlene's bed."

Isabelle would kill anyone who looked at Andy with the merest hint of desire. Not too healthy an emotion, she had to admit. She knew she would have to shape it into something more manageable in the time ahead.

Marc switched on the SUV's engine. "Have you traced Detective Wright yet?" he asked Jam. "We need to find her. Maybe Claire wants to do more than keep tabs on her."

Silence, followed by the quick tapping of keys. A nervous laugh. "Here," said Jam. "Her phone says she's here. Across from our building."

Marc's decision was immediate. "We're on our way."

He pulled away, driving through the thinning Friday night traffic. They made good progress through the city, until they hit red lights on the Brooklyn Bridge.

"Must be an accident," Marc said. "Or roadwork."

Isabelle looked in the rearview mirror, but there was no way they could turn around. Multiple lights blinked at her, inching forward, closing them in.

She called Andy on the car's media system. "Hi. You're on with Marc and me."

"Hi. Hi, Marc."

He mumbled a response.

"Are you okay?" Andy sounded on edge. "Jam just told me that Claire might have been tailing Wright."

"Yes."

"And Wright is across from our building."

"Yes. We're trying to get there, but there's a snarl-up on the Brooklyn Bridge."

"Don't worry. René and I will handle it." A moment's silence. "We found evidence that Claire knew about Kate's affair with Hampton."

Isabelle puffed up her cheeks. "That's bad news."

"I know. It gives her motive."

"Be careful, please. We'll get there as soon as we can."

"Don't worry," said Andy. "We got this. I promise. Marc?"

"Yes?" he answered.

"Your first priority has changed. Please keep an eye on Kate, but make sure not to engage her. Just stay on her when she switches on her phone. She's going into a meeting with Kuznetsova so it should come on pretty soon. Kate should know to have it on when its Ma Soeur business. I'll text you the address as soon as I have it. René and I are going to make sure Wright is out of harm's way before Claire does something stupid."

"Andy…"

"I have to go," Andy said hurriedly, as if she knew what Isabelle was going to ask.

"Andy!" Isabelle called. "Please."

"What?"

"Just do one thing for me. If ever tonight you feel like sleeping, like going into the dark, open your eyes and look up. Just do that for me. Promise?"

"That doesn't make sense."

"I know. But promise?"

"Okay. I promise."

❖

Marc's phone pinged with a text message seven minutes later. He looked at the phone.

"Fuck."

"What?" Isabelle said, although she suspected she already knew.

They were speeding from the roadwork on the Brooklyn Bridge as if fleeing a crime scene.

Marc avoided her gaze.

"Marc. Where is Kate's meeting with Natalya?"

"Roman's Diner, near Ma Soeur, where they apparently always meet," he said. "Neutral ground."

Isabelle looked at the passing traffic and closed her eyes for a second, calming herself. She realized that everything she'd dreamed about the past few months would collide tonight, regardless of what she'd done to prevent it from happening. All paths would converge at a single point. Tonight would bring everything—everyone—that had brought her to Ma Soeur into a single space of chaos, into the realm of potential loss; at the doorstep of the most basic of mathematical truths: one minus one, equals zero.

Three minutes later, she got a call from a number she didn't recognize.

"Are you alone?"

"No." The voice was familiar, strong, talking over the sound of the Eagles singing in the background.

"I want to tell you something, but I need it to remain between us," the woman said.

Isabelle thought about it, and then agreed.

❖

Andy and René slipped out Ma Soeur's back door. There was no need to make Detective Wright nervous by walking right up to her vehicle. Who knew if the woman had an itchy trigger finger.

"Which car?" Andy asked Jam on her earpiece.

"City says she drives a black Mustang. Classic. Sixty-eight."

Andy saw the sleek body tucked in between two Japanese sedans. It was parked in such a way that the driver could keep an eye on Ma Soeur's front door without being noticed.

"Got it," she said.

René pulled her beanie tight over her head and pushed her hands into her coat pockets. She marched next to Andy, keeping pace with Andy's long strides.

The evening had turned into early night, heavy with sudden clouds after a day of clear skies. The snow could come down at any moment. The air was frigid, the earth holding its breath, waiting in anticipation for the first flakes to fall.

Andy approached the Mustang from behind.

She walked by, then turned.

The vehicle was empty.

"She's not here," she called to Jam.

"What? Her phone says she was there just now. I couldn't keep an eye on her the whole time. You guys got me working alone here, because you don't trust anyone."

Andy could hear furious typing. "Hang on a sec, let me ping her phone again."

"Did Kate take her car to the meeting?" Andy asked.

"She must have. She wasn't here. We all know that."

"So Wright wouldn't have seen Kate leave the building. Maybe she spotted her car passing by? Or maybe Claire lured Wright out of the car?"

"Wright's phone is dead," Jam said. "But Kate's is on. She's at Roman's Diner."

René looked at Andy. "The diner is due east. Shall we hope Wright is on her way there? Maybe the cops were also keeping tabs on Kate's phone?"

Andy nodded. It was their best bet. She started running. She felt an eerie calm descend on her, as if what should be happening was finally playing out in front of her. She glanced at her watch. Two minutes after eight.

"Maybe you should let René go in, Andy," Jam said in her ear. "Actually, please let René go in."

"No way. I'll be fine. You keep on looking for Claire. Chances are she's around here somewhere if she's been following Wright, and I don't want her to be the one to blow my brains out."

Up ahead, she saw the red and white lights of the diner. A family spilled from its doors, speaking German. They looked at Andy and René running toward them suspiciously.

Andy schooled her face into something resembling a smile. Slipped in the door left open in their wake, into the warm, welcoming space of Roman's Diner.

CHAPTER FIFTY-THREE

Andy slowed her hurried stride into a calm saunter. No need to cause panic. She directed René to go right through the restaurant, while she went left. It took ten seconds to spot Wright, hiding behind a menu. She was three tables away from Kate and Kuznetsova, who were sitting where she and Isabelle had sat earlier that day.

There was no sign of Claire. Hopefully, René would locate her.

Wright spotted Andy at the same time Kuznetsova did. How Kuznetsova managed the setup so that Kate was sitting with her back to the room, Andy could only guess. Probably showed up first.

Kuznetsova's face broke into an easy, fake smile. "Andy. How nice to see you? Where's the redhead?" she called.

Andy smiled, waved.

Kate's surprise turned into anger, then puzzlement as Andy slipped into Wright's booth.

Andy felt the tightening coil of tension inside her stomach. She resisted the urge to feel for the butt of her gun, seeking the reassurance of the cold steel.

Wright was also supposed to die in this very same diner. Was tonight the night?

How could it not be the case?

Andy watched as René sat at an empty table not far from her, giving her a quiet, reassuring nod.

"Well, hello, Andy. Came to warn your mother?" Wright asked.

"No. You."

Wright frowned.

"Remember what we told your earlier? About you being careful in diners? Well, this is it." Andy motioned to the door. "Please come with me. It's for your own safety, I promise you."

"No way. You just want to get your mother out of here."

"We can wait right outside. I'll make sure Kate comes with you as soon as she's done here. I promise you that."

"Get the fuck out of my face. I have a warrant to arrest your mother on suspicion of murder."

Andy wanted to drag Wright out of here but knew it wouldn't happen without causing a scene. "Remember when you asked what Ma Soeur was, Jane?"

Wright's face grew dark at the mention of her name.

"We dream the future," Andy said, leaning across the table, her voice a whisper. "We try to stop bad things from happening. And Isabelle dreamt that you were going to die tonight in this very diner."

Finally, she'd manage to capture Wright's attention.

"What do you mean you dream the future?" Wright snapped.

From the corner of her eye, Andy saw the door swing open. It was Claire.

Fuck.

Claire spotted her immediately.

Her face told her everything she needed to know. Claire knew that Andy knew, that Ma Soeur knew, who killed Arlene Hampton, and she didn't care. She had nowhere left to hide.

No. She didn't want to hide any longer.

René had also spotted her. She got up from her table.

"Andy, I'm talking to you," Wright said, then grew silent as she followed Andy's gaze.

Claire changed direction to move through the set of tables next to the booth, trying to navigate a path between Andy and René. She bumped a girl's arm as she was biting into a piece of pancake.

Was Wright still the target?

No. This was a different Claire, her anger redirected.

"Kate!" Andy turned around. "Watch out!"

Claire's face tightened as if she was trapped. She pulled a gun from her pocket.

She was five, four paces from Kate and Kuznetsova.

A middle-aged couple saw the gun, jumped up, and screamed, blocking René's path as she tried to get to Claire.

"Get Wright!" Andy called to her. She charged through the tables, diving at Claire.

Claire fired, kept on firing.

Andy felt the sting from two bullets in her vest. A third in her neck. An explosion of warmth flooded her skin.

She was on top of Claire, wrestling for the gun.

"You cheating whore," Claire shouted at Kate.

She slipped from Andy's grasp.

Andy felt lightheaded. Her actions slowed. She fell to her knees, the floor slippery with her blood. She was at Kate's table. Kuznetsova was crouching under the surface, her face ashen.

Kate was slumped in her seat. Her eyes stared at Andy. Dead.

Claire got up. She sank to her knees when the sound of shots rang out again.

René was dragging Wright to the exit. She turned to fire one last round before she left.

Why wasn't she aiming at Claire? What was she…? Andy blinked rapidly as she struggled to her feet again. She strained to look where René had been shooting.

She was firing at Tea Guy, Kuznetsova's bodyguard who had been closing in from the other side of the diner. He must have shot at Claire. At her?

Andy was between him and Kuznetsova. He lifted his gun to fire again.

Her legs were too weak to hold her. She fell onto her back.

People were screaming, running out of the restaurant.

Andy lifted her head, her vision blurring. She closed her eyes. Felt the pop of another bullet in her chest, into the vest.

Isabelle's words drifted to her from the edge of consciousness. *"If you feel like sleeping, open your eyes and look up. Just do that for me. Promise?"*

She opened her eyes. Stared straight at the single throwing knife stuck to the bottom of the booth's table. She reached out and threw it at Tea Guy with every ounce of power she had left.

❖

Isabelle ran into the diner as an elderly man came crawling out of the restaurant. Did Andy…was she…did she spot the knife Isabelle had left there this morning?

"Please, God," she prayed. "Please."

"Isabelle!" Marc yelled behind her. "You can't go in there—"

She ignored him, the door slamming closed behind her.

It was quiet inside Roman's Diner, the scent of blood hanging in the air, permeating her clothes, her skin. The fear was equally palpable, as if it had a life of its own. As if it was a living, breathing animal.

Behind her, the door opened then closed. Probably Marc. She didn't look. She ran to where she knew Andy would be.

Outside, the sound of sirens was closing in.

"Andy! No!" She kneeled in the pool of blood and pressed two fingers to Andy's neck wound.

How much blood had she lost?

She looked to her right. Kuznetsova's bodyguard was dead, Andy's knife in his chest. Beyond him lay Claire, motionless.

"You got him, baby," she said. "Just like I knew you would."

There was no response. She bent down to kiss Andy. Her lips were cold.

She was vaguely aware that Marc did a scan of the diner, René and Detective Wright in his wake.

She looked left. Natalya Kuznetsova stared at her from where she sat in the booth seat next to Kate, having abandoned all efforts to administer CPR. She shook her head in something like remorse.

So many people gone. Some many lives lost. She closed her eyes, unable to hold back the tears.

"Andy, sweetheart," she whispered. "Please just hold on. Just two more seconds."

Outside, the sirens came to a halt. René bent down next to her. "Ambulance is here. You called them earlier? Before all of this?"

"Yes."

"Smart woman."

Isabelle felt Andy's pulse weaken under her fingers. How it slowed to a gentle, almost imperceptible thrum before René dragged her away to make room for the EMTs.

CHAPTER FIFTY-FOUR

"Tell me again," Jane insisted.

She was angry. It raged inside her. These people...Ma Soeur and their bullshit stories. Dreaming the fucking future. How fucking ridiculous.

She'd said nothing to Lieutenant Monaghan when he'd arrived at the diner. She wanted to digest what Andy Bouchard had told her first. She looked at the woman sitting next to Isabelle Templeton. It was the woman who had dragged her from the diner. René something. Allandale. Yes, that's it. Fucking beast of a woman.

They were in the hospital cafeteria, awaiting news on Andy Bouchard.

"There is nothing to tell," the redhead—Isabelle—said in a quiet voice. "I don't know what happened. I arrived when it was all over."

"And you? What were you doing there?" Jane pointed to Allandale. Allandale had dragged her out of the diner, only to charge back in immediately. By then Natalya Kuznetsova's bodyguard and the chestnut-haired woman who'd started it all were already dead.

It was all a terrible mistake, the Russian had said. Her bodyguard must have thought the woman who killed Kate wanted to attack her. "A giant mistake. I'm so sorry," she'd said to Isabelle before Jane had managed to split them up.

Kuznetsova had this thing in her eyes, something like respect, and not for Jane being a cop—no—for Isabelle.

Dreaming the future. Dreaming the *frigging* future. Ridiculous.

Jane studied Isabelle. She seemed calm, but below that placid exterior Jane could see that she was drowning. Her despair, her potential loss, was etched into those green eyes. She was looking for a way out, but there was nowhere to go.

Some things you couldn't escape. You could only go through them.

"I was at the diner to look for Kate Bouchard, to tell her that you were looking for her. That's all," Allandale finally spoke up.

"And you did this at the exact moment Kate Bouchard's fiancée tried to kill her. The same fiancée who murdered Arlene Hampton out of jealousy?"

"Yes." Allandale shrugged, trying to look all kinds of stupid, but with little success.

"And this woman, Claire, was targeting me as well because I was about to arrest Kate Bouchard on murder charges."

"We think so. Or she wanted to follow you to see what you were up to," Allandale said. "I'm not too sure."

"And what—"

"Stop talking!" somebody called from behind her. "Immediately."

Jane turned around. Fuck. It was the lawyer, Caroline Diaz.

"Detective, you should know better than to interrogate my clients without me being present."

"We were just talking."

"Bullshit."

Diaz looked haggard and angry. "We have nothing more to say. Have you even offered my clients medical assistance, or just dragged them aside so you could interrogate them?"

She sat next to Isabelle. Gathered her to her chest, ignoring Jane completely. "It will be okay. Andy will be okay. I promise. Don't worry."

❖

Isabelle didn't want to go home. She had made herself comfortable across four chairs next to the ICU as she waited for Andy to wake up. René was next to her, sitting upright, fast asleep.

Jam said Ma Soeur was a mess. Nobody knew what was going on, with both Claire and Kate dead. Caroline had stepped into the breach, trying to repair the damage done by what had happened at the diner.

She was desperately fending off not only the media, but also a federal investigation into Ma Soeur, continuously casting the murders at Claire's hand as those of a spurned lover and nothing more. And yes, she was convinced there was nothing sinister about Kate meeting with a Russian mobster. Kate was probably trying to get Natalya Kuznetsova into bed, nothing more. She had a history of cheating. She'd been a wonderful woman, but she had her flaws. Nobody would deny that.

Ma Soeur's board wasn't too happy about tarnishing Kate Bouchard's image, but there was no other solution to their problems. They couldn't afford an in-depth investigation into Ma Soeur's books or its global reach and influence.

Isabelle thought René would hate the fact that Caroline had moved into Kate's top floor office, but she'd opted to stay here, happy for Caroline to take control.

Isabelle shifted on the chairs in an attempt to alleviate the pressure on her right hip. Andy better wake up. She'd lost a lot of blood, her body going into hypovolemic shock.

All Isabelle could remember was her weak pulse, her ashen, cool skin as the EMTs sped her to the emergency room.

Isabelle listened to the gentle hum of people talking at the nurses' station, the constant din of the air conditioning, of the machines counting and measuring and scanning. Finally, she fell asleep.

She woke with a start as someone shook her awake. It was René. Her eyes were bright.

"No. Please no." Isabelle ran out of words. She closed her eyes as the room started to spin around her.

"Andy is asking for you." René gently brushed her hair from her face. "Come on, Templeton. Don't get soft on me now. Get up and go give Bouchard hell for making a lady like yourself sleep on these damn chairs."

CHAPTER FIFTY-FIVE

Andy stood at her mother's grave, staring at the yellow roses she'd placed there. The green leaves stirred in the slight breeze, the buds still wound too tightly to bother with the cold wind sweeping across the city today.

Andy had known she'd be here one day, staring at a life well lived, but she'd always imagined it would be later. That she'd be older and stronger. Less in need of a mother. Less in search of what could have been possible between them.

But it was done. Katherine Andrea Bouchard had used up her last life. Her last little bit of luck. As a dreamer, she'd been wounded once, in Milan in 1988. She was still very young, constantly flirting with danger, intoxicated by the possibility of what Ma Soeur could achieve.

Andy stared at the words on her mother's headstone. *Datum perficiemus munus. We shall accomplish the mission assigned.* The motto of Ma Soeur. Kate rested in a row of Ma Soeur women who had come and gone before her, dating back to 1631. Some of the graves had been moved from Avignon, in France, when Louis XV prosecuted Ma Soeur for coming to the aid of one of his mistresses.

She touched the headstone. Murmured the words all of Ma Soeur had chanted as Kate was buried. *Dei sub numine viget. Under God's spirit she flourishes.*

Deo ac veritati. For God and truth.

Dominus vobiscum. The Lord be with you.

Rest. You have fulfilled your destiny.

May She guide you.

May the Sisterhood prosper.

She touched the small cross around her neck. "Old woman. Why did you have to go and cheat on Claire?" she whispered.

Claire was not buried here. By Ma Soeur's laws, she would lie in a second, adjacent graveyard, with a stone carrying only her name, along with the rest of the handful of Ma Soeur women who had betrayed her guiding principles.

Andy touched the granite slab, cold and unyielding. Murmured the motto again.

It provided no solace.

"Kate." She inhaled deeply and felt the prick of tears behind her eyes. "Mom."

It was one of the laws of the universe Andy could never fathom. Why your mother remained your mother, regardless of what hurt she might have caused.

She tapped the headstone with a single finger. "I'll come and talk to you again. Try to behave till then, eh?"

She turned, shrugging deeper into her coat. The car door swung open as she approached the vehicle. Isabelle got out. She slipped her hand around Andy's waist, as if wanting to carry her.

"I don't need help," Andy said.

"I hear you."

Andy gingerly stepped into the SUV and fastened the seat belt.

Isabelle got behind the wheel. She started the engine, looking at her expectantly. "Caroline wants to see us."

"Now?"

"Yes. I think she wants to know if it's okay for her to take over Kate's position. If she has your approval."

"Why even bother. I'm not interested. Not remotely."

Isabelle nodded, her eyes soft.

Andy knew what she was thinking.

"Have you thought about us? Staying?" Isabelle asked.

Andy shook her head. "No."

"At some point you will have to, sweetheart."

Andy wished she wouldn't smile at her with those eyes that knew everything, leaving Andy with so little choice.

She looked out the window. The day was miserable, the wind picking up speed. She rested her hand against her neck and felt the steady pulse of blood, of life. She remembered Kate's dead eyes looking at her. Isabelle's knife under the table.

Isabelle saved her life.
She owed Isabelle her life.
"*Deo ac veritati*," she whispered under her breath.
Why was the truth always so damn unavoidable?

❖

Caroline was in her element. It was hard not to notice. Andy watched as she wrapped up a phone call to David. He was out with Iona, keeping an eye on a congresswoman who was to be gunned down tonight in what was looking less and less like a drive-by shooting.

Caroline was at ease where she sat in Kate's black leather chair. The chair and the 173-year-old desk were the only furniture that remained as Caroline worked to make the space her own.

Andy felt no resentment. Stepping from the elevator, she'd wondered for a moment what she would feel when she walked in here, but there was only relief that no one expected her to do this job. To take on this enormous responsibility.

Caroline nodded. "Yes, yes. Okay. But make sure no one sees you. Congresswoman Leslie was appointed through our assistance, and she knows it, but we don't need the rest of the world to know. We're going to push her all the way for 2028. We need to keep her safe, but we need to make it low-key. We really don't need any more publicity."

She listened again. "Okay. Thanks, David." She put the phone down. "Andy. Isabelle." She walked around the desk and greeted them both with a kiss on the cheek. "I'm so glad you are well," she said, holding Andy's hands for a moment. "You had us worried there."

Andy shrugged. "It's all thanks to Isabelle and her knife."

"Yes. I've heard." Caroline looked at Isabelle. "That's partly the reason I wanted to talk to you. You make a brilliant team. We would like to hang on to you. Both of you."

Andy sat down. "About the other reason you probably want to talk to us? You don't have to worry about your position. I'm happy for you. You have a good strategic mind. And with René as your second in command, the tactical aspect of the business is covered."

Caroline gave a vague smile. "As brutal and direct as always. What about staying then? May I have an equally positive answer?"

Isabelle reached out and placed her hand on Andy's, her eyes asking the same question.

Andy didn't pull away from her touch. "I don't know. I have no pressing business anywhere else. I don't need to go back to London anytime soon. The Black Sheep is in capable hands."

"If you need time after what happened to your mother, I understand," Caroline offered.

"Time to do what? Mourn a mother I never really knew? It's more like mourning the concept of a mother. What she could have been now that there is no hope that she could finally become that elusive, caring being I'd hoped for as a child."

Andy blinked at her emotional outburst and immediately regretted it. Isabelle squeezed her hand, rubbing her other hand up and down Andy's arm.

Caroline looked away.

Andy had slept with both women in this room. Only one wasn't scared of anything she was throwing at her.

She held Isabelle's hand. Felt the firm, unwavering grip. "I'll think about it and let you know. First I have to do something."

Caroline nodded. "René told me. Take as long as you like. We'll be here waiting."

Andy nodded, then tried to change the topic. "Have we learned yet how Claire managed to kill Arlene Hampton?"

"Jam says the Major Case Squad has arrested a security guard for selling security tags to the Russians and to a woman who fits the description of Claire. We assume she followed Kate to her date with Arlene, perhaps surprising Arlene just after Kate left. We'll never really know. Wiping the CCTV that night also killed all evidence of her arrival. I'm guessing, however, that she came up through the basement. It seemed very convenient that those cameras went down a day before the murder."

"And the bullets that killed Kate?"

"Your mother's gun," Caroline confirmed softly.

Andy sighed. "That's that then. Kate's life finally caught up with her."

"Doesn't mean she deserved to die."

"Maybe not, but it doesn't provide much solace, does it?"

CHAPTER FIFTY-SIX

Andy zipped her bag closed. She and René would have to travel for almost two days by car to reach their destination. She didn't want to fly. She couldn't stand strangers around her at the moment.

Isabelle looked at her and smiled. There was no hint of worry in her eyes, almost as if she knew what was going to happen.

"Tell me," Andy asked.

Isabelle tucked her hair behind her ears and closed her laptop. She was finishing her finite math paper.

"Tell you what, darling?"

Andy wished she would stop calling her all those sweet names reserved for lovers. They'd not touched or kissed since she'd left the hospital, yet Isabelle behaved like they were a couple.

She shook her head. "Never mind."

Isabelle got up from the breakfast nook. She was wearing jeans and a T-shirt emphasizing her curves. And damn, did she have those in all the right places. Almost all of Andy's dreams, induced by a raft of pain medication, were of that body. This woman. Their bed.

Heat and desire surged through Andy's body so unexpectedly it took her breath away.

Isabelle came to sit next to her on the sofa. "You don't want to know, so why tell you?"

"So that I can rage against the inevitability of it all." Andy ran her hands through her hair. "Did you know that my mother would die? In the diner? Did you dream it?"

Isabelle didn't flinch. "Yes."

"But you didn't save her."

"I could only figure out how to save you." Isabelle lifted her chin, her green eyes blazing. "And I stand by my decision."

"And Kate?"

"Nobody could do anything for her and she knew it. She accepted it. She couldn't chastise you over Victoria and then change her own destiny."

Andy frowned. "What do you mean?"

"Your mother dreamed of her own death before she died. It was a rare dream. You know she'd largely stopped dreaming years ago already, when she started to run this place. She called me on the way to the diner to make me promise to keep you safe. To look after you after she was gone. I told her that I'd already interfered, with the knife." Isabelle looked her straight in the eye. "She said it was good I did."

Andy blinked back the sudden tears.

Isabelle stared at her bare feet. "She loved you very much. She just didn't know how to say it, and face it, neither of you knew how to listen." Isabelle looked at her, a swell of emotion on her face. "And you still don't know how to listen."

❖

"This is the place." René killed the engine.

Andy surveyed the quiet cabin on the edge of a small, dog-leg shaped lake. The Montana sky was clear. She knew the air would be crisp when she opened the window, just like Victoria James had always dreamed it would be.

Vic had always loved an endless view. She said she couldn't breathe in the city. Funny thing for someone who'd grown up in Chicago with its brooding skies and constant bustle.

René looked at Andy. "Do you think she knows we're here?"

"I imagine so."

René pinched the bridge of her nose and wiped across her eyes. They had driven here through the night, only stopping for bathroom breaks and to swap driving duties.

Andy sat back, watching as the morning air swept gently across the surface of the water.

"I didn't drive out here to look at a house, Bouchard," René said after a while.

"Just wait."

"Wait for what? You better not get cold feet on me again."

Andy knew she wasn't just talking about today, about Victoria. "I know," she acknowledged. "I need to do better."

"Much better. For the sake of everyone who loves you."

Andy looked René in the eye. "I know. I'm sorry."

René cleared her throat and parked her hand across her mouth, resting her elbow on the SUV's windowsill.

"What are we wai—"

The house's back door swung open. A woman appeared. She looked exactly like Andy remembered—medium height, slender, dressed in jeans and a sweater that showed off pert breasts. What Andy could recall ever better, even after all these years, was her eyes. The most enormous, beautiful deep brown eyes Andy had ever seen on a person. They would turn black as she came. And when she dreamed.

Victoria stood, watching them, hands on her hips.

René shifted uneasily in her seat. "I'll stay here?"

"If you don't mind."

"I'll take a nap on the back seat. Just don't leave me here too long. I'm going to freeze my ass off in this lovely Montana weather."

❖

Andy approached Vic with a steady tread. She felt calmer than she thought she'd be. More in control. She came to a halt in front of Vic.

Vic squinted up at her. She'd gotten older. She must be in her late thirties by now. She looked content—happy even—despite the inevitable loneliness, the inability to explain her past to anyone. The turmoil, disappointment, and tension she'd carried in her shoulders and in the downturned corners of her mouth for so long were gone.

Kate had never liked Vic.

Vic was Andy's first true love.

Andy had been Vic's all-consuming obsession.

Andy reached out to hug her. Vic stepped back. "Did you bring her?"

"Who?"

"The redhead? Isa…dore?"

"Isabelle?"

Vic managed a half-smile. "I'm not as good as I used to be. Isabelle, yes."

Andy knew dreamers sometimes dreamed wider than murder and violence. Sometimes the dreams were deeply personal—scary as hell to anyone near them, which meant they kept quiet about them. They carried them inside as a kind of mute, personal treasure.

"No. I thought it was better that I came alone," Andy said.

There was disappointment in Vic's waning smile, a sincere effort to keep it on her lips. Then she dropped it anyway.

"Is she beautiful?"

"Yes. And smart. Strong."

"Does she love you?"

"I think so." Who was she kidding? "Yes."

"But you can't let go."

"No."

Vic took her hand tentatively. "Of me?"

"Yes. And I'm…I'm…"

Andy couldn't say the word.

"Scared?" Vic asked.

"Yes. Of losing someone again. And for what? To chase ghosts again? Fate? To be on the run again constantly. Hunting. Killing."

"You killed someone recently?"

"Yes."

"Come on." Vic turned and walked around the house to a wooden deck. Sat in a chair overlooking the water. Andy sat down next to her.

"Does Isabelle know you're here?"

"Yes."

"Ah."

Andy had a flash of Vic moaning below her, grinding her hips against Andy. Taking Andy in her mouth under a shower, running hot, entering her with her tongue, rendering her helpless in complete submission.

"What do you need from me, Andy? To know that I'm happy? That I release you? That I'm sorry for what I did?" Vic stilled. "That I want you back after you left me just like that?"

Andy thought about her answer. "I need to know that you're okay."

"So that you can move on?"

"Yes." Andy held her breath. "All those people who died in the subway that day…I need to know that you've found some peace. And maybe I need to know that there is life after all of this."

"I don't know about peace. I still regret losing you."

"You knew you were going to lose me, but you did it anyway."

"Yes. Some people are worth it."

"All those people who died…they were also worthy."

"They were not *my* people. For once, I wanted to look after my people. My person. My interests." Vic lifted her knees to her chin and wrapped her arms around her legs. "Don't kid yourself, Andy. You're not here for me. You're here for you." She stared at the water. "You want to make sure we're all okay so you can run again, and you want me to give you permission."

"No. That's not…No more running." Andy placed her left ankle on her right knee. She swore under her breath. Inhaled sharply. "Kate died."

Vic looked at her in surprise. "How?"

"Shot. I was there."

"I'm sorry." Victoria reached for her hand, held it. "I didn't know. I have no contact with anyone at Ma Soeur and there is no way I would have dreamed about Kate." She looked over her shoulder, in the direction of the SUV. "Someone drops by now and then. Not because of me, but to make sure Ma Soeur's secrets are safe." She laughed sardonically.

Andy nodded. There was an entire squad dedicated to looking after the handful of women who'd left Ma Soeur of their own accord. Out of everyone at Ma Soeur, the people in that squad were the truly scary ones. The fanatics.

"Not that they have anything to worry about," Vic said hurriedly. "I don't really dream like that anymore, and if I do it's as if I get trapped inside my mind." She shrugged. "It's better than it was, though. I couldn't speak for a year after coming here. I could only sign or write. People thought I was crazy. A mad, old mountain woman." She squeezed Andy's hand. "But I'm better now. Every day is better. There is hope."

"Do you miss it?"

"I miss you. But the life at Ma Soeur? No. I was never strong enough."

Andy nodded and watched as the sun reflected off the restless surface of the lake, a million shards of yellow light blinding her momentarily.

Vic broke the lingering silence. "Your new dreamer is very powerful. She scares you."

Andy didn't ask how she knew. "Yes."

"She loves you like I once loved you."

"Yes."

"With everything?"

"I fear so."

Vic turned to look at her, resting her head against the back of the deck chair. "You also deserve that, you know? Everything. All of us do. Everything is a gift. An enormously unselfish gift. Don't squander it. Don't be so scared of disappointing her that you walk away from it."

Vic turned her gaze back to the water. "Take everything for as long as it lasts. Trust me. It's better than all the pale imitations you'll find along the way. The only good love is the one that scares you to death."

Andy reached for the words that had been stuck in her throat since they'd arrived here. "I don't know if I can do everything again."

Vic smiled. "I think you can. This woman is special and you know it. And you are capable of so much more by now. She's pushed you somewhere close to the realm of human." She shook her head and chuckled. There was a hint of surprise in her voice, satisfaction even. "Maybe that's why you were terrified enough to come to my front door."

Andy didn't know what to say.

Vic wiped at her cheeks.

"I'm sorry," Andy said. "For everything."

"Me too," Vic said. "But if I had to do it again, I'd make exactly the same decision. I'd choose you."

"I know. And I'm grateful that I'm still alive."

"Then you better not waste it. Don't waste the loss of us."

Vic got to her feet, wrapping her arms around her body, as if she was cold. "You better go. Say hi to René."

Andy got up as well and leaned down to kiss Vic on the cheek. "Thank you. Very much. And I mean it."

❖

Jane looked at the note in her hand. Russo had given it to her earlier today, shaking his head as he'd done so.

"Got a tip-off here about Horace Gibson's death. Two names." He'd bitten into his meatball sandwich, a splash of marinara sauce landing on his striped tie. He'd wiped at it with a fistful of napkins.

She'd asked about the diet and gotten a dirty look. And now she was here, standing across from a known drug den in Queens, her hand on the butt of her gun, Russo covering the back of the two-story shithouse with the front door hanging off its hinges.

"Classy place," she murmured, stuffing the note with the two names back into her pocket. She wondered again whether the redhead and Andy Bouchard had anything to do with this sudden breakthrough in the Gibson case.

"Russo, you ready?" she said into her radio.

"Let's kick some butt," he said.

She adjusted her bulletproof vest, nodded at the uniform to her left, ran up the stairs, and kicked in the door with immense satisfaction.

CHAPTER FIFTY-SEVEN

"Gym time."

Isabelle threw a pair of training gloves at Andy. She'd been moody and noncommittal ever since she'd come back from visiting Victoria, and Isabelle couldn't stand it anymore.

Andy looked up from the book she was reading. "Now?"

"Yes. Now."

Isabelle was restless, blood pounding through her veins in a constant audible surge, a white noise in her ears she couldn't shut up. She was sure she was going to dream tonight. She had raging food cravings Andy had tried her best to accommodate, even if it meant driving out at midnight to look for strawberries.

And she wanted Andy to touch her. She needed Andy to make her come, again and again. She wanted to pound her body against Andy's hard planes, relentlessly and repeatedly.

And not somebody else. Andy.

Fuck it.

"Come. Let's go," she snapped.

Andy got to her feet, dropping the book next to the couch. They were on a mandatory rest period between assignments. They'd both had two sessions with Ma Soeur's psychiatrist already—one of the changes Caroline had made since moving into Kate's office. Each team had to go for a psych eval after finishing a dragon hunt.

"It's ten at night," Andy protested.

"Yes. So?"

Andy had been staying up later and later to avoid going to bed with Isabelle. She would repeatedly wait for Isabelle to fall asleep before slipping into bed. It had happened for five days in a row now and Isabelle had had enough.

They changed quickly and walked to the gym where Isabelle turned and locked the door. She climbed into the ring, watching as Andy did the same. She tied up her hair, then rested her hands on her hips, jutting out her chin.

"Here's the deal," she said.

Andy looked at her suspiciously, her eyes traveling from Isabelle's mouth to her neck to her breasts. Back up again to her mouth.

Good. At least she wasn't dead yet, Isabelle thought with irritation. "You win, and you can go," she announced. "I win, and you stay."

"What do you mean 'go'?" Andy asked.

"Exactly what I'm saying. This is it. The little zero-sum game we've been playing for these past weeks. Mutually assured destruction, but fuck it, I can't stand it any longer. I also have my pride. I keep on waiting for you to wake up and make a decision to stay."

"I'm here, aren't I?"

Isabelle resisted the urge to roll her eyes like a teenager. Andy was here only in name. Something was holding her back. Maybe it was pride, maybe it was the fact that she'd wanted to choose Isabelle, but the decision was stolen from her by Kate's actions and Isabelle's dreams.

"I'm not going to negotiate with you," she said. "I'm going to fight because you don't understand any other language but this." She put up her fists, wrapped in exercise padding.

"That's not fair—"

Isabelle stepped forward and slammed her fist into Andy's bare midriff with everything she possessed. She danced back. "No talking. I'm sick of talking." Two fingers invited Andy closer. "Come on. Come and get it."

Andy squinted, then lifted her fists.

She danced to Isabelle's left. Isabelle remained standing quietly, not moving a muscle.

Andy slowed, frowned. Stepped to Isabelle's right.

Still Isabelle just stood there, waiting.

Andy bent down low and went into Isabelle's body directly. Isabelle stepped back and jabbed sharply at her face, her neck.

Andy reached out and grabbed Isabelle around the waist, driving her into the corner of the ring.

Isabelle kept hitting her with short, sharp, angry jabs.

Andy turned her away from the corner, lifted her body, and brought her down onto the floor with as little force as possible, as if she couldn't get herself to hurt Isabelle.

Andy tried to pin down her arms. "Yield," she demanded.

Isabelle slammed a rogue fist into her mouth, then locked her arms around Andy's head. She brought her right knee up between Andy's legs with considerable force. She knew she was hitting Andy where it hurt, where it had been aching for so many weeks if the damn stubborn woman would just admit it.

Andy inhaled sharply, eyes glazing over, as if the pain was exquisite, desperate.

Isabelle kept her knee between Andy's legs, shifting her hands to Andy's hips. Andy moved involuntarily against the relentless pressure, moaning something Isabelle couldn't make out.

Isabelle rolled Andy over on her back, landing on top of her. Andy looked at her, shaking her head, a swear word hovering on her lips. Isabelle grabbed her hips, increasing the pressure on Andy's clit.

Isabelle rode her without mercy, locking her eyes into Andy's. "Come for me, baby. Come on. Just let go."

Andy's eyes were hazy, unfocused with want. She threaded her left hand through Isabelle's hair and pulled her closer, kissing her hungrily. Her right hand closed around Isabelle's breast, breaking it free from her top. She pinched the nipple, then rolled it between two fingers, pulling at it, causing Isabelle to gasp. Her left hand wandered down the length of Isabelle's body, gripping her butt.

Isabelle lifted herself, slipping her hand into Andy's shorts until she found her clit, swollen and slippery. She pulled at it, tweaked the nub as Andy gasped for air.

"Isa—Oh fuck."

Isabelle rubbed Andy's clit in ever tighter circles. She could feel the first orgasm crash through Andy, how she came again and again as Isabelle would not release her. Isabelle leaned down, burying her face in Andy's neck as she also came unexpectedly, screaming muffled ecstasy into Andy's hair, her neck.

Release, finally.

Isabelle closed her eyes where she rested on top of Andy. She listened to her ragged breathing, how her heart finally settled to a slower, steadier beat.

They remained like that in the ring, no one saying a word.

Someone tried to open the gym door, giving up only after rattling the handle a few times.

Isabelle was too scared to ask, her bravado outgunned by a passion she feared would consume her. Then, finally, she heard as Andy whispered the words she'd been longing to hear.

"Okay, okay," she said.

An almost audible smile.

A sigh.

"I yield."

About the Author

Sydney Quinne writes all kinds of stories for a living. She adores a good thriller, good food, the late-night hum of big cities, and the music of Chet Baker and Miles Davis. She is married and lives where the sun shines most of the time.

Books Available from Bold Strokes Books

Best Practice by Carsen Taite. When attorney Grace Maldonado agrees to mentor her best friend's little sister, she's prepared to confront Perry's rebellious nature, but she isn't prepared to fall in love. Legal Affairs: one law firm, three best friends, three chances to fall in love. (978-1-63555-361-1)

Home by Kris Bryant. Natalie and Sarah discover that anything is possible when love takes the long way home. (978-1-63555-853-1)

Keeper by Sydney Quinne. With a new charge under her reluctant wing—feisty, highly intelligent math wizard Isabelle Templeton—keeper Andy Bouchard has to prevent a murder or die trying. (978-1-63555-852-4)

One More Chance by Ali Vali. Harry Bastantes planned a future with Desi Thompson until the day Desi disappeared without a word, only to walk back into her life sixteen years later. (978-1-63555-536-3)

Renegade's War by Gun Brooke. Freedom fighter Aurelia DeCallum regrets saving the woman called Blue. She fears it will jeopardize her mission, and secretly, Blue might end up breaking Aurelia's heart. (978-1-63555-484-7)

The Other Women by Erin Zak. What happens in Vegas should stay in Vegas, but what do you do when the love you find in Vegas changes your life forever? (978-1-63555-741-1)

The Sea Within by Missouri Vaun. Time is running out for Dr. Elle Graham to convince Captain Jackson Drake that the only thing that can save future Earth resides in the past, and rescue her broken heart in the process. (978-1-63555-568-4)

To Sleep With Reindeer by Justine Saracen. In Norway under Nazi occupation, Marrit, an Indigenous woman; and Kirsten, a Norwegian resister, join forces to stop the development of an atomic weapon. (978-1-63555-735-0)

Twice Shy by Aurora Rey. Having an ex with benefits isn't all it's cracked up to be. Will Amanda Russo learn that lesson in time to take a chance on love with Quinn Sullivan? (978-1-63555-737-4)

Z-Town by Eden Darry. Forced to work together to stay alive, Meg and Lane must find the centuries-old treasure before the zombies find them first. (978-1-63555-743-5)

Bet Against Me by Fiona Riley. In the high stakes luxury real estate market, everything has a price, and as rival Realtors Trina Lee and Kendall Yates find out, that means their hearts and souls, too. (978-1-63555-729-9)

Broken Reign by Sam Ledel. Together on an epic journey in search of a mysterious cure, a princess and a village outcast must overcome life-threatening challenges and their own prejudice if they want to survive. (978-1-63555-739-8)

Just One Taste by CJ Birch. For Lauren, it only took one taste to start trusting in love again. (978-1-63555-772-5)

Lady of Stone by Barbara Ann Wright. Sparks fly as a magical emergency forces a noble embarrassed by her ability to submit to a low-born teacher who resents everything about her. (978-1-63555-607-0)

Last Resort by Angie Williams. Katie and Rhys are about to find out what happens when you meet the girl of your dreams but you aren't looking for a happily ever after. (978-1-63555-774-9)

Longing for You by Jenny Frame. When Debrek housekeeper Katie Brekman is attacked amid a burgeoning vampire-witch war, Alexis Villiers must go against everything her clan believes in to save her. (978-1-63555-658-2)

Money Creek by Anne Laughlin. Clare Lehane is a troubled lawyer from Chicago who tries to make her way in a rural town full of secrets and deceptions. (978-1-63555-795-4)

Passion's Sweet Surrender by Ronica Black. Cam and Blake are unable to deny their passion for each other, but surrendering to love is a whole different matter. (978-1-63555-703-9)

The Holiday Detour by Jane Kolven. It will take everything going wrong to make Dana and Charlie see how right they are for each other. (978-1-63555-720-6)

Too Hot to Ride by Andrews & Austin. World famous cutting horse champion and industry legend Jane Barrow is knockdown sexy in the way she moves, talks, and rides, and Rae Starr is determined not to get involved with this womanizing gambler. (978-1-63555-776-3)

A Love that Leads to Home by Ronica Black. For Carla Sims and Janice Carpenter, home isn't about location, it's where your heart is. (978-1-63555-675-9)

Blades of Bluegrass by D. Jackson Leigh. A US Army occupational therapist must rehab a bitter veteran who is a ticking political time bomb the military is desperate to disarm. (978-1-63555-637-7)

Guarding Hearts by Jaycie Morrison. As treachery and temptation threaten the women of the Women's Army Corps, who will risk it all for love? (978-1-63555-806-7)

Hopeless Romantic by Georgia Beers. Can a jaded wedding planner and an optimistic divorce attorney possibly find a future together? (978-1-63555-650-6)

Hopes and Dreams by PJ Trebelhorn. Movie theater manager Riley Warren is forced to face her high school crush and tormentor, wealthy socialite Victoria Thayer, at their twentieth reunion. (978-1-63555-670-4)

In the Cards by Kimberly Cooper Griffin. Daria and Phaedra are about to discover that love finds a way, especially when powers outside their control are at play. (978-1-63555-717-6)

Moon Fever by Ileandra Young. SPEAR agent Danika Karson must clear her werewolf friend of multiple false charges while teaching her vampire girlfriend to resist the blood mania brought on by a full moon. (978-1-63555-603-2)

Quake City by St John Karp. Can Andre find his best friend Amy before the night devolves into a nightmare of broken hearts, malevolent drag queens, and spontaneous human combustion? Or has it always happened this way, every night, at Aunty Bob's Quake City Club? (978-1-63555-723-7)

Serenity by Jesse J. Thoma. For Kit Marsden, there are many things in life she cannot change. Serenity is in the acceptance. (978-1-63555-713-8)

Sylver and Gold by Michelle Larkin. Working feverishly to find a killer before he strikes again, Boston Homicide Detective Reid Sylver and rookie cop London Gold are blindsided by their chemistry and developing attraction. (978-1-63555-611-7)

Trade Secrets by Kathleen Knowles. In Silicon Valley, love and business are a volatile mix for clinical lab scientist Tony Leung and venture capitalist Sheila Graham. (978-1-63555-642-1)

Death Overdue by David S. Pederson. Did Heath turn to murder in an alcohol induced haze to solve the problem of his blackmailer, or was it someone else who brought about a death overdue? (978-1-63555-711-4)

Entangled by Melissa Brayden. Becca Crawford is the perfect person to head up the Jade Hotel, if only the captivating owner of the local vineyard would get on board with her plan and stop badmouthing the hotel to everyone in town. (978-1-63555-709-1)

First Do No Harm by Emily Smith. Pierce and Cassidy are about to discover that when it comes to love, sometimes you have to risk it all to have it all. (978-1-63555-699-5)

Kiss Me Every Day by Dena Blake. For Wynn Evans, wishing for a do-over with Carly Jamison was a long shot, actually getting one was a game changer. (978-1-63555-551-6)

Olivia by Genevieve McCluer. In this lesbian Shakespeare adaptation with vampires, Olivia is a centuries old vampire who must fight a strange figure from her past if she wants a chance at happiness. (978-1-63555-701-5)

One Woman's Treasure by Jean Copeland. Daphne's search for discarded antiques and treasures leads to an embarrassing misunderstanding, and ultimately, the opportunity for the romance of a lifetime with Nina. (978-1-63555-652-0)

Silver Ravens by Jane Fletcher. Lori has lost her girlfriend, her home, and her job. Things don't improve when she's kidnapped and taken to fairyland. (978-1-63555-631-5)

Still Not Over You by Jenny Frame, Carsen Taite, Ali Vali. Old flames die hard in these tales of a second chance at love with the ex you're still not over. Stories by award winning authors Jenny Frame, Carsen Taite, and Ali Vali. (978-1-63555-516-5)

Storm Lines by Jessica L. Webb. Devon is a psychologist who likes rules. Marley is a cop who doesn't. They don't always agree, but both fight to protect a girl immersed in a street drug ring. (978-1-63555-626-1)

The Politics of Love by Jen Jensen. Is it possible to love across the political divide in a hostile world? Conservative Shelley Whitmore and liberal Rand Thomas are about to find out. (978-1-63555-693-3)

All the Paths to You by Morgan Lee Miller. High school sweethearts Quinn Hughes and Kennedy Reed reconnect five years after they break up and realize that their chemistry is all but over. (978-1-63555-662-9)

Arrested Pleasures by Nanisi Barrett D'Arnuck. When charged with a crime she didn't commit, Katherine Lowe faces the question: Which is harder, going to prison or falling in love? (978-1-63555-684-1)

Bonded Love by Renee Roman. Carpenter Blaze Carter suffers an injury that shatters her dreams, and ER nurse Trinity Greene hopes to show her that sometimes love is worth fighting for. (978-1-63555-530-1)

Convergence by Jane C. Esther. With life as they know it on the line, can Aerin McLeary and Olivia Ando's love survive an otherworldly threat to humankind? (978-1-63555-488-5)

Coyote Blues by Karen F. Williams. Riley Dawson, psychotherapist and shape-shifter, has her world turned upside down when Fiona Bell, her one true love, returns. (978-1-63555-558-5)

Drawn by Carsen Taite. Will the clues lead Detective Claire Hanlon to the killer terrorizing Dallas, or will she merely lose her heart to person of interest, urban artist Riley Flynn? (978-1-63555-644-5)

Every Summer Day by Lee Patton. Meant to celebrate every summer day, Luke's journal instead chronicles a love affair as fast-moving and possibly as fatal as his brother's brain tumor. (978-1-63555-706-0)

Lucky by Kris Bryant. Was Serena Evans's luck really about winning the lottery, or is she about to get even luckier in love? (978-1-63555-510-3)

The Last Days of Autumn by Donna K. Ford. Autumn and Caroline question the fairness of life, the cruelty of loss, and what it means to love as they navigate the complicated minefield of relationships, grief, and life-altering illness. (978-1-63555-672-8)

Three Alarm Response by Erin Dutton. In the midst of tragedy, can these first responders find love and healing? Three stories of courage, bravery, and passion. (978-1-63555-592-9)

Veterinary Partner by Nancy Wheelton. Callie and Lauren are determined to keep their hearts safe but find that taking a chance on love is the safest option of all. (978-1-63555-666-7)